FORGOTTEN DARKNESS

THE SHADOW DEMONS SAGA, BOOK 8

SARRA CANNON

Cover by Ravven

Get new release updates and exclusive content when you sign up for my mailing list.

❋ Created with Vellum

For George & Andrew
Because you're the ones my heart would refuse to forget.

BREAK THE GIRL

THE EMERALD PRIESTESS

"What have you done to her?"

My sister Magda leaned over the girl on the stone table and pushed her blonde hair back from her face. Sweat gathered along the girl's temple, and her chest rose and fell with each labored breath.

"Everything I can think of," I said. I shook my head and paced the dusty floor. "She's resisting all my best spells. Nothing seems to break her."

"Maybe she simply can't be broken," Alexandra said.

The way she was touching the girl—almost reverently—sent a fresh wave of anger through my body. Did no one understand just how dangerous she was? How much she had done to ruin all our plans?

"She can, and she will," I said through clenched teeth. "Even if I have to cut her heart from her body, I will see the end of her before I'm done."

Alexandra turned to me, her eyes flashing red. "You can't

kill her. You know that," she said. "The High Priestess wants her alive, and she's already upset with you for taking the girl and bringing her here, of all places."

"If I had taken her anywhere else, the High Priestess would have already stolen her from me," I said. I barely had control of my voice, but rage wasn't going to do me any good in this argument. I was duty-bound to honor my priestess, and after what I'd tried to do by reopening the sapphire gates without her permission, I was already on thin ice.

Still, Harper was mine. I had been the one to capture her when no one else had been strong enough.

"If you harm her powers in any way, the High Priestess will have your head." Alexandra leaned over the girl again, this time stroking her scarred arm.

"I didn't bring you here to admire her," I snapped, pulling my sister's arm away. "I brought you here to help me figure out a way to break her mind. If I can't take her memories away, I have no hope of bringing her over to our side."

"And you tried your fractured stone spell?" she asked, as if I were some kind of fledgling witch who didn't know the first thing about stealing memories.

"Of course," I said with a sigh. "That was the first spell I cast on her."

"And what happened?"

"I was able to capture some of her memories," I said. "She was so weak and confused, I thought surely it was going to work. But over time, she somehow regained the strongest of them. I tried again, cutting into her flesh a little deeper the second time and bleeding her for hours."

"And?"

"And nothing. As the wounds healed, many of her memo-

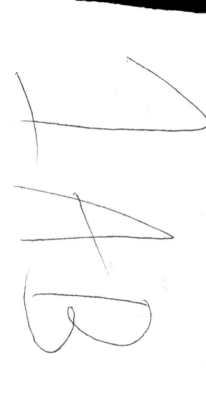

ries returned," I said. My jaw hurt from the constant stress of grinding my teeth.

I'd had her in my dungeons now for months, casting every spell I could find and torturing her in the most painful ways I could imagine. She would sometimes forget who she was completely, but over the following days, she would always remember.

"Her memories of that demon boy are the strongest," I said. "Nothing I have done to her so far has been able to remove him completely from her mind. It's infuriating."

Magda smiled, and I wanted to slap her. This was not the kind of place where anyone was allowed to smile. This was a place of nightmares.

"Maybe it's not her mind you should be worried about," she said.

I narrowed my eyes at her. "What do you mean?"

"Maybe it's her heart that refuses to let go," she said, absently touching the ruby snake pendant at her breast. "You never have understood matters of the heart the way a real mother might. Break her heart, and maybe you finally break the girl."

Fire ran through my veins. Magda threw motherhood in my face every chance she got, but arguing with her now would do me no good. Maybe she was right about the girl's heart, after all.

I studied Harper. She didn't look like much lying there on the cold stone table, her body bruised and covered in scars. She was so young and weak now that it was hard to imagine she had ever been strong enough to defeat my sister Eloisa, Priestess of the Sapphire Gates.

But I knew that deep inside that petite body, this girl held a power stronger than any this world had seen in decades. Maybe centuries. She could have done so much for the Order of Shadows. She could have been one of our greatest accomplishments, but my sister Eloisa had never been the smartest among us. She had taken the girl's powers for granted and assumed she was nothing more than an annoyance.

Eloisa's pride had gotten her killed, but I was the one who had outsmarted this so-called heroine. She may have ruined my plans to reopen the sapphire gates, and yes, she may have even killed one of my precious daughters, but she was mine now. The power locked away inside her was mine to rule. All I had to do was figure out how to break her and turn her to my side.

I had to find a way to convince her that she had been mine all along.

Maybe Magda was right. Maybe I had been going about this whole thing all wrong. Spells and torture were not working as I had hoped, but perhaps it was her love for her friends and for the demon that would finally bring her to her knees.

Besides, killing the demon would be a pleasure. He'd been torturing my hunters, and I simply wouldn't stand for it.

Yes, maybe this was the way.

Break her heart—her spirit—and I break the girl.

A sudden calm settled over me. I walked toward the girl on the stone table, her body shivering with fever, and leaned close to her ear.

"You're such a fighter," I whispered. "Let's see what happens when you think you have nothing left to fight for."

SHE WAS NOWHERE

JACKSON

Darkness fell upon the mountain, creating shadows I could slip through undetected. The hunter wasn't far. I could smell her rot from here as she made her way up the crooked path toward her lair.

This had to be it. She'd performed her duties in the fishing village earlier, scoping out the remaining demons. I'd watched her for hours as she studied them in their work, spying on them from the edge of the small village. None of the demons had noticed her, but I'd been tracking her for days.

I knew when she had found her target, a younger demon who had revealed the strength of his power as he helped his father unload the day's catch. He'd unloaded an entire ship's worth of boxes in a matter of minutes, not showing any signs of fatigue as he cast his magic. He had smiled and tilted his head toward the eastern sun. His joy had made my heart ache.

Despite the ruin of most of the villages here in the Northern Kingdom, there were still those who chose to live on their own terms, refusing to leave their homes behind out of fear. This village was one of the few that still thrived along this part of the coast, and the demons here were determined to protect their own.

For decades they had succeeded, casting powerful wards around the village that kept many of the hunters out. But now that most of the Outerlands had been picked clean or abandoned, the hunters had started studying these demons, watching their routines and finding their weaknesses.

This young demon couldn't have been older than sixty years. He was just coming into his true power, and he foolishly flaunted it. Their safety had made them complacent, and the emerald priestess's hunter had her eye on him.

She'd smiled as she watched him, her rotting lips stretching over her blackened teeth. She'd pulled a small glass box from her robes and opened it carefully. Her lips moved as she spoke words of power that didn't reach my ears.

I had never seen this part of the process and was terrified when the young demon on the docks frowned and clutched his heart. There was almost no visible sign of the magic she had cast on him, but in the heat of the sun, I could just make out a wave of energy flowing from the hunter to the demon. Whatever she'd trapped inside that box had made its way to the young demon, entering his body and marking him.

Just as quickly as the energy had reached him, the hunter pulled it back, closing it into her box with a small emerald key.

So, this was how they marked their targets. Some dark magic reached out to unsuspecting demons, its fingers seeking them out and reaching deep inside them, placing some kind of mark on their souls.

I knew that sometime in the near future, the hunter would

return to this village in the dead of night. She would open her box of horrors and summon him from his bed and into a nearby field, likely close to where I was now hiding among the ginger reeds. She would open a portal to some emerald gate in the human world, and the Prima there would suck the demon through, enslaving him inside the body of a newly initiated human girl. After that, there would be no saving him until the emerald priestess herself was killed.

No easy task, but if I had anything to say about it, the witch was going to die. And soon.

I made my way around the shadowy mountain-top, following the hunter back to her lair. I'd made an art out of tracking hunters over the past few months since Harper had been taken from us.

God, I miss her.

Life had no purpose without her by my side. When I'd stood outside the priestess's door that night, kneeling in Harper's blood, I thought I would have her back in days. I needed her back.

But need was not enough.

The emerald priestess had hidden her away somewhere no one could find her, and no matter what I did or who I killed, I hadn't been able to save her.

Being in the castle was difficult. She was everywhere, and she was nowhere. Her absence was a constant knife in my heart.

So, I left as often as I could. I hunted. I killed. I destroyed those who worked for my enemy, and their deaths were a drug that numbed the pain, if only for a while.

Already a dozen hunters had died at my hand.

After tonight, it would be thirteen.

I stayed far enough back that the hunter couldn't see or sense me, moving slowly and as quietly as the grave. My weapons were strapped to my belt and pants: Fifteen different knives and daggers. More than twenty small potions. I'd even brought an enchanted gun for when things got interesting.

But my most powerful weapon was the necklace wrapped around my left wrist. Harper's locket and her mother's pendant hung from the broken chain. I kept her most treasured items close to me at all times. They gave me purpose and kept the fear at bay. I would move heaven and earth to find her, and I wasn't going to let anyone stand in my way.

I paused near a large white boulder, shifting back to my human form and crouching low to the ground. I listened, no longer hearing the subtle flapping of the hunter's robes in the windy night. She had stopped. Her lair had to be close.

I waited, taking stock of my weapons and drawing my favorite dagger into my hand. I uncorked a swiftness potion and drank it quickly, ignoring the bitter taste of the elven root. With any luck, the hunter would be in chains before she'd even realized I was there.

When I was certain the hunter was no longer on the move, I crept out of my hiding place, following the trail. Hunters practically floated above the ground, leaving no footsteps and making them difficult to track, but I'd followed enough of them over the past few months to recognize the places where their robes had trailed along the ground, disturbing the dust and rocks and weeds along the way.

I caught sight of her trail just a few feet away and walked with nearly silent footsteps until I saw the mouth of her cave.

Many hunters lived in caves like this, carved into the side of mountains. They often had traps and wards in place to protect their homes. Many used illusions to conceal the fact that there was a cave at all, but I had the rare ability to see through illusions, making me particularly suited to tracking these hunters.

I reached inside a small leather satchel at my side and grabbed a handful of enchanted dust, one of Rend's most recent creations. I crouched in front of the cave's entrance and opened my palm, blowing the dust in front of me and searching for any sign of traps. As I suspected, the outline of a spell appeared with a brief shimmer across the middle of the entrance.

From the looks of it, this spell was nothing more than a sort of simple tripwire. If I crossed it, the spell would alert the hunter to my presence and likely unleash some sort of cave guardian, like a demon dog or a shadow guard.

It was the kind of spell I knew how to disarm. I settled my dagger back in its sheath and pulled out a special set of tools I had crafted by hand. Essex had made a special leather holster for my tools. It was nearly weightless and took up almost no space in my pocket, but when I untied the leather strap and unrolled it, the tool belt tripled in size.

I removed a simple knife with a jagged saw edge along the tip and another one that had a hook on the end. I held my breath and carefully worked at the trap. One wrong move or slip of my hand and the thing would go off, killing the element of surprise. But my hand was steady, and my skill was improving.

It was amazing what you could learn to do when love was on the line.

I disarmed the trap in less than a minute, smiling as the shimmering tripwire disappeared, leaving the entrance defenseless. I replaced my tools and put the leather roll back into my pocket, reaching once again for my favorite dagger.

I stood, my back pressed against the solid rock wall. I took a deep breath to calm my rapidly beating heart. Would this hunter know more than the others? Was this finally going to be the one who would provide some clue as to where the emerald priestess had taken Harper?

I brought the locket to my lips and kissed it for good luck before I stepped inside the hunter's cave and all hell broke loose.

DIE WITH HONOR

JACKSON

The moment I stepped into the cave, the entrance closed behind me with a slam. The hunter stood in the center of the large room, her eyes locked on my face. She laughed, the sound echoing all around me.

I spun, realizing too late that she'd been expecting me. I wasn't sure where I'd messed up, but there was no doubt she had known I was coming.

I shifted to shadow and tried to find any exit around the black magical barrier that had slammed shut around the mouth of the cave, but I was trapped. There was no way out, not even a sliver of light or space to slip through.

I shifted again and pressed my back against the barrier, lifting my dagger as I faced the hunter.

"It was only a matter of time until you came after me," she said. "But I am smarter than my fellow hunters. I won't be killed so easily, demon."

"We'll see about that," I muttered.

My eyes searched the cave, looking for any sign of an exit or weakness that could be used against her. We were on her turf, but I could handle a single hunter. All I needed was time.

I saw no exit, meaning the barrier at my back was the only way out. I had a feeling the barrier wasn't going anywhere until she was dead.

The hunter carried no weapons that I could see, but a hunter's real weapons had nothing to do with steel or daggers. The power they wielded was dark magic, given to them by their priestess when their humanity was stolen.

I gathered my own power into my core, drawing from the magic that infused the very air here in the Shadow World. But before I cast, I saw a shadow slink across the ceiling of the cave. My eyes followed the movement.

We were not alone.

My jaw tightened. In my confidence and carelessness, I had walked right into a trap. The only way out of this was to fight, and from the looks of the shadows now slinking down the walls, I was going to have my work cut out for me.

The shadows gathered at the hunter's feet, a slithering mass of darkness that covered the surface of the rock. She lifted her hands and pushed them forward, sending her small army of shadow-snakes toward me.

The snakes coiled, ready to strike. I planted my feet and gathered my power into my hands, letting it build through my body until my fingertips were covered in frost. With a great push forward, I sent a solid thread of ice across the ground.

The coiled snakes froze in place, their shadows solidified and encased in a thick blue ice.

The hunter screamed and sent a poisonous ball of green acid soaring across the space between us. I lifted my palm just before the magic reached me, a shield of frost protecting me from the blast.

The acid corroded my shield, and several drops splashed against my arms, burning deep into my skin. I ignored the pain and shifted to black smoke, twisting toward the ceiling and coming down behind the hunter. I retook my human form and shot black ropes of shadow from my hands. I wrapped them around her neck and twisted, pulling her backward against me. She sputtered and gasped, her long fingernails scratching at her own neck, trying to break free of my magic.

Her body jerked, and she vomited. Acid cascaded down her chin, burning into my ropes. I drew back as she flew forward, free of my grasp. She cupped her hands against her mouth and blew into them, a thick fog of gas filling the room. She pushed the fog toward the ground, the dark magic melting the ice around the snakes.

I sheathed my dagger, needing both hands to cast. I raised my palms in front of my body and began moving them in a circle. A sheet of ice formed, spinning in the air in front of me. I breathed in and when I released my breath into the sheet of ice, twenty spikes formed on its surface. I focused my attention on the shadow-snakes slithering toward me.

I tapped a finger on the sheet of ice and the first spike shot forward like a bullet, piercing the nearest snake's body. The shadow writhed and twisted against the ice and then disintegrated with a hiss. I repeated the motion, tapping on the sheet of ice until all twenty spikes had been deployed. I missed a few of my targets, but I'd managed to kill at least a dozen of the snakes.

There were only a handful left, but they were moving too fast. I didn't have enough time to conjure a second sheet of spikes. Instead, I shifted to smoke just as the first of the snakes reached me, its fangs embedding into the rock where I had just stood.

I moved toward the entrance of the cave, getting as far away from the snakes as I could, but just as I shifted back to human form, the ground under my feet began to rumble. I swallowed and pushed my fear down into the depths of my being. I couldn't afford to be afraid right now. I had to be strong.

Dust fell around me as the walls of the cave shifted. My eyes widened as the rock actually moved, four large boulders rolling forward and joining the hunter in the center of the cave. The rocks shifted into small statues about half the height of the hunter. They each wore a single emerald around their necks.

I cursed. How the hell had she managed to tame four rock golems?

The hunter's eyes glowed a deep green as she looked at me.

"You should give up now, demon, while you still have your life," she said. "The emerald priestess would prefer to use you to open a new emerald gate than see you dead at my hands."

I studied the golems. They were only minor rock golems, not fully matured. Still, they would not be easy to kill. I needed to keep my focus on the hunter. If she died, whatever power she held over them would be destroyed.

Getting to her would be the hard part. Rock golems were notorious defenders and protectors. They wouldn't give her up easily.

"It will be tough for her to open any new gates without her

hunters," I said. "And I've made it my mission to kill every last one of you."

The hunter narrowed her eyes and the side of her mouth twisted into a gruesome smile. "Miracashi. Melomorra." The moment the foreign words touched her lips, the rock golems rushed toward me, their bodies rolling across the stone floor so fast my eyes could hardly keep track of them.

I managed to shift, but before I could fly above their heads, the first golem reached up and touched its stone hand to my shadow. My entire body solidified in an instant and fell to the ground.

I could still see and hear, but I couldn't move.

Panic ripped through my heart. My power had been encased in stone once before, and the sensation that held me to this form was eerily familiar.

I pushed against it, struggling to shift, but unable to reach my magic.

The golem turned me over so that my back was against the floor. I looked up into its dark stone eyes, hatred burning in my heart. How could this have happened? I'd been so careful, taking every precaution to make sure I had not been followed.

But this hunter had known I was coming.

Either that or the emerald priestess had gotten tired of me killing her slaves. Maybe she'd equipped all of her remaining hunters with their own personal rock golem guards.

If that was true, things just got a lot more difficult for me.

The hunter moved to stand over me, her stink filling my nostrils. "The emerald priestess will be so pleased to know you are still alive," she said. "Your power will be useful to the Order of Shadows."

I only had one last trick up my sleeve, and I poured my

whole heart into it. My power was dull, but not gone completely. I could still feel it building inside of me. I used every ounce of energy I had to send tiny streams of frozen power through the minuscule cracks and weak points in the stone around my hand. When I felt the ice reach my fingertips, I closed my eyes, needing every bit of my concentration to pull this off.

I pushed my power through those small cracks, forcing the ice to expand. The rock around my hand exploded. Shards of stone flew through the air. I reached for the bag of potions still strapped to my leg. I quickly felt for the small round bottle among the glass tubes and let out a breath of relief as my fingers closed around it.

I smashed the vial, glass piercing my skin, allowing the liquid inside the bottle to seep into my veins.

I sent up a silent word of thanks to the vampire Rend, who had insisted I take a negate magic potion with me. I knew how to make a handful of potions, but Rend was a master alchemist, his skill and power much more potent than my own.

The potion flowed through me as fast as a streak of lightning, and the stone around me disintegrated in a cloud of dust. The rock golems lunged toward me, but I was too fast for them. I shifted to smoke and flew straight into the air, passing over their heads and aiming straight for the hunter and her snakes.

She shrieked and floated forward, searching the dark cave for me. I gathered my energy in the air and formed a single dagger of thick ice, grabbing for the silver dagger at my hip at the same time. I reformed behind the hunter and plunged the ice dagger into her back, hoping to hit what was left of her rotting heart.

She screamed and fell to her knees. The dagger melted in

my hand, but I already had my silver dagger at her throat. What remained of her snakes attacked, their fangs sinking into the flesh at my ankles and calves, but I forced my mind against the pain.

Something clanked against my dagger, and I noticed for the first time that the hunter wore a necklace strung with four emeralds around her neck.

I smiled. So, this was how she was controlling the golems: one matching stone for each of them.

I used my free hand to yank the strand of emerald beads from her neck. I held them in my hands, allowing the power of my ice-magic to cover them. The four rock golems stopped instantly, their stone bodies freezing in place at my command.

I held my dagger close to the hunter's neck, allowing the blade to sink into her corroded skin just enough to keep her from moving. With a deep breath, I forced freezing magic through my veins, focusing on the lower half of my body. Ice crackled as the snakes drew the magic in through their fangs and froze in place.

"Where is the emerald priestess keeping her?" I asked, my teeth gritting against the pain in my legs. "Tell me and I will spare what is left of your life."

The hunter's shoulders slumped forward, and she practically leaned into my blade.

"You are a true warrior," she said. "But after all the killing, you have yet to learn the most important truth."

"What truth?" I asked.

"No hunter will ever tell you the secrets of the emerald priestess," she said. "The moment any hint of it left our bodies, we would disintegrate in an instant. It's part of the magic that keeps us loyal. How can you not have recognized this by now?"

The air left my body, as if she had kicked me in the stomach.

I'd spent months tracking and torturing hunters, praying for one of them to break down and give me some clue as to where I could find Harper or the emerald priestess. None of them had spoken a word to me of their whereabouts, and I had cursed their loyalty to a priestess who had offered them nothing but sorrow. I had wondered why none of these former witches had been willing to turn on a woman who had stolen their lives from them.

"You're going to die, anyway," I said, leaning close to the hunter's ear. "Make the sacrifice of your life—of who you were before she turned you into this rotting pile of flesh—mean something. Die with honor and tell me where I can find your priestess."

The hunter drew in a shuddering breath, and a drop of burning acid fell on the back of my hand.

She was crying.

"I used to be beautiful," she whispered. "I was young, and like you, I was in love. My priestess did not approve of my love and had promised me to another. If I tell you something, you have to promise me one thing."

"Anything," I said, my heart pounding.

"Find Kristie. Find my mother. Tell them I'm sorry," she said. "Please, tell Kristie I love her and that I died clinging onto what was left of my humanity."

"I will find them," I said. "I promise you."

"When Priestess Evers took me from my home for refusing to follow her plan for my life, she brought me to a place near her home," she said, her words coming rapidly. "An institution filled with other girls. She meant to add me to her collection."

Her body began to decay as the truth poured forth from her. Acid pooled at my feet, and I stepped back, removing my dagger from her throat.

"What collection?" I asked quickly. "Where?"

The hunter turned to face me, her skin almost melting from her bones. Tears of thick acid streamed down her face, and for a brief moment, I could see the girl she once was.

"I don't know where it is," she said. "But she has a collection of them. Hundreds of them. That's where you'll find your Harper, if she's still alive."

The hunter fell to her knees as the rest of her body disintegrated into a pool of acid, corroding the rock beneath her.

I collapsed onto the ground, tears in my own eyes. "No," I shouted. "Don't go yet. I need to know where she is. I need to find her."

I pounded my fist against the stone, knowing it was no use. The hunter was gone and could tell me no more.

I'D LIKE TO SEE YOU TRY IT

AERDEN

The sound of steel hitting steel pulled me from my nightmares. My body tensed, every muscle aching from weeks of sleeping on the harsh stone floor. Around me, demons groaned and mumbled as they sat up and rubbed the sleep from their eyes.

"Get up, prisoners," the guard shouted. "It's another day in paradise."

I narrowed my gaze. This guard was one of my least favorites. Karn. He was mean to the weakest among us, using any excuse to serve a few extra lashings on those who deserved it the least. His soul was dark, and I hated him with intensity.

Anyone who would prey on the least fortunate didn't deserve to be in charge of prisoners. Especially prisoners who were mostly innocent of any crime worse than simply trying to survive in a world ravaged by the Order of Shadows.

I'd heard Andros speak of the deterioration of the kingdom, but I never expected this level of destruction and depression. I'd had a hundred years to come to terms with the fact that my king and family had abandoned me to my fate, but understanding how the king could abandon everyone who didn't benefit him in some way was beyond me.

I hadn't spent much time above ground in the King's City, but what I had seen here in his prison told me all I needed to know.

The king was no longer concerned with justice or the well-being of his people. He had either lost his mind or been turned by greed and fear. Either way, I didn't care to serve him.

There was once a day when I was in training to become the captain of the King's Guard. But that was a long time ago, when I was someone else. Someone I barely remembered these days.

"What are you staring at, prisoner?" Karn said.

I realized he was talking to me. I lowered my head, letting my long, dark hair cover most of my face.

"That's right. You aren't worthy to look upon my face," he said, a sick kind of joy in his tone. "Maybe I'll place you in the front of the line today. Let you learn to really pull your own weight around here."

I didn't answer or speak back to him, but I swore that one day, when he least expected it, I would repay his kindness.

"Let's go. We don't have all day," he said, turning his attention to the other demons in the room.

About twenty-six of us were crammed together in a cell that should have held no more than ten demons. My second day in the dungeons, I'd been dragged from my cell adjoining Lea's and brought here, where I was forced to work in the quarries, mining gemstones.

I hadn't seen Lea since that day, but there wasn't a moment when I didn't think of her.

Was she okay? Were they treating her well?

And how was I going to escape so that I could get her out of there?

I didn't trust her father. Especially not now that I'd seen with my own eyes how much he valued his own people these days. A lot could really change in a hundred years.

The guards sneered and pushed as we filed out of the cell toward the mess hall. I kept my head down, not wanting to draw attention to myself. So far no one in this godforsaken place had recognized me. None of the guards seemed to know who I was, and I intended to keep it that way.

If these guys found out I was the son of the king's closest advisor and a former slave of the Order, it could cause some real trouble for me. I wanted to be as invisible as possible until I figured out the right moment to escape.

For the past few months, I'd been paying attention to every detail of our routine. Every shift change. Every key ring. Every guard's uniform, name, and disposition. Nothing went unnoticed. After a century locked inside someone else's body without the ability to talk or control anything around me, I'd gotten very good at observation.

But so far, no plan had emerged. Without magic or weapons, I was powerless.

I just had to be patient and hold on. I had to wait for the perfect moment when the routine was off, or all the guards were looking the other way.

They had pulled me away from Lea just when I was starting to finally remember what it was to hope. I still thought of the way it felt to touch her cheek with the back of my hand.

The way her black hair fell across her shoulder when she tilted her eyes toward mine.

Those memories were the only thing that allowed me to keep my head down and be patient.

Someday, I would find my way back to her. Even if I had to kill every guard in the castle.

I shuffled through the line and carried my daily portion of food to the stone tables lining the room. I chose a seat at the very end, away from any of the others. Just like every day. I didn't speak to anyone, and I kept my eyes hidden. The less they knew of me the better.

The four demons sitting closest to me were debating about the uses for the gemstones we'd been mining. I kept my ears open and my head down as I shoveled the cold paste they called food into my mouth.

"But why would the king need so many sapphires?" an older man named Trention said.

Trention was one of the few demons I recognized in this place, though he didn't seem to recognize me. He used to be a top scholar in the castle and the headmaster of the city's school. It was a prestigious position that took hundreds of years of study to obtain, and I couldn't help but wonder why such an intelligent and decorated demon had been thrown in the dungeons with criminals. I'd never heard him say.

"I don't see why it matters what color stone we're mining," a demon with eyes as dark as the Black Cliffs said. I'd heard others call him Soran. "It still hurts like hell at the end of a long day, no matter if it's sapphires or rubies."

"For all we know, the king is stacking them up in his chambers, so he can sleep on them at night," a tall demon named

Priyo said. "The old demon lost his mind a long time ago, if you ask me."

"It matters because the sapphire quarries haven't been mined this hard in centuries," Trention said. "Most demons don't even know the quarries just outside the gates exist. Over the years, the king and his guard have been very careful to keep them hidden so that other demons wouldn't steal them. But some of the other stones like rubies or amethysts are much more useful. Rubies are the basis of most communication spells and are used for things like powering lights. Amethysts are used for healing and growing crops, but sapphires? What use would the king have for a hundred thousand sapphires?"

I wondered if any of them knew about the fall of the sapphire gates in the human world. Could that have anything to do with why the king suddenly needed a stockpile of sapphire stones?

Most of us weren't even halfway through the pitiful bowl of food we'd been given before the guards started clapping their hands and shouting at us to fall into line to be shackled.

Many of the demons in the room groaned and protested, but as always, I kept my head down and did as I was told. I was uniquely suited to being a slave, after all, and if there was one thing I was still good at in this world, it was following directions.

And biding my time.

Let them think I was docile and weak. What did I care? I just wanted them to ignore me, and so far, it was working.

As a guard named Thoriare passed by, I held my hands out. He slammed a silver shackle on each of my wrists. The shackles were all connected by a strong link of chain that kept us in line and bound to one another as one long group. The material the chains were made of had the unique property of blocking any demon's magic so that we couldn't cast. Down here in the dungeons, our magic was blocked by spells, but outside the gates in the sunlight, they needed these shackles to keep us in line.

Still, they seemed to trust us with tools to mine, and as we marched through the dark corridor that wound under the streets of the King's City and out toward the mines, I gripped my pickaxe tightly in my hand.

As the sun came into view, I lifted my face and let its warmth wash over me. This was my favorite part of the day. Many of the others complained about the physical labor of having to mine all day without a break, but I loved it. I enjoyed being outside when the weather was nice. I loved the feel of the axe in my hand, even though this one was nothing like my old weapon.

This was a quarter as heavy as the weapon I'd favored as a young demon and only had a small pick on the front end instead of a broad axe-head, but it was close enough to give me comfort in these dark times.

And since the power of my magic had seemed to abandon me, I knew my unique ability to fight well with a weapon in hand-to-hand combat would become useful someday soon. The more chances I had to strengthen my muscles, the better.

Karn hadn't followed through on his threat. He seemed to have forgotten about me again and was walking down the line, scrutinizing every demon's movements. I'd seen him in this type of mood before, and it made the muscles in my jaw tense.

I kept one eye on him as I reared back and swung down hard against the blue stones. I thought back to the conversation in the mess hall about the stones, and a part of me wondered if our time in the sapphire quarry had more to do with punishing me than anything else. Was this the king's way of saying he wished I'd never been rescued? That he wanted to punish me for stealing his daughter away from him?

But Lea's leaving had not been my fault. I'd never expected my brother to abandon the kingdom to come after me. I thought he would marry her and forget me. I never dreamed they would both risk everything to save my life.

But I'd also never dreamed that I could be saved.

If life had taught me anything so far, it was that no matter what situation you found yourself in, you should never lose hope. Even the most desperate of no-way-out scenarios can be defeated as long as there is someone out there who loves you enough to risk everything to save you.

Karn passed by me and continued down the line. I relaxed slightly. He was looking for trouble, but at least he'd decided not to pick on me today.

I kept swinging, concentrating only on the feel of the warm sun on my face and the satisfaction of feeling my muscles stretch and tighten. I may have been a prisoner, but nothing about this compared to the torture I'd endured as a slave to the Order. Nothing compared to not being able to control my own power. To not be able to feel my muscles or my body. For a hundred years, I was nothing but a battery.

Here, at least, I was a demon with my own true form and no one else's voice in my head.

In front of me, the scholar, Trention, winced and grabbed his arm. His axe fell to the stones with a thud. On instinct, I reached out to help steady him.

He coughed and nodded. "Thank you," he said.

"You okay?" It was the most I'd said to anyone in weeks.

He touched a hand to his shoulder and groaned. "It's just a cut on my shoulder," he said. "It's been bothering me lately, but I'm sure I'll be fine."

I wondered just how old he was. By my guess he had to be no less than five or six hundred years old. A demon of his age and stature didn't need to be out here working.

Trention glanced nervously in Karn's direction. He steadied himself and attempted to pick up his axe, but it dropped right back down to the ground and he cried out. He tripped on a protruding stone and fell backward. I used my axe to keep my balance and reached out for him.

"Sit down a minute," I said. "Take a rest."

He laughed and held his hand to his shoulder. "I don't think the guards will look too kindly on any one of us taking a break," he said. "Get back to your work and leave this old demon alone before you get yourself into some trouble."

"Don't worry about me," I said.

He narrowed his eyes and tilted his head to the side. "You don't like to draw much attention, do you? Keep mostly to yourself. You're always hiding your face until we get out here in the sun, and then you seem to worship it as if you'd lived a thousand years in the darkness."

I raised an eyebrow. Apparently, I wasn't the only observant one in this place. If he only knew just how close he was to the truth.

I didn't confirm or deny his observations. I simply stepped back and lifted my axe, letting it soar over my head and embed into the hard sapphire stones at my feet. A large piece chipped off, and I tossed the gemstone into a large steel wagon a few feet away.

The old man coughed again and when I looked up, his skin

was covered in sweat. His face had grown pale. I stretched the chain, so I could move closer to him, setting my axe down at my side.

"You're burning up with fever," I said, touching a hand to his head.

He shivered and drew a shaky breath. "I'll be fine," he said. "Perhaps it's time for this old man to pass on, anyway. If I hadn't been thrown in the dungeons, I may have chosen to pass my spirit on to my daughter by now."

The sorrow in his voice echoed in my heart. I knew that kind of pain and regret, and it wasn't fair to hear such an esteemed demon have such regret. He should have been able to choose the time of his passing. He had earned that.

"Stand up, prisoners," Karn shouted. His whip snapped against the blue stones, and I stood to face him, careful to keep my head down and my hands ready. "What's going on here? No one gave you permission to carry on a conversation."

"I'm not feeling well," Trention said. "This young demon was encouraging me to get back up and get to work."

"Was he now?" Karn said, stepping closer to me.

I forced a deep breath, reminding myself that right now patience was a virtue. And I could be patient. I'd been practicing for what felt like an eternity.

Karn turned his attention away from me and snapped his whip close to the old man's head. "And what made you think you could take a break?" he asked. "I don't care if you're half-dead. You don't stop mining without my permission. Now get up, old man. And you, get back to work."

I backed away and retrieved my axe but kept one eye on the old man. He tried to use his axe as leverage to stand, but he was weak and sick.

It was rare for a demon to be so torn up with fever. Demons were immortal, but sometimes wounds didn't heal, and infection set in. If I had to guess, there was some kind of nasty wound under the old demon's tunic.

"Stand up," Karn said again.

Trention struggled to stand, and it took every ounce of my patience not to offer my hand to him. But I knew that offering my help would only make it worse for both of us.

"Now, or I'll give you six lashes," Karn said.

By now, our little section of the chain had started to draw attention. Most of the demons on the line tried to keep swinging their axes just enough to look like they were still working, but their eyes were on us, and just like me, they were all pulling for Trention to stand. No one wanted to see the eldest among us get six lashes.

Six lashes from Karn was likely to kill him, and I'd be damned if I could stand by and let that happen.

Don't intervene.

I knew that the worst possible thing I could do would be to stand in Karn's way, but something bigger than my patience had already taken control.

Trention attempted to stand one more time, but rocked forward and then back again, falling down with a groan.

Karn lifted his whip and before I was even aware of my actions, the sharp sting of leather burned a path across the skin of my back.

A gasp rippled through the group of chained men as I twisted my body and grabbed the end of the whip. I quickly wrapped it around my arm and pulled the guard forward, anger searing through my veins.

With my other hand, I reached for the handle of my axe,

lifting it with such accuracy and speed that the tip of it grazed Karn's neck before he even realized what was happening. A spot of blood formed on the collar of his uniform.

Karn jerked toward me, his eyes wide. He yanked against the whip, but I held fast, already acutely aware that I held more strength in one hand than this guard had in his entire body.

"How dare you stand in the way of my punishment, prisoner," he said through gritted teeth. "Let go of this whip before I end your life."

"I'd like to see you try it," I said, pushing the tip of the pickaxe deeper into his neck.

Shadows zoomed toward us as the other guards realized what was happening. My stomach knotted at the loss of my anonymity, but I could not regret my actions. I couldn't stand by and watch an innocent demon be tortured.

"Seize this prisoner," Reynar, the head guard, said. If Karn was one of my least favorites, he had nothing on Reynar. He was the worst of the worst, and I shuddered at the things I had seen him do to some of the other prisoners.

Two of the guards grabbed my arms and pulled me backward. I released my grip on the leather and let it unwind itself from my hand as they hauled me several steps back.

"What happened here?" he demanded.

"I found the old man sitting on the job, and when I went to punish him, this prisoner stepped in the way and threatened me." Karn dabbed a rag on his neck, soaking it in blood.

Rage surged through me, but I didn't try to pull away from the guards. I was outnumbered and shackled to more than twenty other demons. There was no hope of escape, and from the look on Reynar's face, I was about to be punished in a way I'd remember for many days to come.

He stepped forward, standing between me and Karn. "It seems you have forgotten your place, prisoner," he said. "What makes you think you have the right to stand in the way of any demon's punishment?"

"Justice gave me the right," I said. "That used to be a word the King's Guard understood."

His nostrils flared, and he held his hand to his hip where his dagger glinted in the sun's rays. "You should think about who you're talking to before you open that mouth of yours again," he said. "You are a prisoner and traitor. What could you possibly know about justice?"

"I know it's not right to whip a demon who's ill and needs medical attention," I said. My brain told me to keep my mouth shut, but all thoughts of patience and invisibility had been replaced with rage.

"I could have you sentenced to death for threatening a guard," Reynar said. "Are you really willing to sacrifice your life for this old man?"

I lifted my chin and tensed my jaw. "I would rather die serving justice than live serving a king whose mind has been twisted by greed and power and fear. I would rather stand up for those less fortunate than prey on the weak."

A rumble erupted through the group of shackled demons.

Reynar lifted his hands and chains of lightning shot forth. The guards at my side dropped my arms and backed away as the magic slammed against my body. Pain ripped through me, every muscle crying out in agony.

But I stood my ground, refusing to fall to my knees. I locked my eyes with his and concentrated instead on memorizing every inch of his face. Someday, when I was free again, I would revisit this man and let him know what happens to those who find enjoyment torturing the innocent.

Reynar's eyes darkened. He took a deep breath and poured more of his power into the lightning. My knees started to buckle, but I would not fall.

Years of torture had taught me more than just patience. I found that it had also taught me endurance. He wanted to hurt me for my defiance, but if he wanted to play that game with me, he would find that it would take a lot more than lightning to even scratch the surface of what I'd already endured in my lifetime.

"Fall, damn you," he shouted. He pushed himself to the limit of his power and then staggered backward, the spell faltering as he tightened his hands into fists.

He reached down and grabbed the handle of my fallen axe. In the slow and clunky movements of someone who was not used to wielding a physical weapon, he lifted the edge of the blade to my neck and stared into my eyes.

"If you think I wouldn't end you right here, you have obviously underestimated my hatred for scum like you," he said.

"If you think you're capable of such a thing, you're the one who has misjudged this situation," I said.

Before he could press the tip of the axe deeper into my skin, I twisted my body and planted my foot directly in the chest of one of the guards who'd been holding me. Careful to not get tangled in my chains, I lifted them over my head and spun again, knocking the second guard several feet back.

As I came around, my hands gripped the top and bottom of the axe's handle and I twisted it around until the blade sank into Reynar's chest just above his heart. The fear in his eyes told me how much of a mistake I'd made. I hadn't meant to show them the extent of my power, but after all this time of holding back, I'd finally reached my boiling point.

And I was certainly going to pay for it.

Part of me wanted to sink the blade into his corroded heart and see the end of him.

But a stronger part of me wasn't ready to die just yet. And death would most certainly be my sentence if I murdered a guard out here in the presence of so many witnesses.

"That's enough." A powerful voice boomed across the quarry of stones.

I stared into Reynar's eyes and smiled. "You lucky bastard," I said, my voice so low no one else could hear me.

"This isn't finished between us," he said through clenched teeth.

You're damn right it isn't.

Ezrah, one of the ten lieutenants of the King's Guard, shifted to smoke and reappeared at my side. "Release this guard, prisoner," he said.

I dropped the pickaxe and stepped away, the chains around my wrists clanging together as I walked.

"I want this prisoner put in solitary confinement and brought before the Council," Reynar said, standing. Sweat dripped down his forehead and his color had turned pale. He lifted his chin, but he couldn't wipe the fear from his eyes.

"This prisoner is protected by someone on the Council, soldier," Ezrah said. "He will spend a week in confinement and then return to the dungeons."

"This is outrageous, sir. Did you see what he did to me? To my men? I won't—"

"You will," Ezrah said. "Or you will be removed from the king's service immediately."

Reynar's face nearly turned purple, and I had to suppress a smile.

I was still going to pay for this moment in a million tiny ways, but at least for now, I was protected. I was alive.

"Yes, sir," Reynar sputtered. "But—"

"We can discuss this later," he said. "For now, I will take this prisoner back to his cell and see that he is properly punished."

"Lieutenant—"

"Enough," Ezrah said again. "This matter is finished. Get the prisoners back to work."

Reynar cleared his throat and glared at me.

Yes, I would pay for this. But it would be worth it.

As Ezrah unlocked the shackles that restrained my wrists, I dared a glance at the old man. His eyes met mine for a brief moment and he nodded, the beginnings of a smile playing at the corners of his lips. I nodded back, and then quietly followed Ezrah through the corridors to the containment cell.

"I told you to keep your head down," Ezrah said as he locked me inside.

"I was," I said.

"You call standing in front of the whip and threatening the worst guard on the block keeping your head down?" he asked, his hands gripping the bars of the cell.

"I couldn't stand there while he whipped that old man. He's a scholar, for Christ's sake," I said.

Ezrah shook his head. "You talk like a human."

I shrugged.

"I'll do what I can to mitigate the damages here, but you

can't do something like this again," he said. "If you want to have any shot at getting out of prison and into the King's City again, you have to play by the rules, no matter how unfair or awful they may be. Trust me, I've wanted to whip Karn myself a few times, but punishing him or stopping him would betray my position, and we have to always remember there is a greater war at stake here."

"Doing things for the greater good means nothing if all the people on the bottom still suffer," I said.

"Please, Aerden, you have to hang on just a little while longer," he said. "I need more time."

I shifted my weight and lowered my head. He was right. What I did today was stupid, and it put everything in danger. If the king or any of his guards found out about Ezrah's loyalty to Andros and the Resistance, all hope would be gone.

"I'm sorry," I said. "It won't happen again."

"I will have to whip you," he said, his voice filled with sorrow.

"Get it done, then," I said.

I removed my tunic and turned around, gripping the bars as the whip slashed against my back. I winced, but I endured the lashings with as much dignity as I could. Every time he lifted the weapon, I imagined the face of the first witch I saw when I was taken from this world and bound to slavery in the human world.

Priestess Winter.

I saw the greed and hunger in her eyes. To her, my only value was in the power that ran through my veins.

I pictured Harper ripping the woman's heart from her chest and the way Priestess Winter looked as she disintegrated to dust.

And I remembered the way it had felt to finally break free.

No pain or torture could ever take that moment away from me. That was the moment my life was given back to me. And there was no prison in any world that could hold me now.

Not for long.

When he was finished, he used a cloth to gently wipe the blood from my wounds.

"Have you seen her?" I asked softly.

"Three days ago," he said.

"How is she?"

My heart raced at the thought of Lea. I understood what it was like to be alone in the dark for long periods of time, but Lea deserved so much more. She wasn't used to being locked in a cage.

"She's having a rough time, but you know her. She's tough. She'll make it through," he said.

"Tell her I..." I paused, unsure of what message I could send that would possibly help her through this dark time. I wanted to tell her I loved her. I never should have waited this long.

I wanted to tell her that I would do anything—including sacrifice my own life—in order to save her from suffering.

"Tell her the light is never as far away as it seems," I said finally.

Ezrah nodded. "I will," he said. "Aerden, please keep your head down. Karn and Reynar will both have it out for you after this. I'm sorry I had to be the one to cause you so much pain."

His voice ached with regret.

"Pain is an old friend, Lieutenant," I said as he closed the bars between us. "It simply reminds me what I'm fighting for."

THIS IS MY FIGHT

JACKSON

"Where have you been?" Illana asked, catching me at the top of the stairs as I returned to the castle in the Southern Kingdom. "You've killed another one, haven't you? You're turning into a monster, Denaer. I hardly recognize you."

"My name is Jackson now," I said. I ran a hand through my hair, not caring that there was still blood streaked across the edge of my palm.

Of all people, my own sister should have understood how difficult this was for me, but losing our brother all those years ago had not broken her the way it had broken me. She had gone on living her life, while mine had stopped completely.

It was Harper who had brought me back to life, couldn't she see that?

"You have to stop," Illana said, touching my arm and gasping at the wound. "You're hurt again. It's too dangerous to keep going out like this alone."

I pulled away and winced as I put my weight on my left leg. The shadow-snakes had done a real number on me, and I needed time alone to focus and heal before the poison spread too far.

"Don't tell me what I have to do," I said. "You especially have no right to tell me how to act when it comes to trying to save someone I love."

She recoiled, her face crumpling and her lips falling open. She shook her head. "Denaer, that isn't fair at all."

"At least I'm out there risking my life to save them and bring them all home," I said. "What did you ever do? You abandoned our brother, just like everyone else. You did nothing to save him. Nothing to help me. You have no idea what it's been like for all of us."

"And you think it was easy living in the castle without you?" she asked. "Watching our mother and father struggle every day with the sorrow of losing both of their sons? Having to be everything they needed us to be just to try to keep our family together? To keep our sanity?"

I swallowed and drew my hand into a tight fist. I didn't want to argue with my sister, but she had no idea what she was talking about.

"I'm sorry if your life inside the safety of the King's City was so hard for you," I said. "I'm sure having everything you ever wanted delivered to you on a silver platter was just torture."

Tears glistened in her eyes and she turned her head to the side to hide them. "I love him, too," she said. "And I love you. I was scared, Denaer. You have to understand that. We all were."

"It's Jackson," I said sharply. "I will never be Denaer again. I've been through too much to even remember who he was."

"Jackson, I'm sorry," she said softly. "I honestly didn't think I had a choice all those years ago. I didn't think there was any hope for our brother, but I'm here now. That has to count for something."

"Why are you here?" I asked. "I mean, other than being kidnapped by the emerald priestess and needing us to save you. Why did you leave the castle in the first place?"

"Because I needed to see you both," she said, blinking. "I heard rumors that Aerden was free, but our mother denied it. I needed to see for myself."

I shook my head at the irony of the situation. She left the castle, risking her life to see Aerden, and now he was locked away in the dungeons of that same castle. Maybe whatever god they prayed to in the human world truly did have a wicked sense of humor.

"Too little, too late," I said through clenched teeth.

I walked past my sister, heading toward the steps that would lead me back to Harper's room. I could hardly stand after the difficult journey home. I needed to rest and go through the things I had found inside the hunter's lair.

She hadn't given me much, but it was the most information I'd gotten from any of the hunters so far. The emerald priestess had a place where she took these girls who had disobeyed her. She had some kind of collection, and I needed to figure out what that meant.

I had to find a way. I had to get her back.

I had to get all of them back. At least Aerden and Lea were safe in the King's City. Andros, the leader of the Resistance Army, had a man on the inside acting as one of the King's Royal Guard. He'd sent word to us that Lea and Aerden were captured and thrown in the dungeons. They were prisoners, but they were safe.

Until we had a plan in place, that would have to be good enough.

But where the hell was Harper?

Thoughts of what she must be going through haunted me day and night. I hadn't really slept in as long as I could remember.

Illana touched my arm, jerking me from my thoughts. I took a deep breath and turned to her. This wasn't her fault, but she had never once fought for those she loved. She couldn't understand what this was like for me.

"You have to stop this madness," she said. "You need to take some time away from this constant search. You're killing yourself, De—Jackson."

"I can't rest until I've found her," I said. "If you can't understand that, then you might as well go home."

Her eyebrows twitched as she studied my face. "You don't mean that."

"Don't I?" I asked. "You're only going to put yourself in more danger if you stay, so unless you plan to help me, there's no reason for you to stick around. You'd be safer back home in the King's City where the Order can't get to you."

A tear fell down her cheek, and she shook her head. "I miss the brother you used to be," she said. "If this is the demon you've turned into, maybe I should go back."

"Then go," I shouted.

Her head fell into her hands, and she turned and ran from the room, her shoulders shaking with sobs.

I grunted and rammed my fist into the nearest wall as hard

as I could, relishing the feel of blood as it snaked down my knuckles and onto the floor.

I hadn't meant to make her cry, but the last thing I needed right now was someone lecturing me about what I was doing. It was my job to find Harper.

And if I was even a split second too late, she might be lost to all of us forever.

What would happen to the world if she was gone?

My sister said she was grateful our brother had been freed, but she didn't seem to understand that none of that would have been possible without Harper.

For more than fifty years I had searched for a way to free my brother from slavery. I sought out wise men, mystics, oracles, even dark magic users, searching for answers. There had to be a way to free him from his bindings as the Prima demon of Peachville. But no one, not even the wisest and oldest of them had answers for me. Nothing I tried made any difference.

Until her.

I leaned my head against the cool stone and closed my eyes. I could still picture the way she looked down at me from the window of her bedroom at Shadowford that first day. Her blonde hair fell over her shoulder and the sun glinted on the glass, covering her in golden light.

Something inside me changed that day. She was the one, and I knew it. The one hope I had of ever saving my brother.

I never expected her to save me, too.

I couldn't lose her. I would risk everything to save her, and it was killing me that it had already been four long months.

God, what were they doing to her?

I slammed my hand against the stone again and pushed away from it. I had to find another way.

Killing hunters wasn't working. If they couldn't betray their priestess without dying for the crime, I would never get more than just a few quick confessions as their bodies turned to ash and acid. It wasn't enough. I needed to find someone who knew where to find the emerald priestess's collection. But who? Where?

I climbed the three flights of stairs to the north tower, the pain so great now that I couldn't even focus enough to shift to my demon form.

I took a deep breath and paused outside the large wooden door. I rested my palm flat against it, feeling the smooth grain of the juniper tree against my skin before I pushed through as quietly as I could.

When the sky came into view through the open archways in the tower, I was shocked to see that the moons had risen, and the suns were gone. It had taken me more than a day to get home after killing the hunter.

More time wasted, with almost nothing to show for it.

This room had become like a sanctuary to me. A place I came to pray to whatever god might be listening.

The candles had long worn down, so I conjured fresh ones, placing them in the holders spread evenly throughout the room. It was a simple rotunda with no furnishings except for the carved table that held the cocoon and a simple wooden stool.

I sat down and pulled the stool up as close to the table as it would go. I reached into my pocket and took out a folded piece of paper that had become so weathered and worn that the image I'd drawn onto it had become smudged and torn at the edges.

I unfolded the square of paper, fresh tears finally falling freely.

I ran my thumb along the edge of the sheet, touching Harper's crown and staring down at the silver eyes of our son. I couldn't see our faces in the picture. I had only drawn us from the back, but I was sure that there were smiles on our faces. It was the only hope I had left of the future.

No matter what we were going through now, someday this would be our life. I had to believe it.

The paper fluttered to the floor, and I clasped my hands together as I bent over the still cocoon.

"Zara," I whispered. "I need you to wake up. Please. Come back to us. I need you."

I rested my forehead against my hands.

Zara was the last one to see Harper before she was taken. She was there when Harper fought the emerald priestess.

What happened that night?

What did the emerald priestess do to Zara? How did she defeat Harper?

Not having any of the answers was eating me alive.

I was the one who had promised to protect her. How did I lose sight of her during the battle? I hadn't even realized she was gone until it was too late.

"Zara, if you could just tell me what happened," I said. "Maybe you could give us some clue about where they took her."

I had no idea if Zara could hear me. The shaman had said that Zara was still alive but going through some kind of mystical transformation. No one knew how long that transition might take. It could be weeks, or it could be decades.

All I knew was that I wanted her back.

I wanted Brighton Manor back, and I wanted it to be full of family again. Many of us were living here in the castle now. Mary Anne and Essex. Angela, Harper's half-sister, had stepped in to rule the kingdom in Harper's absence. My sister Illana was here, and sometimes Lea's best friends—Mordecai, Erick, Joost, and Cristo—were often here for short periods of time.

I was grateful for them, and I was glad we had a place to live, but it wasn't the same. This place was empty without Harper, but we'd been a family back at Brighton Manor.

We'd been happy.

Our time together hadn't lasted nearly long enough. I would have given anything to go back to those times before the emerald priestess took it all away.

"Jackson?" A small voice echoed in the chamber just outside the tower room. "Are you in there?"

"I'm here." I sat up as Mary Anne walked into the room.

"I thought I might find you up here," she said. Her normally bright blue eyes were clouded with worry.

It was a look I'd seen a lot over the past few months.

Everyone was worried about me. They thought I was being reckless and stupid, acting on anger alone instead of stepping back to make a plan.

But where had their plans gotten them?

Harper was still missing. My brother and Lea were still locked away in the dungeons with an entire army guarding them. Courtney was still dead. And Zara? I wasn't even sure if she could hear us from inside her cocoon, or if she would ever return to us.

"Illana told me you killed another hunter," she said.

I tensed, waiting for the judgment that I knew would follow. No one approved of my plan to try to bleed information from the hunters. They all believed it was far too dangerous for me to keep chasing after them, but what they didn't understand was that I needed this. I needed something to keep from going insane, and tracking hunters was the only outlet I had these days.

Besides, the fewer hunters there were in the world, the better.

"You're injured," she said, reaching for my arm. "You should go see Angela."

I waved her away. I would deal with my injuries in a minute. For now, I just wanted to sit here and rest.

"Did she give you any useful information?" Mary Anne said. It wasn't really a question.

"None of them do," I said, not wanting to talk about what I'd learned. Not until it meant something real.

"Then why do you keep hunting them?"

"Because I want them all dead," I said. "I want the emerald priestess to know that I'll hunt down every single witch in her covens if that's what it takes."

"You don't mean that."

"Oh yes, I do."

"What about Eloise and her daughters?"

I closed my eyes and shook my head. "You know what I mean."

"It's hard to know what you mean these days, Jackson," she said. "I can see from the way your whole body just tensed up that this isn't what you want to hear, but I've been letting this go on too long without saying anything. I can't do it anymore."

"Can't do what?"

"Watch you tear yourself apart," she said. "I can't watch you practically destroy yourself looking for her. You're not even sleeping, are you?"

"I don't need sleep," I said. "I need Harper."

I cleared my throat and adjusted my position in the chair. It was one thing when my sister lectured me, but it was much worse coming from Mary Anne. My sister had never met Harper. Not really. Harper had saved her life and they'd never even gotten the chance to speak to each other.

Illana couldn't understand what this loss meant to all of us, and she certainly didn't have any place telling us how we should be acting.

But Mary Anne was a part of this family. She'd been extremely close to Harper, and I knew she missed her just as much as I did.

I didn't want to hear her lecture me about this.

"Jackson, you need to slow down," she said. "I know how much you're hurting, but you have to understand that we're all hurting. We all love Harper, and we love you, too. We miss her just as much as you do."

I turned away.

"I can't slow down," I said. "I have to find her."

"We will find her," she said. "But we need to do it together. We can beat them, Jackson, but only if we work as a team. A family. Alone, we're nothing compared to the Order."

"I can't listen to this," I said, standing. "This is my fight, Mary Anne. I'm the one who needs to find her. It's my fault she was taken. I should have been with her. I should have been looking out for her."

"You have to stop blaming yourself, dammit. You're just sitting around wallowing in this self-pity, and frankly, I'm tired of it," she said.

Her harsh words threw me off balance.

"Wallowing? I've been working my ass off, looking in every wretched corner of the Shadow World for clues. I've been contacting every person and demon I know in the human world, looking for answers. I've killed more than a dozen hunters. What have you done?" I shouted.

Unlike my sister, Mary Anne was unaffected by my anger. She seemed to have been expecting it. She crossed her arms and stared at me, moving her feet into a wider stance.

"If you spent any time at all with us, you would know the answer to that," she said. "Essex and I have been making important contacts with as many of the emerald gate Primas as possible, gathering some information about where the emerald priestess might live."

"And what exactly have you found out with this peaceful exploration?" I asked. I hated the sound of my own voice, but rage was always on the tip of my tongue these days. I didn't seem to have any other tone to use.

"We're putting together a profile, Jackson. We're getting closer every day."

"Well, while you're safe here putting together your little notes, I'm out there risking my life trying to find her."

"Which is exactly the problem," she said. "You have to stop running off without telling us where you're going. You have to stop going off alone without help. You're going to get yourself killed or captured, and then where will we all be?"

I swallowed and turned away. The truth of her words only made me angrier.

"What else am I supposed to do?" I said, trying to cut the edge of anger out of my voice. "I can't just sit here while she's being tortured or hurt. While she's forgetting us."

My voice wavered on the word.

There had been shards of green stone strewn across the floor of the hallway at Winterhaven. They'd been covered in blood, and as much as I didn't want to admit it at first, I knew that blood was Harper's.

Rend had taken the shards to a mystic woman in New Orleans who had performed a special identification ritual on them shortly after Harper disappeared.

Yes, the blood was Harper's, but there had been something else inside those shards of glass.

There had been memories.

Harper's memories.

They had oozed from her wounds like blood.

What if she was out there somewhere right now and she didn't even remember who I was? What if I rescued her and she didn't even recognize me?

I lowered my head, not wanting to face the possibility of it.

How could I sleep not knowing the truth? How could I slow down?

"I'm not asking you to stop looking for her," Mary Anne said. "I'm just asking you to acknowledge the fact that you're not alone in this. We are stronger together than we are alone, Jackson. You know that's what Harper would say if she were here."

She was right.

Harper would fight for us to stick together and work as a

family. She was always bringing us together, which was the only way we'd been able to defeat the sapphire priestess in the first place. Together, we were stronger.

But this was different.

Without her, everything was different.

"Look, just promise me that you'll let me know before you go out on another rogue mission to track down a hunter or some kind of obscure clue," she said. "I could go with you. Or Essex."

"I don't want to put anyone else in danger. Why can't you understand that?" I said.

"Why can't you understand that you're being ridiculous?" she said, stomping her foot. "If you keep running off without thinking things through, you're going to get hurt."

I shook my head. "Drop it, Mary Anne," I said. "I'm tired and it's been a long couple of days. I just need some time alone."

"You're always alone these days," she mumbled.

She placed a hand on the edge of Zara's cocoon and patted it gently. Without another word to me, she spun on her heel and walked out the door.

When she was gone, I bent over to retrieve the tattered piece of paper from the floor. I looked again at the promised future and folded it neatly, carefully tucking it away in my pocket.

I walked over to the open window and stared out at the gardens the king had loved so much. The white roses glistened in the moonlight and the hours passed, each one taking me farther from the promise of hope.

I HAVE NEVER BEEN ANYTHING ELSE

LEA

A door creaked open, and a sliver of light crept down the hallway. I squinted even though it was still dim. I hadn't seen light in several days.

I lifted my head from my arms but didn't move to straighten my legs. I'd managed to find a comfortable position a few hours ago, and my legs had long since gone numb. I doubted I'd be able to move them even if I tried. The stone floor of the dungeons was unforgiving, and after months of living on them, I'd learned to change positions every four or five hours just to avoid sores on my skin.

It wasn't exactly a glamorous existence.

"Hello?" I called out, but my voice was hoarse and unrecognizable. No one had bothered to bring food or water in days. If I'd been human, I'd be long dead by now.

Footsteps sounded on the stone, and a woman appeared. My heart sank. It had been a week since Ezrah had come to see me. I wanted news, not more of this crap.

I didn't recognize this particular woman, but they were all the same: maidservants sent by my father to test my loyalty. I wanted to tell her to turn around and go back to wherever she'd come from.

But she carried a large stone mug and a loaf of brown bread on her tray.

My leg twitched beneath me. I tried to swallow, but it was like trying to force sand down my throat.

I eyed the tray, my teeth clenched with longing.

"Princess, my name is Anastia," she said. "Your father sent me to have a word with you."

I settled back against the prison wall.

How many times would I have to play this game?

He'd sent many different women over the past few months, and they all asked the same questions. They asked what I knew about the Order of Shadows. Where they could find the Resistance Army. What I knew about Harper and her mission to kill the priestesses.

What no one in this castle seemed to understand was that it was my mission, too. And nothing he did would force me from that path.

But damn, that bread looked good.

My stomach ached with hunger.

The cloaked woman—Anastia—set the tray on the floor, just far enough from the bars of my cell to keep it out of reach in case I lunged for it. I hated to tell her, but there was no lunge left in me at the moment.

She pulled up a dusty wooden stool, letting the legs scrape against the dirty stone floor. The sound carried throughout the prison, but there was no one here for it to bother but me.

Imprisonment might not have been so bad if they had left

me next to Aerden. At least I would have had someone to talk to. Someone to touch through the bars to remind me of my life.

But my father must have known it would be too easy for us if we stayed together. He'd separated us only days after he'd first put us in chains, sending Aerden to the main prisons above and keeping me down in the lower dungeon alone.

I'd been alone for so long, I'd lost count of the days.

"What do you want?" I asked. I'd grown tired of this game. It was the same every week. They asked questions, and I refused to answer them. I had nothing to offer a mad king who would sentence his own daughter to this fate, leaving me in the dungeons to rot.

"Where is the girl? Harper?" she asked.

I opened my eyes and studied the woman. This was a new question.

They usually wanted to know her plans, not her where-abouts. *What was going on?*

"I didn't realize she was missing," I said. "For all I know, she's locked down here in these dungeons, just like me."

I moved my arms and tried to straighten my legs. Pinpricks of pain shot through them, like a thousand fire ants dancing inside my veins. I longed to be able to shift out of this form.

Anastia shook her head and stood. She leaned down to retrieve the tray, but I forced myself up and grabbed hold of the bars with both hands.

"Please," I said, hating the sound of desperation in my voice. "I don't know where Harper is. The last time I saw her, she was at home at Brighton Manor in the human world. She was alive and well at the time. Has she gone missing?"

Why hadn't Ezrah told me about this?

Anastia paused and gently set the tray of food and water

back on the stone floor. She didn't sit down, but at least she hadn't left.

"You heard that Brighton Manor was attacked?" she asked. "Burned to the ground?"

I nodded. "I heard."

"Who would have done this?" she asked.

"The emerald priestess," I said. *They already knew the answer to that question, so why even ask it?*

"You're sure of this?"

"I don't know for certain, but when I left, she's the one we all assumed had stopped time," I said. "Part of why I left in the first place was to find out for sure who was behind the attack on Harper's city in the south."

One eyebrow went up and she stepped closer.

"Harper's city?" she asked. "Isn't it her father's city?"

"Her father's dead," I said.

"Yes, but Harper never had an official coronation," she said.

"No."

"It's our understanding she has a sister, as well," Anastia said. "A half-sister who is actually older than she is, is that right?"

I nodded.

Why did they insist on asking me questions they already knew the answers to? Besides, I was the one who'd been locked down here for months. If they really wanted answers about Harper, they were in a much better position to find them than I was.

"Then why did you call it Harper's city?" she asked.

"Because when her father died, he told her he intended for her to rule," I said.

I had no idea where this line of questioning was going, or how long I was expected to play along with it, but as long as the questions didn't seem to betray any information that would put my friends in danger, I didn't see the harm in it.

I eyed the tray again.

"Are you thirsty?" she asked.

I gripped the bars tighter, thinking that if the woman was standing a bit closer, I would like to put my hands around her neck and squeeze as hard as I could. She had to know I was thirsty. Wasn't that the point of her torture?

"What would you do for a drink of water?" she asked. Her eyes actually glimmered in the low light. She was enjoying this.

"What would you ask of me?"

A smile tickled the corners of her mouth, and she straightened.

"All your father wants is to know that his daughter has returned to him," she said. "He still adores you, despite your numerous betrayals."

I bit down on my tongue to keep from lashing out at her. It took an enormous amount of effort. Holding my tongue wasn't exactly in my nature.

She leaned over and retrieved the mug from her tray, holding it just out of my reach. Taunting me.

"Do you feel you are ready to be the king's daughter again?" she asked.

"I have never been anything else," I said.

She narrowed her eyes and pulled the mug back. "Perhaps a few more days without food and water would help you to realize the extent of your betrayal."

"No," I said. I cleared my scratchy throat and pressed my

face against the bars. My hair was matted and tangled against my head. "Please. I'm thirsty."

She turned toward me, holding the mug closer. "Are you ready to rejoin the royal family?" she asked. "To turn your back on those who seek to betray the king's wishes? Are you ready to hear of his plans and join him in his quest to restore the Northern Kingdom to its former glory, no matter what it takes?"

If I said yes, would you give me that freaking mug?

I swallowed, my throat sore and dry. There was no way I was going to turn my back on my friends. Not now. Not ever.

But that didn't mean this woman had to know that.

"Yes," I said, hating the desperation in my voice. "I'm ready."

She smiled and handed the mug to me.

I reached for it, my mouth already imagining the cool, fresh taste of water. But as I brought the stone mug to my lips, I realized it was completely empty.

I tipped it over, praying for even one drop of water. None came.

I dropped the mug to the floor and slid down the bars to the floor. Tears welled up in my eyes, and I suddenly felt so incredibly tired and weak. I hardly recognized myself.

Shame made me shiver.

Anastia bent over to retrieve the fallen mug and placed it on the tray.

"Maybe next time, you'll mean it," she said.

She turned on her heel and walked away, leaving me in darkness once again.

SOME PART OF HER

JACKSON

The garden was drenched in sunlight. It was the kind of day Harper would have loved, and it broke my heart to know there could still be so much beauty in a world where she was being held prisoner.

I turned away and walked into Harper's bedroom. There were traces of her everywhere. Even though we'd been spending most of our time at Brighton Manor before our fight against the emerald priestess, she'd also been coming to the castle a lot during those months.

I moved to her bedside table and ran my fingers across a blue ribbon she'd left behind. I missed her so much it hurt every part of me.

The door to her room opened and Tuli stopped short, nearly dropping the vase of white roses she was carrying.

"I'm so sorry, Jackson. I didn't know you'd be in here," she said. She lowered her head, her cheeks flushed. "I can come back another time."

"No, it's fine," I said. I left the ribbon on the table and walked back to the balcony.

There were no doors or windows on this side of the room. Instead, beautiful stone arches opened up to a balcony that overlooked the gardens. How many nights had I watched her stand in this very spot and stare at the flowers, talking about her father?

"You miss her, I know." Tuli set the vase on the table in the center of the room and joined me on the balcony, the cool breeze blowing her hair back. "I miss her, too."

"Thank you for all the work you've been doing in the castle since she disappeared," I said. "I know Harper would appreciate it."

Tuli blushed again. "When she comes home, I want her to know that her things have been taken care of," she said. "I want her to see that we've been thinking of her all along."

I smiled and forced back tears.

"Is there anything else I can do for you?" she asked. "I made some pastries this morning. I can bring a basket up for you, if you'd like."

"No, thank you," I said. "I appreciate it, but I'm not hungry."

"You haven't been eating enough lately," she said. "You need to keep your strength up."

I shook my head. I had no appetite. I couldn't think of food or sleep. All I could think about was bringing my family back together and getting revenge on those who had torn us apart.

"Thank you for your concern, but I'm fine," I said. I wanted everyone to stop worrying about me. All our attention should have been focused on finding a way to save the others.

Tuli curtsied and lowered her head. "I will leave you to

your thoughts," she said. "If you need anything, please call for me."

I nodded as she straightened and left the room.

I paced the floor in front of the bed, trying to decide what I should do now. I thought about what the hunter had told me before she died. She said that when she'd disobeyed the priestess, she'd been taken to an institution of some kind to be added to the emerald priestess's collection. What did that mean, exactly?

I had to find someone who knew more.

I walked over to the bag I'd stashed in the corner of the sitting room. I'd promised the hunter that I would find her mother, so I had grabbed everything I could find in her lair and stuffed it into the bag, hoping I would be able to find some clue as to who this hunter used to be when she was still human.

I opened the top of the enchanted bag. It was one Essex had crafted for me. Like the tool kit, this bag was enchanted with a special spell that allowed me to carry a large amount of items in a small container.

I removed the hunter's things, looking through trinkets and stones and setting each thing aside after I'd studied it. At the bottom of the bag, I found a photograph inside a roughly carved wooden frame.

I took the frame over toward the table, placing it directly under the light as I sat down to study it. The picture was of a young girl, no more than seven or eight years old, sitting on her mother's lap and smiling at the camera. From her eyes, I was sure this was my hunter as a child.

I cracked open the frame and pulled out the photograph, turning it over in my hands. On the back, the writing was faint and faded, but I could just make it out.

Juliana Rodriguez. Age 6.

I breathed a sigh of relief. I had her name. Finding a record of her might be impossible, since I knew the Order had a habit of altering legal records to hide their activities. But her mother would likely have the same last name, and now I had her picture. If I had to search every single emerald gate town in the world, I would find her.

And maybe this woman would somehow lead me one step closer to finding Harper.

I set the photograph on the table and packed a new bag for myself, grabbing a map of the emerald gates and stuffing it in the outside pocket.

I left the castle without telling anyone where I was going. Mary Anne and the others were concerned about me, but what they didn't understand was that I kept them at arm's distance to protect them. The places I had to go were dangerous, and I'd already lost too many of my friends. I couldn't afford to lose anyone else. They were safer here in the castle.

I made my way down to the garden of white roses and crossed through the portal into the human world. On the other side, I paused briefly at the two graves there by the lake.

Harper's father—lost to us during the final battle against the sapphire priestess—and Courtney—taken from us by the emerald priestess's daughter Sophie just a few months earlier.

As I stood for a moment to honor the dead, I sent up a silent prayer that no more graves would ever have to be added to this site.

I shifted and flew through the woods toward the ruins of Brighton Manor. Inside the shed behind the burned house, I found my old motorcycle. I couldn't afford to travel in demon form for very long in this world. It would leave too much of a trail.

I would have to drive.

I hated to lose the time, but Mary Anne was right. I needed to be more careful. The emerald priestess had set a trap for me, and I had walked right into it. I'd nearly died at the hands of that hunter and her rock golems. I would have if it hadn't been for Rend's potions.

I couldn't afford to be so careless.

As I drove past what remained of Harper's old house, I held back tears, a part of my heart mourning all that we had lost in the months since the emerald priestess first attacked.

Seeing this place made me miss Harper more than ever, the ache so deep it physically hurt to leave it behind.

"Where are you?" I whispered into the wind, hoping that somewhere, some part of her still listened for my voice.

COINS FOR THE FERRYMAN

HARPER

Voices seemed to come to me through a tunnel, their echo reaching me in waves of awareness. One second, I could hear them as if they were standing beside me, and the next, they disappeared entirely into the darkness.

My eyelids were so heavy, I wasn't sure I'd be able to open them. It felt as if someone had placed weights on them. Coins for the ferryman.

Was I dead?

I tried to push against the darkness, searching for any memory of what had last happened to me, but the thick blackness was too deep and dark to see anything. Nothing came at all. I felt as though I'd been asleep for years.

As I struggled toward awareness, the pain came with it. My skin burned as if someone were holding a flame too close. I reached back, trying to pull myself from the fire, but my hands were bound at my sides.

My legs struggled against the bindings too, a sudden panic rising inside me, primal and desperate. Angry. I needed to be free. Why was I being held down?

My eyes snapped open. Or at least I wanted them to snap. My body wasn't entirely cooperating with me. My eyelids struggled to open, letting in just a tiny sliver of light that burned just as much as the flames on my skin.

Only, there were no flames.

When I was able to look around, there wasn't much of anything here in the room. Pristine white walls. A pristine white hospital gown covering my body. My hands and feet were bound with leather straps.

Other than that, there was nothing at all. No one.

The only color I could see was in the depths of the cuts that ran up and down my legs and arms, ugly red scars that were swollen and bruised around the edges.

I strained my neck to see more, but my view was extremely limited. There wasn't even a single window in this room. White walls. White floors. A white ceiling with a single metal lamp hanging in the center.

Where the hell was I?

My eyes fluttered closed against the brightness of the room. I focused on the cuts along my body. I tried to remember them. I tried to remember what had happened to me.

It seemed like the kind of thing that should have been easy to recall.

Not being able to come up with a single memory—not even a brief picture of my life before this moment—hurt worse than the chains on my arms or the cuts or the headache pounding in the base of my neck.

Something terrible happened, and I couldn't even remember it.

Behind me, a door creaked open and someone stepped into the room, their shoes squeaking against the floor. I struggled to turn my head to see her, for some reason expecting a harsh, unsmiling face with eyes full of hate. Instead, a pretty young woman wearing a white nurse's uniform and a soft smile came into view. She had a clipboard pressed against her chest as she leaned over me.

"Well, my goodness, look who's awake," she said. She placed a hand tenderly on my shoulder. "How are you feeling, Harper?"

"Where am I?"

She shook her head and quickly jotted something on her white papers. "Now, now. Let's not get ahead of ourselves here, shall we?"

I didn't know what to say in response. Asking where I was seemed like a perfectly normal question, and one I desperately needed to know. Would she rather I asked why the hell my hands and legs were chained to this bed?

"I asked how you were feeling," she repeated.

I cleared my throat, trying to figure out what in the world this woman expected me to say.

I feel like I just woke up from being dead, thanks. May I have a glass of water?

"I have a little bit of a headache," I said, instead.

Her smile returned. "I can get you something that will help with that."

"Thank you," I said.

"Is there anything else I can get for you?"

I tried to lift my hands. "You could take these off for starters," I said.

She instantly frowned, her blue eyes darkening. She even clucked her tongue at me as if I should be ashamed for asking in the first place. "Those are for your own good," she said. "I trust you won't ask me to release you again."

I narrowed my eyes at her. Was she serious?

"If there's nothing else, I'll get some medicine for that headache," she said.

"Wait."

She paused and cocked one hip to the side, frustration clear on her face. "Yes, dear?"

"I would hate to get ahead of myself," I said, letting a bit too much sarcasm into my tone, "but how did I get here? What happened?"

She pressed the clipboard tight against her chest and pursed her lips. "Don't you remember, dear?"

I really wanted to tell her to stop calling me dear. She was speaking to me as if I were a child. My headache was pounding so hard now, I could hardly think straight, and it agitated me. I obviously didn't remember, or I wouldn't have asked her.

"No, I'm sorry, I don't remember much at all," I said, trying to control the frustration in my voice. Whoever she was, this woman seemed to have some level of power over my current situation, and I wouldn't get very far by making her angry.

I could have sworn a small smile teased the corners of her lips before she feigned sympathy. She placed a cold hand on my forehead and looked into my eyes.

"You were in a fire," she said. "You were the only survivor, poor thing."

My insides twisted, and I struggled to lift my arms. *A fire?* I closed my eyes and leaned back against the hospital bed. I could see the flames burning in my memory. I could feel their heat lapping against my skin.

When I opened my eyes, I had to blink back tears.

"Please," I said. "I need to know what happened. Where am I?"

She shook her head and stroked my hair.

"You really don't remember anything?" she asked softly. There was an excitement in her tone, as if she wanted me to say yes. As if she didn't want me to remember.

I shook my head, a sense of absolute dread igniting in my stomach and burning its way toward my throat.

The nurse took a deep breath and pulled her hand away. "You accidentally set the fire," she said. "Your entire family was trapped inside. Everyone close to you."

She leaned down until her lips were nearly touching my ear.

"I'm sorry, Harper," she said. "You killed them all."

THIS WASN'T ABOUT ME

LEA

I paced the floor of my cell, my brain in overdrive. I was going insane locked up in this place.

It had been months, and my father had not come to visit me once. Instead, he kept sending servants who pushed me to declare my loyalty. But how could I be loyal to a father who would sentence me to this darkness?

When I'd faced him on the day his soldiers first brought me to the castle, my father had called me a traitor, but he was the one who had betrayed us all. I couldn't get the image of his face out of my mind. Those deep red eyes and his wild hair. His hunched shoulders. How could such a powerful demon diminish so much in just a few decades?

For years I'd been arguing with Andros about my father's ability to rule this kingdom. Andros had been waiting for me to make the decision to lead the Resistance into war against the king, but I'd refused to be a part of it.

Fighting the Order of Shadows was one thing, but fighting against my father? How could he ask me to do that?

But after months in the depths of my father's dungeons, I'd finally realized why Andros was so insistent. Why the entire Resistance Army was so set on war as the only option.

My father was gone. The demon I loved as a shadowling was unrecognizable that day in his throne room. I didn't know if it was the stress of watching his kingdom turn to ruins or the loss of his only child that had hurt him more, but there was no doubt in my mind that I'd been a part of his deterioration.

In the beginning, I followed Jackson because he was my betrothed. I felt a duty to go with him while he searched for the truth about his brother. But over time, as his love for me seemed to disappear altogether, I stayed because the fight had become my own.

It was bigger than rescuing Aerden from the Order of Shadows. If that was all that mattered to me, I would have come back here as soon as I realized it was an impossible task.

No, I stayed because it was the only choice. I didn't understand how any demon could stand by and let the Order of Shadows destroy our world. How could my father see what was happening and do nothing to protect his people?

I wanted to hate him.

I wanted to kill him.

But even after everything he'd done, I still loved him. Something deep inside of me wanted to believe that he was still in there somewhere, making the choices he thought were best. He was just misguided.

After seeing him that day in the throne room, however, I realized there was more to it than that.

It was more than just stress or age. Something was terribly

wrong. If I could see that so clearly when I'd only been in his presence for a few minutes, why couldn't everyone else see it? Why didn't my mother do anything to help him?

I needed answers, and all this dark cell provided was solitude and sorrow.

It had been days since I'd seen anyone, and being alone with these thoughts was a brand of torture I'd never experienced.

I slumped against the damp wall of the cell and slid down to the floor. *What was I going to do?*

If only Aerden were still locked in here with me, maybe we could have come up with a plan to escape or at least to make some kind of a difference here in the castle. I missed him terribly, and I worried about him more than I worried about myself.

He'd been a slave for so long. I couldn't imagine what it must be like for him to gain his freedom only to be locked up again by his own king. It was all my fault.

And Jackson?

I closed my eyes and lowered my head. *Was he okay? Had something happened to Harper?*

It's amazing what the heart will try to make you believe when you're alone with your darkest thoughts. If Harper was truly gone, what did that mean for us? What if there was hope that we could still find the love we'd once had for each other?

Those were the worst, darkest thoughts during these long hours of solitude.

I knew that things would never be the same for Jackson and me. His heart belonged to Harper, whether she was dead or alive. And if she was dead, I wasn't sure he'd even survive the loss of her.

If she was still alive, he would spend the rest of his days looking for her.

Whatever he'd once felt for me was gone. Why couldn't I just accept that?

The lock on the dungeon door clicked, and I stood quickly and walked to the front of my cell, waiting. It would either be another servant—in which case I would be ridiculed and tortured with the vision of food she'd never let me eat—or it would be Ezrah.

When his face came into view, I nearly wept for joy.

"Thank God," I said. "Any news?"

He closed the door to the main room and passed the handful of empty cells to get to mine. He reached inside his cloak and took out a piece of bread and a small bottle of water. "I'm sorry I couldn't get more," he said.

I ripped the bread with my teeth, devouring it in seconds. I emptied the bottle, and my body begged for more.

As a demon I could go for a very long time with no food and water, but it wasn't the most pleasant experience. My stomach grumbled, arguing with the pitiful offering.

"I appreciate this," I said. "Ezrah, why didn't you tell me something had happened to Harper?"

He avoided my gaze. "You have enough to worry about down here," he said.

"Where is she?"

"No one knows, exactly," he said. "Jackson and the others fought the emerald priestess. She was trying to reopen the sapphire gates using Zara's blood."

I shook my head, tears forming in my eyes. "Are they okay?"

"Courtney is dead," he said. "Killed by the priestess's

daughter. Zara is in bad shape, and no one knows if she will live or die. She's in some kind of cocoon for now."

"What about Jackson and Harper?"

"Harper was taken by Priestess Evers. No one saw it happen, but there was a lot of blood." He shook his head and sighed. "Jackson's doing as well as can be expected. He looks for her all the time. He's killed all the hunters he can find, talked to everyone he thinks might have information. As far as I know, he's not any closer to finding her."

I closed my eyes and pressed my forehead against the bars. My family—my true family—was going through hell, and I was locked away like some dog. I should have been there to help them fight. I should be out there right now helping them bring her home.

What torture was the priestess putting her through?

I shuddered. Wherever Harper was, she was probably in a much worse position than I was. We had our differences, but Harper was a good person. She didn't deserve that.

"What news do you have for me?" I asked, hoping for even one happy thing. "How is Aerden doing?"

Ezrah smiled briefly. "He asks the same about you every time I see him," he said. "You seem to never be far from his thoughts, Princess."

"Is he still working in the quarry?"

Ezrah nodded. "The prisoners mine sapphires every single day, and I heard the gems are being delivered to an outpost about three day's journey from here."

"For what purpose?" I asked.

"I can't be sure," he said. "But the Council has been meeting more often lately. They lock themselves away in the council room for hours and come out tired and angry. They're planning something."

"But they can't agree on it," I said, pacing. "If they agreed, they wouldn't be meeting so often. Any idea what it might be?"

He shook his head. "It has to be something big," he said. He glanced at the door again. He wouldn't stay long. He never did. "All mining operations have increased in the past few months, and the builders have been working late at night to build the walls of the city even higher."

I grasped the bars between us. "Higher?"

"I heard someone say their orders were to make it twice as high as it stood before."

"But why?"

"The only thing I can imagine is that the Council is expecting the city to be attacked."

"By the Order?"

"I don't know," he said. "Do you think a wall of any height could keep the Order out?"

I shook my head. "If the Order wants to get inside this city, a wall isn't going to keep them out for long. It's madness."

Ezrah's features darkened, and he glanced at the door again.

"What is it?" I asked.

"We need to know what's going on in those Council meetings, Princess."

I closed my eyes and let my face rest against the bars of my cell. We'd been through this conversation several times, and it never got any easier.

"You don't know what you're asking me to do," I said.

"I understand how hard this is for you, but you have to think of your people," he said. "You have to think of the Resistance. With you at the king's side, we would have access to everything the Council discusses. We would know every move the king planned to make."

"It's not in my nature to play games," I said. "I can't pretend to be okay with all that my father and his Council have done over the past century. I can't go up there and play the part of the loyal daughter, Ezrah. It will destroy me."

"You are stronger than you think," he said, grasping my hand. "We need this information, and you're our best hope of obtaining it."

I took a deep breath to calm my beating heart.

"They'll ask things of me in order to prove my loyalty," I said. "They'll want information on the Resistance Army. The Southern Kingdom. They'll want me to tell them everything I know about anyone who might oppose the king. What am I supposed to tell them?"

"Whatever you must," he said. "We are at war, Princess. And we're losing. Every day the King's City grows stronger and the villages of the Outerlands grow weaker and more vulnerable. Soon there will be nothing left of your own people. They will all be slaves to the Order of Shadows. Do you mean to tell me that you would rather rot away in the safety of this dungeon than do what you must to save those who need you most?"

I turned away from him, my heart aching. "Of course not," I said.

"Then now is the time to act," he said. "I know it is a great sacrifice for you, but war often calls for our greatest sacrifices. You've seen what's happened to the Shadow World in the years you've been gone. Imagine how much worse it will be if the Resistance is captured or defeated? We need your eyes and ears in those Council meetings."

I pushed back tears. I didn't want to do what he asked, but he was right. This wasn't about me or what I wanted. This was about what the people of my kingdom needed most from me, no matter the sacrifice.

"What do you need me to do?" I asked.

Ezrah let out a sigh of relief and leaned closer. "The servant Anastia who came to you last time is on her way down here as we speak," he said. "Tell her what she wants to hear. Make her believe that you have been broken by this place. Make her believe that you have realized the error of your ways and will do whatever is necessary to make things right with your father."

My knees trembled. He was asking me to betray everything I believed in and turn my back on my own fight for freedom. Even if it wasn't real, I would have to make them believe it was real. I would have to bite my tongue at every turn and convince them that I didn't care about the humans and demons who were currently suffering at the hands of the Order.

"Can you do this, Princess?"

"I have no choice, do I?" I asked.

"You are my princess. The rightful heir to this throne," he said. "As hard as this may be, you have a duty to the demons you are meant to lead. The question isn't whether you have a choice, Princess. The question is whether you will choose to save yourself or to save your people. That is the only choice that matters."

Footsteps sounded on the stone stairs outside the dungeon. Ezrah turned and searched for a place to hide.

"Wait," I said softly.

He looked at me, his eyes questioning.

"Promise me you'll tell him why I've done this," I said, thinking of Aerden. "Tell him I'll do everything in my power to get my father to release him."

"I will tell him," he said. He started to turn away but stopped. "I almost forgot. Last time I spoke with Aerden, he gave me a message for you. He said to tell you that the light is never as far away as it seems. Does that mean anything to you?"

I shook my head, not quite sure what Aerden must have meant by that. *What light?*

The door to the dungeon creaked open, and Ezrah slid into the shadows near one of the empty cells. Anastia appeared in the doorway. She carried the same wooden tray she'd brought last time, and I wondered if she'd actually brought water in the goblet this time, or if she meant to torture me further.

As she approached, I swallowed what was left of my pride. I shoved my anger and my bitterness down into the depths of my heart and locked them away for another time.

I fell to my knees, forcing tears into my eyes. If I had to play the part of the remorseful, broken princess, I was going to be so freaking good at it, they would be kissing my feet by the end of the week.

THE GIRL I USED TO BE

LEA

The servant took her sweet time, her footsteps shuffling across the floor. She carried the wooden tray like a shield against her breasts. Her lips were pressed into a thin line, and her eyes widened as she caught sight of me.

"Stand up," she said.

"I'm not worthy to stand in the presence of my father's servant," I said. A lump formed in my throat at those words, but I swallowed it down to the pit of my stomach. "Please, forgive me for all that I have done."

I bowed my head and clung to the bars of the cell.

"I understand now what my betrayal has done to my father," I said, my words carried by sheer determination. My people needed me right now, and I was going to get out of this dark place if it killed me. "My father was right to send me down here. I just needed time to see it clearly."

The cloaked woman—Anastia—narrowed her eyes at me. "How am I to believe this sudden change of heart?"

I chose my next words carefully. She was testing me.

"You've left me down here for months with nothing but my own thoughts," I said. "In the darkness of this cell, I've come to realize that my father is the only one who has ever deserved my loyalty. Instead, I turned my back on him to follow a demon who betrayed me and this kingdom by falling in love with another."

I shook my head, true tears falling like rain across my cheeks. I hated the taste of the lies on my tongue.

"I have been blind and selfish," I said. "I deserve much worse than the darkness of this dungeon. I see that now."

Anastia set the tray on the floor. She knelt and lifted the cup toward me.

I looked at her, questioning. She nodded, and her yellowed teeth showed through a crack in her lips as she smiled. She actually believed me.

I took the cup in my trembling hands, surprised to find it full this time. Still, I couldn't allow myself to drink. It took the greatest willpower of my life not to suck it down and soothe my cracked throat, but I wanted freedom more than water.

If I was going to do this, I was going to be good at it.

"I don't deserve to even drink the water from his wells," I said. "Not until I've had a chance to kneel before him."

One eyebrow raised, Anastia glanced at the cup.

"Pour it onto the floor in sacrifice," she said. "Prove your loyalty to your father's name."

Damn.

I held the cup out from my body and tipped it over, letting the sweet, cool water fall to the stone floor.

"I would pour a thousand goblets of water onto this floor before I would take a single drink without his blessing," I said, hoping I wasn't going too far with the dramatics. "I have wronged my father, and I will do whatever it takes to prove to him that I am truly the daughter he once lost."

Anastia reached through the bars and took hold of my wrist. Her touch on my skin surprised me, and the cup fell to the floor with a clang that echoed through the dark dungeon.

"Princess Lazalea, you have no idea how long the king has been waiting to hear this," she said. Her eyes actually glistened with tears. "It will take some time for your father and mother to forgive what you have done, but believe me when I say that they want nothing more than to have their daughter returned to them. Are you willing to kneel at his feet and confess to him your sins? Are you willing to turn your back on your old life and rejoin your family in this castle?"

I nearly cried from joy. Apparently, I'd missed my calling as an actress.

I had a feeling I would have to draw on this new talent a lot over the coming months. Even if they set me free from this dungeon, I knew that becoming my father's daughter again was not true freedom. It was just a different form of imprisonment.

Up there, I would have to face every memory that had burdened my heart for decades. I would have to pretend to embrace a life I had mourned over since the day Aerden disappeared.

It would be like shedding my own skin and stepping into the girl I used to be.

But I hated that girl. She was weak and vulnerable. She had no idea how cruel the world was outside the walls of this castle. She believed in love and fairy tales. She trusted in the future she'd been promised, not understanding that it could all be taken away in an instant.

That girl was unprotected and naive, and I hated her. I'd murdered her and buried her so deep I swore they would never find the body.

But in order to do what Ezrah was asking me to do, I'd have to resurrect her and make the people in this city believe she had never died in the first place. I would have to strip my heart bare of the armor I'd worked so hard to create.

I was a warrior. Give me a bow, and I would kill a room full of hunters before I let them bring me down. But up there, I would have no bow. No weapons. This was a game of the heart, and I'd never done anything in those kinds of games except lose.

I'd rather face the emerald priestess herself with one hand tied behind my back than have to face the girl I used to be, with her wide eyes and her unguarded heart.

"I'm ready," I said, swallowing back fresh tears. This was war, and if I was going to be the leader my people needed me to be, I'd have to be willing to face anything.

Even if it killed me.

I DIDN'T HAVE THE LUXURY OF BEING BROKEN

LEA

T he nurse and five guards escorted me to the baths. They marched me through the halls like a prisoner in the home where I'd lived for over a hundred years.

I kept my head down as I passed the curious demons of my father's court, their whispers too soft to hear. I could only imagine what they thought. *The traitor princess has returned in shame.*

Did they even know what we had accomplished in the human world? Were they aware of how many demons we'd saved from the clutches of the Order of Shadows?

They probably had no idea. The king would never have allowed that kind of news to be spread throughout the city. We had done what the king himself was too cowardly to do. We made him look weak and powerless, and there was no way he would let that happen. Not here.

I watched their faces as I passed. They were prisoners here, just like me, whether they admitted it to themselves or not. In their eyes, they were the privileged few, chosen by the king to be saved from the Order. Didn't they even care about their fellow demons still fighting for survival in the Outerlands? Had any of them seen the destruction of the once-thriving villages near the Black Sea? The poverty and hopelessness of those in the mountains?

I may have been labeled a traitor, but at least I knew the truth. Even decades in the darkest of dungeons couldn't make me forget.

Or forgive.

I eyed everyone we passed, wondering how many of these demons had helped convince my father that closing the city was the right decision. I had no doubt in my mind that someone had been manipulating him. The father I used to know wouldn't have been such a coward.

Someone was advising him to follow a path of darkness rather than glory and battle.

But who? That's what I wanted to find out.

My father's closest advisor was Jackson and Aerden's father, Naman, and I didn't want to believe he could be capable of such cruelty against his people.

Still, he'd abandoned his own son to the Order. He couldn't be trusted. None of them could.

But something told me there was another player in my father's decisions. Someone who had turned his mind to fear rather than strength. Whoever that person was, they were the real traitor. I intended to find them, and I intended to kill them.

When we reached the bathing pools, the nurse stripped

the tattered clothing from my body, leaving me naked in front of the guards. She wanted to shame me, but shame and I had already become close friends over the past few months. I refused to let her break me. Ezrah was right. I didn't have the luxury of being broken. Too many depended on me, and I wouldn't let them down.

Three of the guards looked away, showing at least some hint of honor. But two stared brazenly at my nakedness, their eyes hungry and filled with lust. I didn't try to cover myself. Instead, I memorized their faces. I kept my chin up as I walked into the warm pool.

I bent my knees, letting the water rush over my body.

I needed to be strong. To do whatever it took to spy on my own father and figure out what was really going on in this castle. But as I disappeared into the water, I gave myself this one moment to be weak and scared.

The dungeons had been hard on me, but at least there I could use my anger as a shield. I could be myself and speak my mind, even if I was only speaking to the shadows.

Up here in the castle, I would need to lock my true thoughts away. I'd have to hide my anger and my bitterness. I would have to hold my tongue.

If life in the dungeons had been difficult, life in the castle was going to be pure hell.

I stayed under the water, letting the tears flow where they would disappear and never be seen. How was I going to survive this all over again? How was I going to do this on my own?

I acknowledged my fear, and then I locked it away. I pushed up from the water, breaking free from the surface to reclaim my strength. I'd been through worse than this. I was a warrior.

I would smile and lie and cry tears made of diamonds if they wanted me to, but I would also be making plans. As I washed the stink and filth from my body and combed through the matted mess of my hair, I made a promise to myself.

Someday I would rule this kingdom.

No, it wouldn't be the life I had dreamed of. There would be no Jackson. No tiny shadowlings running through the halls, their laughter filling my tender heart.

But it would be the life I needed. The life my people needed me to live.

I'd resisted it for so long, thinking that my father would come around. That he would join the fight once he saw how bad things had gotten. But his time was up. I didn't care if it took me decades. Someday I would bring him down and take my place on the throne.

I emerged from the bath a determined woman with a mission etched into my hardened heart.

"That's better," Anastia said, draping a robe over my shoulders. "If only it were that easy to wash the stink of betrayal from your soul."

I swallowed my anger. I practiced holding my tongue.

It was going to take a hell of a lot of practice.

"I will do whatever it takes to prove myself again," I said softly.

"It may take more than you're capable of, my dear, but we shall see," she said. "Let me escort you to the tailor. She's waiting to fit you for a new wardrobe of dresses and finery. No more of this disgusting leather you wore in the human world. If you're going to be a princess again, you'll need to look like one."

I followed her to a room deep in the castle. I didn't say a word as the tailor measured me, poking and prodding at my skin, lifting my arms into the air and studying my naked body as if I were nothing more than a doll. *Let them dress me up and parade me around like a dutiful princess.* The more I looked the part, the less they would see me for what I really was. A wolf in sheep's clothing. A snake in the grass. I would learn their secrets and make them trust me again.

And when they least expected it, I would destroy them all.

THE SAME STORY

JACKSON

I sat in a corner booth of the small diner and pulled out my pencil and drawing pad. I was early and wasn't expecting the woman for another thirty minutes. It had taken me longer than I hoped to find her, and I prayed it would be worth it.

With Eloise's help, I had gone through the rosters of every emerald gate town, searching for any witch with the last name Rodriguez. As expected, there was no record of a Juliana Rodriguez, but there were ten others with the same last name spread across three different towns.

Over the past week I had visited each of these towns, tracking down each woman and comparing her to the picture I'd found in the hunter's lair. I wasn't sure how much time had passed since that photograph had been taken, but so far, none of the women I had found had even remotely resembled her.

This time, though, I'd recognized her the moment she stepped out of the school where she worked in the small town of Alpine, Utah. She'd been talking to a student and when her face broke out into a smile, I knew I'd found the hunter's mother. The picture was an exact match.

There was no record of a Kristie Rodriguez or anyone else with the name Kristie in the Order's roster of witches in this town. I hoped the mother would be able to tell me who she was. Maybe she had been the girl's best friend or an aunt or something.

I'd wanted to approach the hunter's mother immediately, but talking to her on school grounds would have been too dangerous. Most covens of the Order of Shadows ran their training programs through the cheerleading teams of the local high schools, which meant the schools were always crawling with members of the Order.

Instead, I'd left a copy of the photograph tucked inside a few letters in her mailbox. I watched from the shadows across the street as she walked out to check her mail, her face going almost white when she spotted the picture. She glanced around nervously, clutching the picture to her chest as she ran inside.

On the back, I had written the name of this diner and a time.

If I was lucky, she would come alone.

"What can I get for you?" A waitress stopped by my table and pulled a menu from her pocket. She set it down in front of me. "Would you care to hear our specials? We've got some fresh meat loaf cooking now if you want to wait for it."

I shook my head. "I'll just take a cup of coffee," I said. My stomach was too knotted up to even think about eating anything.

From my research, I had learned that Alpine was actually

one of the older emerald gates in existence, dating all the way back to the mid-1800s. Typically, that meant the Prima demon was one of the most powerful. If the Rodriguez woman had gone to her Prima and told her about the photo, there would be a shit-storm headed my way.

To calm my nerves, I opened my drawing pad to a fresh page and closed my eyes. I took a deep breath, opening myself to any visions that might be lurking on the edge of my consciousness.

I tried to make time every day for meditation and drawing, praying that something would come to me that would lead me to Harper. So far, I'd spent a lot of time drawing scarab beetles and stone guardians. Terrifying, but not particularly helpful.

The waitress set a cup of steaming coffee down in front of me and glanced over my shoulder. "Are you an artist?" she asked.

"Something like that," I said. I took a long sip of black coffee, welcoming the warmth as it traveled down my throat.

"I used to have a ton of those notepads or whatever you call them," she said. "Back when I was in high school, I was hardly ever without one in my bag."

"Did you grow up around here?" I asked.

"Born and raised," she said. She smiled and leaned against the table with her hip. She was an attractive woman who looked to be about thirty, and her eyes were kind.

"I don't suppose you were on the cheerleading team, were you?"

She raised an eyebrow and laughed. "Who? Me?" she asked. "Nah. Never did understand why girls want to prance around in tiny little skirts in the freezing cold."

I smiled and raised my cup. At least I wouldn't have to

worry about her trying to stab me in the heart with a silver dagger. "Well, thanks for the coffee," I said.

"Sure," she said. "Let me know if I can get anything else for you."

I nodded and glanced at a car pulling into the parking lot. When Maria Rodriguez emerged, my heartbeat kicked up a notch. She glanced around, pulling her sweater tighter across her body. She looked nervous and scared, which immediately put me at ease. If she had called her Prima, she wouldn't be so twitchy.

A bell sounded over the door when she walked in. I was the only customer in the whole place on a Monday at ten in the morning, so it didn't take her long to figure out that I was the one who'd sent the photo.

She cleared her throat and nodded at the empty seat across from me.

"Have a seat," I said. "You're Maria?"

She nodded again, her leg jumping under the table. "What's this about?" she asked, pulling the photograph from her pocket and sliding it toward me. "Where did you get this?"

"I found it," I said. I didn't want to give away too much information until I'd found out how much she remembered. "Do you recognize this photograph?"

She squeezed her eyes shut and set her elbows on the table, letting her head fall into her hands. "It doesn't make any sense," she said. "When I saw that picture, it was like something in my heart recognized it, but I swear I've never seen that photograph in my life. How is that possible?"

I glanced around to make sure no one was paying any attention to us. "What if I told you the young girl in that photograph was your daughter?"

Maria looked up. There were dark circles under her eyes, as if she hadn't slept at all last night.

"I'd say you were crazy," she said. "I don't have any children. We wanted to, but..."

Her voice trailed off, and a tear rolled down her cheek. She swiped at it and took a quick breath in and out.

"Listen, I don't understand what you're trying to do here, but I don't appreciate strangers leaving things in my mailbox and demanding that I meet them on the edge of town," she said. "I had to call in sick today just to be here."

"Then some part of you must know how important this photograph is," I said. I slid it back toward her. "Maria, I'm telling you the truth. I'm not sure how long ago this picture was taken. Maybe twenty-five years ago. Maybe more. But the little girl in this picture is your daughter. Her name was Juliana."

Maria's mouth dropped open and she quickly lifted a hand to cover it. She shook her head, her tears flowing freely now. "That was my mother's name," she whispered. She picked up the photograph and stared at it again. "I always said that if I ever had a daughter, I would name her after my mother."

She shook her head.

"This is me, and I don't understand how it's possible I'm sitting there with a child I've never seen before in my life."

"But you have seen her," I said.

She looked into my eyes, confusion and fear written across her features. "I don't understand."

"Maria, you know what the Order is capable of," I said, my voice a low whisper. "They can make people disappear. They can alter your memories. They can do anything they want, and you would be powerless to stop them."

Her hand trembled. "What do you know of the Order?"

"Plenty," I said.

She clamped her eyes shut and her hand gripped the photograph tighter. "I can't be talking to you," she said. "If they find out—"

She dropped the picture and started to stand, but I grabbed her hand.

"Maria, please wait," I said. "Sit down. All I am asking for is five minutes of your time. After that, if you don't believe me or want to hear what I have to say, you can walk out that door and forget this whole thing ever happened."

She pulled her hand away but sat back down.

"Hi," the waitress said, walking over to us. "Would you like anything? A cup of coffee, maybe?"

"No," Maria said. "I'm fine."

"Okay, well, I'll be back in a few minutes if you want to order."

Maria nodded, but kept her eyes on mine the entire time.

"You have five minutes," she said.

"The Order has taken someone from me, too," I said. "The emerald priestess has her locked away somewhere, and I need to find her. I was hoping you might be able to tell me something, anything about where to find the priestess or where she takes these girls once she's kidnapped them."

"We shouldn't be talking about such things out here in the open," she said, glancing around. "If my Prima found out I was here, she would punish me in ways you cannot possibly understand."

"I do understand," I said. "I have seen with my own eyes the things the Order is capable of, and believe me when I say I know the risk you took to be here. But that also means you must know there is truth to this photograph. There has to be some part of you that recognizes this girl. Maria, she was your child."

She closed her eyes again, not even bothering to wipe away the tears that flowed freely down her cheeks. "I spent the entire night staring at that picture, trying to remember this little girl," she said. "I searched old family photographs and journals. I tried to remember anything. Maybe she was a cousin or a little girl I used to teach in school. I tried to convince myself that she couldn't be who I thought she was."

I held my breath, waiting for her to continue.

"But there was something in my heart that knew the moment I looked into her eyes," she said. She picked up the picture and clutched it to her chest. "This really is my daughter, isn't it? Why don't I remember her? Do you know where she is?"

My heart broke at the sound of her grief. If I hadn't come here, this woman would never have known she had lost a child to the Order. I hated to have to tell her the truth, but this was my best chance to find out anything about the emerald priestess.

"I saw her," I said. "A few days ago. She gave me this photograph and asked me to find you."

Maria placed her hand over her mouth to stifle her sobs.

"The reason you don't remember her is because the emerald priestess stole her from you," I said. "Juliana told me she fell in love with the wrong person, and the emerald priestess didn't approve. When she disobeyed her coven, she was taken away and all memories of her were wiped from your mind, as if she never existed. But your heart remembers her. You know I'm telling you the truth."

"For years, there's been this hole in my heart," she said. "I couldn't explain it or understand it, but it was as if a piece of me was missing. It all makes sense to me now. I need to see her, please."

"I'm sorry, Maria," I said, unable to meet her eyes. "Juliana is dead. She wanted me to tell you that she died with honor."

I couldn't bear to tell her what had become of her child. Most witches in the Order didn't even know about the hunters. They saw them on the other side of the portal when the gates were opened during initiations, but most of them had no idea that the creature on the other side had once been human.

"No," she cried. She wrapped her arms around her body and rocked back and forth, sobs shaking her shoulders. "My baby girl. Why? Why would they do this to me? I have been nothing but faithful all these years."

"Because this is what the Order of Shadows does," I said. "They take whatever they want and think nothing of the lives they destroy in the process. Please, Maria, I need to find the emerald priestess. I'm sorry that you lost your daughter, and I'm sorry that you had to find out this way. But I have lost someone too. Someone very special to me. If you know anything about where the emerald priestess lives or how I can find her, I'm begging you to tell me."

Maria wiped her face on her sweater and shook her head. "I don't know anything," she said. "The emerald priestess never shows herself to us in person. She only visits our Prima when they have business to discuss. She's very private. None of the other witches in the coven have ever even seen her. I have no idea where she lives."

I ran a hand through my hair. It was the same story I'd heard a thousand times.

"What about your Prima?" I asked. "Do you think she would know where to find her?"

"She would never tell you even if she did," she said. "She is extremely loyal to the emerald priestess. Her family line goes back many years, and their family has always been very strict and devoted. She would never betray our priestess."

Maria wiped a napkin under her nose and crumpled it in her hand. She smoothed the photograph against the table and traced a fingertip across her daughter's face.

"Can I keep this?" she asked.

"Of course," I said. "I'm so sorry I had to tell you about this. It might have been easier for you to never have known."

She shook her head, wiping away a stray tear. "It's better to finally understand why my heart has been in pieces for so long," she said. "It's better for me to be able to see her face and know that she was mine, even if I can't remember our time together."

I set a five-dollar bill on the table and packed away my drawing pad.

"Thank you for telling me what you could," I said. "I'm very sorry for your loss."

I stood, but as I passed by her, Maria grabbed my hand and met my eyes.

"I hope you find her," she said. "Your loved one."

"Me, too," I said.

As I walked away, I added Juliana Rodriguez to my mental list of names to avenge. Someday, when I looked into the eyes of the emerald priestess just before I killed her, I would think of the names of those she had wronged, and I would know that they could finally rest in peace.

I started my bike, but before I could drive away, the waitress ran out of the diner, waving something in her hand.

"You forgot this," she said.

It was a drawing pad, just like mine, but I remembered putting it away.

"I think you made a mistake," I said.

She shook her head. "No, I didn't."

For the first time, I looked down and noticed the name tag pinned to the woman's shirt.

Her name was Kristie.

SHE ALWAYS DOES

JACKSON

I put the extra drawing pad in my bag and drove off, but as soon as I had a chance, I stopped and studied it. The notebook was mostly empty except for a few doodles and sketches in the front, but near the middle I found an address scribbled on the bottom of the page.

Maybe this trip wouldn't be a bust after all.

I found a place to wait until night had fallen. Whoever she was, Kristie was taking a huge risk meeting me like this. If the Order found out, they'd kill her for sure. Especially if she had something valuable to tell me.

Once the house was covered in shadows, I shifted and flew around back. It was a small house with faded vinyl siding and an overgrown yard. Not exactly the kind of house witches of the Order lived in.

I knocked on the back door, and it opened almost immediately.

"Come in," she said. "I made fresh coffee."

"Thanks."

I walked inside and looked around. I didn't think this woman was affiliated with the Order, but I also didn't want to walk straight into another trap. But the house felt quiet. There was no other energy here.

Kristie poured two cups of coffee and set a bottle of powdered creamer on the table. "I'm sorry I don't have any milk," she said. "I work so damn much the stuff always ends up going bad before I can use it."

"This is fine," I said, pouring some of it into my coffee. "Thank you."

"Sugar?"

"Sure," I said. I took a seat and waited until she joined me.

"Do you mind if I smoke?" she asked. "I've worked double shifts every day for a week. I could really use a night to relax, if you know what I mean."

I smiled. "Go ahead," I said. "Can I bum one of those?"

She raised an eyebrow and offered me the pack. I hadn't smoked in a long time. Harper hated it. But hell, I could use a night to relax, too.

We sat there for a while smoking and drinking our coffee, making small talk about her work at the diner and why we liked to draw. She seemed nervous, her hand sometimes trembling as she reached for her cup. I didn't want to rush her.

"You're probably wondering why I asked you to come here," she said. "I was half-scared you'd think I was trying to make a pass at you and you'd skip town without giving it a second thought."

"I saw your name tag," I said. "Juliana mentioned a woman named Kristie before she died. She made me promise to find you, but the only clue I had was a photograph of her with her mother."

Kristie's eyes fluttered, and she drew a quivering breath. "I'm glad she's dead," she said, her forehead wrinkling as she began to cry. "I'm glad she's finally at peace."

"She is," I said. "How did you know her?"

She sniffed and straightened, as if deciding she was going to be strong. "Shit," she said, laughing. "I never cry."

"It's okay," I said. "Just take your time."

"I loved her," she said. "We were best friends since we were little girls, but as we grew older, it turned into something more. Neither of us planned on it, really, but it just happened. I loved her so much, she became a part of me. Do you know what I mean?"

"I know exactly what you mean," I said.

I hadn't expected this at all. When Juliana told me she'd loved someone the Order didn't approve of, I'd assumed it was a man. Maybe a high school boyfriend? I never expected to find out she'd loved a woman.

"We told each other everything," she said. "Or at least I thought we did. But I guess I knew all along that she'd been keeping something from me. Her mother was part of the power-group in town. That's what I called them, anyway. The women who make all the rules. Juliana never talked about it, but a part of me knew there was more to it than just money and politics. I wish she had just trusted me back then."

"It wasn't about trust," I said. "She was probably protecting you. When a girl is put into their training program, she's given a tattoo on her lower back. It's a tracking device. When the Order wants to, they can see and hear anything going on in that girl's life. She couldn't tell you the truth."

Kristie's eyes went wide, and she shook her head. "That stupid tattoo," she said. "I hated that thing. It was this giant cat, like a bobcat or something. Whenever I asked her about it, she said she liked cats, but I hated it."

She lit another cigarette.

"Things were good between us back in high school. We had to keep our relationship secret from our parents and our friends, but I didn't care. I just wanted to be with her," she said. "But after Julie turned eighteen, everything changed. She was different. She stopped hanging out with me, and when I confronted her, she told me that if I loved her, I would forget her. She said she had things she needed to do, and that it was dangerous for us to be together. I thought she was just scared to tell her parents the truth."

I drank the last of my coffee and poured another cup.

"We couldn't stay away from each other, though." She smiled at some passing memory. "I loved her so much."

"When did they take her away?" I asked.

She closed her eyes and leaned forward against her hands. "After she graduated from college, her mother kept pushing her to date this guy we all hated," she said. "He was older. An attorney in Salt Lake City who came from old money. Julie despised him. She refused to be with him, but they just wouldn't stop pushing."

She hid her face from me, her shoulders shaking.

"She came to me in the middle of the night with a bag slung over her shoulder," she said. "She told me we needed to leave and never come back, but I hesitated. My whole life is in this town. My family, my job. I thought she was nervous about people finding out she was gay. I wish she'd just told me the truth. I wish I'd gotten in that car with her and never looked back."

"They would have found you," I said. "This isn't your fault."

"I should have fought for her," she said. "Instead, I told her to go home and we'd talk about it in the morning. I told her everything would be fine."

Kristie began to sob, and I moved to sit beside her, putting an arm across her shoulder.

"I never saw her again," she said. "I went about my life, and I forgot about her, as if she'd never even existed or meant anything to me. I heard her mother talking about it earlier in the diner. She said there was a hole in her heart she couldn't explain. That's how I felt, too. I thought I was going crazy until one day, there she was in my dreams. And I knew she was real. That's when I started to remember her."

"Did you say anything about it?"

She shook her head, wiping away her tears. "No, I didn't dare," she said. "I just started watching. I started listening. You'd be amazed at how openly people speak to each other when they think the diner's mostly empty. It's like they assume the waitress is bound to some confidentiality clause, like a priest or a lawyer. I did my best to seem invisible, and I listened."

"So, you know about the Order?"

"I know," she said. "I know everyone in town who's a member. I know details of their meetings and the things they've done. Things people wouldn't believe."

"I believe," I said. "I've been fighting them for a very long time."

"You're part of that group who killed the sapphire priestess, aren't you?" she asked.

"You heard about that?" I asked.

She took a drag of her cigarette and nodded. "Some witches in town are excited, hoping they'll be free someday, too. Others want to kill you with their bare hands."

I laughed. "I'll bet."

"I'm sorry about your girlfriend," she said. "I can tell from your eyes how much you miss her. How much you love her."

"We have something in common, then," I said, and she smiled. "Do you know something that could help me find her?"

"I don't know," she said. "I can't tell you where to find the emerald priestess. I've never even seen her myself. But I can tell you this. Whenever there's a problem here or if someone disobeys the Prima, someone always comes."

"What do you mean?"

"She sends someone. A daughter," she said. "It's not always the same lady, but someone always comes to deal with the problem. They always have red hair, and they always wear the same scarab beetle bracelet around their wrist."

I nodded. The bracelet was good information to have, but I wasn't sure how it helped me right now. "Thanks," I said.

"I'm just telling you that if you've been searching for her all this time and you can't find her, maybe you could try something new," she said. "Maybe you could bring her to you."

My lips parted, and I stared at Kristie. She was right. All this time, I'd been searching for information on where the priestess lived and how I could get to her. Never once did I consider drawing her out and making her come to me.

"She might not come in person," Kristie said, "but if you

make her angry enough, she'll send one of her daughters. She always does."

I smiled, a plan forming in my mind. "Thank you," I said. I crushed my cigarette into the ashtray and stood up. "I have to go, but thank you."

She walked me to the door. "I may not have the magic or skills to fight them myself, but I want to see them dead just as badly as you do," she said. "Make them pay for the things they've done."

"I will," I said. I opened the door. "And I want you to know that before she died, Juliana said she wanted me to tell you how much she loved you. She wanted you to know she died saving what was left of her humanity. In the end, she died free."

THE IMAGES THAT HAUNTED ME

HARPER

I squinted against the light that poured into the room as the door opened. They'd kept me in darkness for days, only coming in to ask questions and give me more drugs. That nurse had told me I killed my whole family, and then she'd locked me away in this room all alone.

What kind of person did something like that?

What was this place?

I pressed my back farther into the corner, turning my head and shielding my face. My entire body trembled.

I didn't want to be restrained again and pumped with sedatives. I just wanted to go home.

"Harper, sweetheart, are you feeling any better today?"

The nurse's voice was calm and gentle.

I opened my eyes and angled my head toward her slightly to get a better look. I hadn't seen this nurse before. I studied her, searching for any sign of needles or restraints.

Everything about this place terrified me. The visions. The

nurses. The needles and pills. I was scared to tell them when I wasn't feeling well, because all they did was make me feel worse by injecting me with more medicine that made me groggy and disoriented.

"I'm feeling good," I lied.

I'd had a headache for days. Weeks, maybe. I'd completely lost track of time. How long had I been here?

The nurse was younger than the others, her face smooth and beautiful. Not a wrinkle in sight. She wore a pristine white uniform with long sleeves and a skirt that settled somewhere just below the knee. White tights covered her legs. Her dark hair was pulled into a twist at the base of her neck and covered at the top with the type of white nurse's hat that went out of style more than fifty years ago.

She smiled and crouched beside me.

I pressed my back harder into the wall behind me, wincing.

"The doctor said if you're feeling up to it, you might be ready to come outside and join the other girls sometime soon," she said with a glance toward the open door. "Everyone is anxious to meet you."

I swallowed against the dry sandpaper of my throat and tried to find my voice.

"Other girls?"

She raised an eyebrow and tilted her head. "Of course. You didn't think you were all alone in here, did you?"

I closed my eyes against the pounding headache that drummed against my skull.

I'd been alone for as long as I could remember. All I knew anymore were these white walls and the nightmares that haunted my sleep.

"Harper?" The nurse touched my arm, and I flinched, pulling back sharply.

I stared at her, waiting for her to pull a needle from her pocket and jab it into my arm. I gritted my teeth, preparing for the pain and the horror of the endless nightmares that always came when they forced me into a deep sleep.

Tears stung my eyes, and my entire body tensed.

"I'm not going to hurt you," she said softly.

I dared to draw a breath, my trembling body resisting the fullness of it. How could I trust her? My only memories of this place so far were of women who looked just like her holding me down so they could sedate me. Women who told me I'd done horrible things and was a danger to myself and others.

"Where am I?" I whispered, daring to ask the one question the nurses had refused to answer.

"You're in a safe place," she said with a sad smile. "We're going to take care of you here, I promise."

I closed my eyes. A tear escaped and fell down my cheek, leaving a hot trail across my skin.

She hadn't answered my question. Not really. And I was too tired to protest. Too afraid to ask again.

The nurse reached out and ran her hand along my hair, pushing the matted blonde mess behind my ear. "I know you've been through some hard times," she said. "It can't be easy to lose everyone close to you, but now that you're feeling better, we're hoping the healing can begin. Do you think you're ready to see the doctor, Harper? To talk about what happened?"

My eyebrow twitched involuntarily as I stared at her. I looked deep into her dark-brown eyes, trying to make sense of her words.

How could I possibly talk about something I didn't even remember?

I glanced toward the doorway and watched as several girls who looked about my age passed by. One glanced inside, and then quickly snapped her head away. All of them were wearing knee-length gray dresses, their feet bare against the tile floor.

I closed my eyes and thought of the oppressing loneliness of this room. The images that haunted me night after night.

After a few seconds, I looked up at the nurse.

"Are you ready to join the others now, Harper?" she said.

I swallowed again, wishing for water.

"Yes," I said, my voice like sand against my throat.

The nurse smiled, her teeth white against the red of her lips. "Wonderful," she said.

She stood and reached for my hand.

Taking in a deep breath, I put my hand in hers and let her help me to my feet. My knees wobbled, and I steadied myself against the padded wall. The nurses had kept me in restraints for days before they locked me in this room. How long ago was that? Days? Weeks? The room had no windows and no clock. No way to mark the passage of time.

It felt as if I'd been here for a lifetime.

"Come on, now," the nurse said, coaxing me from the safety of the wall. "Let's get you cleaned up. Dr. Evers has been dying to speak with you."

I took the journey one step at a time, the door in front of me like a gate to another world. Would I find answers beyond that doorway? Would someone be able to tell me who I was? Would anyone know why I couldn't stop dreaming of a guy with green eyes?

I was terrified to know if he was still alive or if he'd also died in that fire. I was terrified to know the full extent of what I'd done.

Maybe it was better that I didn't remember.

I slowed, my stomach reeling at the thought. Had I killed everyone I loved? Was that why I couldn't remember? Because the horror of it was so great, my mind had refused to see?

A part of me knew it had to be true. I dreamed of fire constantly. I saw it every time I closed my eyes. Every night I watched the beautiful white house burn in the flames. Sometimes, I could swear I still smelled it in my hair.

I reached up to touch my unruly locks, the matted waves so knotted and dirty I pulled away, embarrassed. I tucked my head down, not wanting anyone to see my face. I didn't want the first glance the others had of me to be of a girl with tears in her eyes.

This isn't me. I don't belong here.

I wasn't sure where the thought came from, but the heat that pulsed under my skin told me that whoever this girl was— with her lowered eyes and trembling knees—she was not me. I had no idea what events had brought me to this place or why I couldn't remember anything, but I prayed that whatever answers were hidden beyond that doorway, I would have the strength to seek them out.

And the courage to face the truth, no matter how horrible it might be.

THERE'S ONLY ONE

HARPER

I sat in a leather chair across from the large mahogany desk, waiting for the doctor. It had taken two nurses over an hour to brush the tangles from my hair, and my scalp still hurt from all their pulling. They'd watched me as I stood under the shower, making sure I didn't hurt myself.

But I didn't want to hurt myself. I wanted to stand in that stream of hot water forever.

After weeks without a shower, it felt like heaven. But the nurses had rushed me along, dressing me in a simple gray dress that matched those worn by the girls I'd seen earlier. They pulled my long blonde hair into a simple ponytail and had me brush my teeth.

Then they had brought me here, telling me to wait.

This room was so different from the rest of the hospital. Where everything out there was white and sterile and harsh, this room was welcoming and warm. A fire burned in the hearth and the lamp on the desk emitted a soft, warm glow. Sunlight streamed in through heavy gold curtains.

The doctor's desk was neat and tidy, decorated only with a leather blotter and a fountain pen. There was the lamp, too, of course, and a picture frame. I couldn't see what it was a picture of, though, and I was too nervous to dare stand up and go around to look.

A plaque across the front of the desk read *Dr. Monica Evers.*

The door opened, and a woman walked in, her dark hair pulled into a bun at the base of her neck. She wore glasses and a simple brown suit with a knee-length skirt and kitten heels. She smiled at me as she came into the room.

"Harper, I'm so happy to see you looking well," she said. "How are you feeling today?"

I stifled a groan. How many times would I have to hear that question?

"I'm fine," I said.

"That's good," she said, taking a seat behind her desk. She opened a drawer and pulled out a large file, opening it and glancing through several pages before she looked up again. "The nurses tell me you've been improving, and they feel you're almost ready to join the rest of the girls in the main ward."

I nodded, although I didn't like the sound of that word. *Ward.* No one had explained to me what this place was, but considering the fact that I'd been locked in a room with padded walls, I had a pretty good idea.

"I know it's been a difficult few months for you since the fire," she said. "But we are here to help you, Harper."

I looked up at her. "Months?"

I thought it had maybe been a few weeks. But months?

"Yes," she said, lowering her glasses onto the edge of her nose and looking at her files. "You've been at the Evers Institute going on four months now."

I shook my head. How was that possible?

"How much do you remember of what happened before you were admitted to this place?" she asked.

"Not much," I said. "I remember a fire. Sometimes when I fall asleep, I dream of a large white house burning down."

She nodded, her eyes sympathetic but watchful. "What else? Do you remember who was inside the house?"

I shook my head. "I've tried to remember," I said. "But there's only one person I see over and over again in my dreams."

She nodded, encouraging me to go on as she lifted her pen to an empty page in her notes. "And who is that?"

"I see a guy with green eyes," I said. "I think he's about my age. His hair is dark and longer on top. But mostly it's his eyes that I see."

She gripped her pen tighter, and a muscle in her jaw twitched.

"Do you remember his name?" she asked.

I lowered my head. Had I said something wrong? "I can't remember anything else."

"It's going to take some time," she said. "You've been through a very traumatic event. Sometimes it takes a while for our memories to come back from something so tragic."

"Why am I here?" I asked. "Is it because I can't remember?"

"I'm afraid it's more complicated than that," she said, pushing her glasses up and setting down the pen. "Harper, there have been some questions about how the fire got started in the first place. The police seem to think you may have been the one to start it, but whether it was intentional or not is something only you can answer. After the trauma of the event, you closed yourself off from the world, refusing to speak or eat. You tried to hurt yourself. That's when they brought you here to us."

None of this sounded familiar. None of it sounded like me.

"How long do I have to stay?" I asked.

"As long as it takes," she said, which wasn't really an answer.

"What will I do here?"

"We'll work together to help you remember what happened," she said. "Hopefully as time goes on, we'll work through the event together, trying to understand it and make sense of what happened that tragic night."

"And what about my family?" I asked. "Surely there's someone out there who is worried about me? Has anyone come to visit?"

Dr. Evers sighed and shook her head. "Harper, I know this is hard to hear, but your parents were both killed in the fire," she said. "Your sister was also killed. You had no other relatives."

"You're telling me I'm all alone now?" I asked. I drew my knees up into the chair, wanting to curl into a ball and go back to my white padded room. I didn't want to hear this. It couldn't be true.

"You're not alone, Harper," she said with a smile. "You have us now. Over time, you will come to see the girls and the staff here at the Evers Institute as your family. You'll see. Things are going to get better. It just takes time."

I wanted to believe her, but something in the deepest part of my heart refused to believe this could be real. Something was off about this whole place, as if I were locked inside a nightmare.

"I'm sure you're tired and hungry," she said. "I'll have one of the nurses escort you to your room, so you can meet your new roommates. What do you think?"

I didn't know how to answer. I wanted to be alone. I wanted to fall asleep and wake up tomorrow in my own bed with my own memories. I didn't want to be in this place.

"Everything is going to be okay," she said, standing and coming over to place her hand on mine. Her skin was cold, and I wanted to pull away. Something about her made my skin crawl. "We're going to take good care of you, Harper. We're a family here. You'll see."

She clutched my hand tighter, and I heard the jingle of a bracelet as it slipped down her wrist. I peered at it, noticing a single charm dangling just beneath the hem of her brown suit jacket.

A tiny emerald scarab beetle.

I'D DONE THIS BEFORE

HARPER

"Come with me," the nurse said as I left the doctor's office. "Let's get you settled in your room. Dinner should be starting soon, so if you're feeling up to it, I'll take you by the dining hall, too."

"Yes, thank you," I said, even though I wasn't sure I felt up to it at all. For some reason, the charm on the doctor's bracelet had completely unsettled me. I felt as if I had seen that image before somewhere, only I couldn't remember where.

I followed the nurse into the stark, bare-walled hallway and around several turns. The dress they had given me scratched at my skin, making everything itch. They had not given me any shoes, and my feet slapped against the tile floors.

Everything seemed so cold in this place, and I longed for carpet and blankets and hot chocolate. I prayed for a hot dinner of soup or pasta, something that would warm me from the inside.

I kept my eyes lowered when we passed other nurses or

other girls in dresses like my own. I wasn't quite sure where I fit in this place, but there was definitely a hierarchy. And I was at the bottom of it. To them, I was the new girl. An outsider.

I couldn't imagine I would ever feel that I belonged here.

When the nurse stopped suddenly toward the end of one long corridor, I looked up, eyes wide as I peered inside the door of a new room. There were four beds lined up in a row with white metal railings at the head and foot of each one. Except for a navy wool blanket folded at the bottom of each bed, there was no color in this room, either. It was bare and cold just like the rest of this institution.

"Go on, then," the nurse said. "Your bed is the one there in the middle."

I walked inside and moved to stand beside the bed, unsure what she expected of me. I had no belongings to put away or to even mark my spot. All I could do was stand here and stare at the bed I'd been given and wonder who occupied the other three. There were a few items on top of each of their beds, but nothing that really told me who they were or why they were here.

The nurse stepped out of the room for a moment, leaving me alone to stare at the walls. I wanted to crawl into the bed and wrap the blanket around my body, shutting out the world.

"Your roommates must have already gone to the dining room," she said when she returned. She handed me a small white bag with my name embroidered in green thread along the edge. "These are just a few things you'll need while you're here. A toothbrush. A comb. A change of underwear. A nightgown. Just set them on your bed, and I'll show you to the dining hall."

She tapped her hand on the bronze numbers nailed to the door of my new room. 1802.

"I'll make sure someone is with you at all times, so you don't get turned around in this place," she said. "But try to remember your room number in case you get lost."

I memorized the numbers, saying them in my head over and over. I hoped I wouldn't forget, but so many things seemed to have slipped through my brain like sand through an hourglass. I remembered bits and pieces of life before this place, but my memories were only fragments, like a jumbled puzzle with no matching pieces.

I tried to memorize the turns as she led me through a maze of hallways where each one looked identical to the last. I began creating a map in my head. Turn left at the end of the hall, and then right. Another right and the hall opened into a much larger room filled with square tables, rocking chairs, sofas, and even a fireplace. Windows lined the far wall, and I breathed in, as if I could smell the fresh air from here.

My shoulders relaxed at the sight of the courtyard just beyond the glass. It was twilight and the sky was painted in dark pinks and oranges. After being locked away with no windows for such a long time, I was grateful for this glimpse of the outside world. It was the first sign of warmth I'd had since I arrived, and it filled me with hope.

We passed through another corridor, and at the end of that hall, she led me through a set of double doors that brought us, finally, to the dining hall. The noise of it assaulted me. Until now, I hadn't even realized just how quiet my life had become. I'd been alone for so long, I'd forgotten the way a room sounded when there were people in it.

The noise seemed to brush against my skin, as grating and

rough as the fabric of my dress. I lowered my head, wanting to disappear as eyes turned toward me. Too late, I realized the nurse had already started walking. She looked displeased, her arms crossed, and her smile faded.

"Harper, I need you to pay attention, please."

"I'm sorry," I mumbled as I hurried to catch up to her.

I tried to ignore the eyes that followed my every move, and the whispers and laughter that rippled through the place as I walked by.

This room was the largest I'd seen in the place, filled with long wooden tables that extended the entire length of the space. Each table had several matching wooden benches lined up on either side, most of the seats already filled with girls. I dared a glance around, noticing that some of the girls were much younger than I was. Possibly as young as seven or eight years old. Others looked about my age or older, but none looked over twenty or twenty-one.

I wondered what happened to the girls here when they got too old for this place. Were they moved to another institution? Or were they allowed to go home?

"Amelia, this is Harper," the nurse said when we reached the front of the room. A large banquet table was set up with plates and several pots of steaming food.

Amelia was a large black woman who smiled when I met her eyes. It was the first truly genuine smile I had seen in as long as I could remember.

"Welcome, Harper. Don't look so scared, girl. Everything's going to be alright now," Amelia said. She sounded so sincere, I almost believed her.

"Thank you," I said, taking the tray she held out toward me. There was no soup, but there was some kind of warm meat and mashed potatoes with gravy. Green beans. My stomach growled.

"Drinks are here," the nurse said. "And your napkin."

I looked around. "What about silverware?" I asked.

"No silverware," she said. "It's not safe."

I eyed my food. How was I supposed to eat this without silverware? I glanced around and noticed most of the other girls eating with their hands, scooping the potatoes into their fingers like children.

I took a napkin and a cup of water and followed the nurse to a table in the far corner of the room. Everyone sitting at the table straightened their shoulders and stopped talking as we approached. With the exception of one dark-haired girl on the end who kept her head down and rocked furiously back and forth, they all placed their hands in their laps and smiled at the nurse.

"Good evening, Nurse Joan," a girl with two short, blonde pigtails said.

"Good evening, Miss Nora," the nurse said. "Ladies, this is Harper. She's new here, and I trust you will all help her to feel welcome. She'll be joining Mary Ellen, Nora and Judith in room 1802. Please make sure she feels welcome. And Nora, will you please make sure she finds her way back safely before room checks?"

"Of course," Nora said.

Dumbly, I stood there with my tray as the nurse nodded and walked away. Panic shot through my veins as she left me. No matter how much I may have disliked her, she was the only thing I knew in this place. I didn't understand the rules or even where I was. How could she simply walk away and leave me here?

"Are you just going to stand there catching flies? Or do you plan to sit down and eat that meat loaf?" someone said. I snapped my mouth shut and looked down into the dark-blue eyes of a girl who looked as if she couldn't have been more than twelve or thirteen years old. "Because if you aren't hungry, I'll gladly take what's leftover. I'm starving."

"You're always starving, Bonnie," Nora said. "And yet you weigh twice as much as any of the rest of us."

The other girls at the table giggled, but Bonnie didn't look amused. Her jaw clenched, and she rose from her seat, the bench scraping the floor.

"You'll shut your mouth if you know what's good for you."

"Oh, sit down and stop your complaining," Nora said. She glanced up at me. "You going to join us, or what?"

I cleared my throat and nodded, setting my tray and cup on the table before stepping over the bench and sitting down.

"Harper, huh? I'm Nora, and this here is obviously Bonnie." She pointed her index finger at each girl as she went down the row. "Judith is in the room with us. Hailey. Meredith. And our resident rocker over there is Mary Ellen. She doesn't say much."

Everyone waved as they were introduced, but Mary Ellen just kept rocking. She didn't even lift her head or look up, and from the looks of it, she hadn't touched her food.

"So, what's your story?" Nora asked, spooning a glob of mashed potatoes into her mouth with her fingertips.

I shook my head, not sure what I wanted to tell her. I certainly didn't want to say that I'd burned my own house down and apparently murdered a family I couldn't even remember. I lifted a chunk of meat loaf to my mouth and took a large bite. My stomach revolted, and I nearly tossed it back up.

"Don't you talk?" Bonnie asked.

I washed another bite of the meat down with a gulp of water and wiped my lips with the back of my hand. "I don't know what to say. I don't know my story."

Several of the girls at the table lowered their heads or exchanged glances before taking bites of food and turning their eyes away from mine.

"What?" I asked.

The only one who would meet my gaze was Nora. For a moment, her eyes dipped toward my arms where my dress lifted just enough to show the scars that marred my skin. Absently, I touched one and ran my fingertip along its upraised pink surface. I quickly pulled the edge of my sleeve down to cover it.

"It's nothing," Nora said. "Just some girls come here with absolutely no memory of their lives before Evers."

"Evers Institute?" I asked. "That's the name of this place?"

"Evers Institute for Troubled Girls," Bonnie said. "If you want the full technical name."

A chill ran across my skin like a ghost passing through me. I felt as if I'd done this before. A strange place. New girls. Something unpleasant tugged on me. When I focused on it too hard, though, a sharp pain exploded behind my right eye. I winced and lowered my head.

"What's wrong?" Judith asked. She was sitting across from me and leaned over to touch my arm. "Do you need me to call for the nurse?"

I shook my head. "I'm fine," I said. "It just hurts sometimes."

"Headaches?" Nora asked.

"Yeah," I said, opening my eyes and sucking in a deep breath. "I used to have them all the time. I think they're getting better, but sometimes I get this shooting pain right here."

I touched my hand to my temple, and Nora nodded.

"I've had that before," she said. "It's from the meds. It should get better."

Behind me, a tray crashed to the floor and everyone at my table turned to look. A girl who looked to be about fifteen or sixteen stared directly at me, her eyes wide and her mouth open.

"Harper?" she whispered.

Confused, I studied her face. "Do I know you?" I asked.

"We've never met, but I know who you are," she said. Tears slipped from her eyes and fell onto her gray dress, leaving dark marks on the fabric. She pressed her fists against the side of her face, her voice growing louder. "If you're here, the world is lost. You can't be here. You don't belong here."

I swallowed, her words like a punch in the gut. What the hell was she talking about?

Nora grabbed my arm, and I spun around.

"Ignore her," Nora said. "Someone needs to shut that girl up or things are going to go very badly for her. You don't want to get caught in the middle of that."

The girl behind me screamed, and everyone in the entire room froze.

I turned around, angling my body so I could see what was going on. Two nurses rushed to the girl's side. One of them inserted a long needle into the girl's neck.

The screaming cut off abruptly and the girl went limp,

falling into the arms of the nurses. They lifted her and carried her away so fast they were practically running.

"I don't understand what's happening," I said.

"Just turn around and eat your food," Judith said in a loud, rough whisper.

The noise in the dining hall gradually returned as girls went back to their food and their conversations, but I couldn't force another bite.

I turned to glance toward the door, but Nora grabbed my arm. When I looked up, she shook her head sharply back and forth. There was a panic in her eyes that frightened me.

I lowered my head and stared at the food on my plate. My hands were trembling, so I hid them under the table, clasping them together in my lap.

"Who was that girl?" I whispered, so low I wasn't sure anyone could even hear me. "What did she mean by that? That I don't belong here?"

"Her name is Robin. She's insane," Bonnie said, leaning close to me. "She's always causing trouble, saying things that don't make any sense. Just ignore it. She probably didn't even know what she was talking about."

Bonnie sounded so sure of herself, I might have believed her. Except for one thing.

As far as I remembered, I had never seen that girl in my entire life.

And yet, she had known my name.

THE TRUTH OF IT

AERDEN

My muscles ached from working all day, but while
the other demons groaned and complained, I sat
in one corner of our cell, enjoying the pain.

I'd spent a week in solitary confinement without food or
water, but today they had brought me back out to the quarry.
The wounds from Ezrah's lashing still pulsed along my back,
and my muscles begged to be stretched. Any normal demon
would consider it agony to be pushed so hard and beaten so
badly, but my heart swelled with gratitude.

This pain belonged to me. Just as my heart belonged to me.
My mind.

My own mind. Everything else here was just temporary.

"How is it you can smile after such torture?" The old
demon, Trention, walked toward me and rested his side against
the stone walls.

I looked up briefly and met his eyes. Had I been smiling?

"I don't know how to thank you for your kindness on

the line the other day," Trention said. "I deserved those lashings, and it pained me to see you have to take them for yourself. When you didn't return to our cell for several days, I was worried something terrible had happened to you."

I held my tongue. I'd already drawn enough attention to myself this week. There was a rumbling among the others already about my display of power and my defiance. I knew I should tell this demon to move on. I wasn't here to make friends.

I nodded and looked away.

"I'm sorry to disturb you," he said. "I just wanted to say thank you for what you did. Your kindness will not be forgotten."

He turned to walk away, his steps slow and pained. One hand clutched his shoulder, and he leaned against the wall for support.

For the most part, everyone here had left me to my own thoughts. Already, though, I'd been getting curious looks throughout the day.

I'd done a good job keeping my head down as Ezrah asked, and I wanted to keep it that way. But for some reason, I had a soft spot in my heart for this old demon.

Growing up as a young shadowling, I had not known him personally, but I had known of him. He didn't belong in a place like this. He didn't deserve this.

"Want me to take a look at that wound?" I asked.

He looked back to me, his head tilted in surprise. "Looking at it won't do much good, I'm afraid," he said. "But you're welcome to see it if you want to. I haven't even had the courage to look at it myself."

I stood and walked over to him, helping him sit down on the pile of rags that was the closest thing I had in here to a bed.

Once he was settled, I pulled the fabric of his tunic off the top of his shoulder. Trention winced and sucked a breath through his teeth. The fabric had stuck to the wound, and when I got a good look at it, my heart sank.

"This is infected," I said.

"Oh, I know," he said. "Been that way for about two months now. I kept hoping it would heal on its own, but the way they have us working every day keeps opening it up. It's hard to lift that axe over my head without upsetting it. If they were smart, they'd just use magic to mine those quarries. I don't understand it."

I didn't want to tell him that they all probably had me to thank for this particular daily task. Someone in charge likely thought it would be fun to watch me have to mine the very type of stone that had held me prisoner for so long.

"I'm guessing you already asked the guards for some kind of ointment or a trip to the shaman?" I asked.

Trention nodded. "A few times, but Karn told me if I asked again, he'd deepen the wound by double," he said. "I have to tell you, I never believed this would be the way my final days would go."

"You were a scholar in the castle," I said.

He looked up, surprised, and smiled. "How did you know that? Most of the demons around here assume I was just some fisherman living out on the Black Cliffs before I came here," he said. "I never bothered to correct them. I figured if they knew the truth... Well, it doesn't matter, I guess, now does it?"

I didn't tell him how I knew, but he seemed to appreciate that someone had finally recognized him.

I wished I had any tools that might help his wound heal, but they didn't give us much inside the cell. No running water. No food or clean cloths. There was only one thing I could think of that might work.

I brought my wrist up to my mouth and bit into the skin at the base of my thumb. When I tasted the sharp sting of blood on my tongue, I held the wound out toward the old man.

He backed away slightly, scared for a moment.

"What are you doing?"

I moved forward and dripped blood across his wounded shoulder. The blue drops soaked into his skin in an instant, the wound drinking it like it had been dying of thirst.

His body immediately relaxed, and he moved his shoulder back and forth. His jaw fell open and he leaned forward, taking a closer look at my face. I turned my head to the side, letting my dark curls hide most of my profile, but he simply reached over and pushed my hair back.

"It's you," he whispered. "I thought I recognized you when you first arrived, but it's been so many years since I had seen your face. I thought it was impossible. When you disappeared, we were all told you had died."

"I'm sorry. I don't know what you're talking about," I said. I'd gone too far. Exposed too much. Healing was a rare ability in the Shadow World. Only a few families held that power in their blood. I'd made a mistake. "I hope that helps your shoulder, but if you'll excuse me—"

"How did you get free?" he asked, reaching out to touch my hand. His voice was reverent and full of wonder. "It's impossible that you could be here in this world or even in this place. No one ever comes back. I don't understand it, but it's you. It's really you."

I shook my head. The last thing I needed right now was for this guy to tell everyone that I was the long-lost son of the king's most trusted advisor. Or that I had been strong enough to somehow escape the Order's slavery.

"I'm telling you, old man, I'm not who you think I am," I said, my voice harsher than he deserved. Softly, I added, "And even if I was, there might be a reason I didn't want everyone to know."

He slowly nodded and glanced toward our other cellmates.

"Your secret is safe with me, Aerden," he said.

I looked up at the sound of my own name. He said it with such reverence it nearly brought tears to my eyes.

"I don't know how you did it, but if you're here it must be true. I'd heard the rumors, but none of us actually believed it," Trention said in a whisper. "But how did you end up here? How could a great warrior such as yourself become a prisoner in your own kingdom?"

"I could ask you the same thing, scholar," I said.

"Does this mean our princess has returned as well?" he asked.

For the hundredth time that day, I thought of Lea and the words I hadn't yet been able to say to her. We'd spent months together in Brighton Manor. I'd had every opportunity to tell her the truth about the heart stone and why I had left the King's City all those years ago.

So why had I never told her?

Because I was a coward. The truth of it hit me harder than Ezrah's whip.

I'd distanced myself from my brother—the only one who'd actually believed there was hope of ever saving me—because I blamed him for Lea's broken heart. But the truth was that Jackson was the one who'd been true to his own heart. He hadn't asked me to pour my own love into that heart stone. I had done that all on my own, thinking it would make Lea happier.

And Jackson hadn't been the one to willingly walk away from his duty to the kingdom. Not until my life was on the line.

I had once been groomed to someday take over the King's Guard. Money and time had been poured into my training, and my people were counting on me. I left because I was too much of a coward to stay and watch my brother marry the woman I loved.

Everything that happened was my fault.

Hearing this demon call me a warrior made me sick to my stomach. I'd spent so much time blaming everyone else, that I'd never realized that I was the one to blame.

How would things have been different if I had stayed? Or if I'd told Lea the truth about my feelings before her engagement? If I had faced my fear and been true to my heart, I might never have spent a hundred years in slavery. Lea might already be the Queen of the North, leading this realm to victory against the Order.

My fear was the cause of so much pain, my heart couldn't even comprehend.

I turned away from the old demon, holding back tears. I hoped he would walk away and leave me to my thoughts, but he stayed, placing his hand on my arm as if we were old friends.

"I'm sorry to have upset you, warrior," he said.

"Don't call me that," I said. "I am nothing. I'm not respon-

sible for my freedom. I was rescued by the ones strong enough
to stand against her."

"And the others?" he asked. "Those who were also held
captive by the sapphire priestess? What of them? I had a
daughter who was taken many years ago. My youngest."

"If the human who hosted her was still alive, then your
daughter is free," I said.

He clutched my hand and held it tightly in his own. "A
true priestess of the Order of Shadows is dead. There is hope,
after all."

I thought of Lea. Everything that had kept us apart—our
duty to the kingdom and my slavery—was gone. If I could
prove to her that I was worthy of her love, would she ever find
it in her heart to love me back?

In that moment, though a prisoner in the deepest depths of
the king's dungeons, I vowed that somehow, I would face my
fears and restore my power. Somehow, I would become the
demon she deserved.

I placed my other hand on top of his and met his eyes.
"Where there is still life," I said, "there is always hope."

LIKE A REAL PRINCESS AGAIN

LEA

"When can I see my father?" I asked.

I'd been waiting for days, locked away in my room. Granted, it was a lot more comfortable here than the dungeons. At least I had food and water, but I was still a prisoner here. They still didn't trust me.

"Soon, Princess," Anastia said. "Your mother has appointed three handmaidens to your service. Ellain, Presha, and Margot."

The girls walked into the room, each one bowing to me in turn.

"For what reason?" I asked.

"For whatever reason I say," she snapped. "Why do you have to be so defiant?"

I lowered my head. I was still learning my way around this new me.

Of course, this wasn't new. Not really. I was a curious shadowling, questioning everything and breaking the rules when I thought I wouldn't get caught. Even then, before my heart had been broken and all my deepest, strongest loyalties tested by fire, I had been a defiant girl.

I'd never liked being bathed and dressed by maidens, and I didn't want to invite them into my chambers. It seemed like an invasion of my privacy rather than a benefit to being royalty. I didn't want someone in my chambers at all times, waiting on my every need and desire. I wanted to be alone and free to think or speak to whoever I damn well wanted without a dozen pairs of eyes staring back at me, watching my every move. Judging my every choice.

Over the past several decades, I'd gotten used to that privacy. I'd built so many walls around myself that no one dared to even think about disturbing me when I didn't want to be disturbed.

Yet, like a mouse caught in a wheel, here I was again: a princess in a castle with three young girls staring at me like I was some kind of mutant.

"Go ahead," I said to the girl in front of me. Her eyes were about as wide as they could get, and I could tell she was trying very hard not to stare at the bruises and cuts on my wrists and neck.

Did they know I'd been kept in the dungeon? Would the people of the King's City know it? Or would they be fed some lie about how I'd been captured by an enemy and had fought my way home after all this time?

If I knew my father, there would be many lies. Make them believe whatever it is you most desperately need them to believe, and never let yourself be made vulnerable by the truth. This is how I was raised, and I used to have an appreciation for that type of manipulation.

But somewhere along the way, I'd started to crave the actual truth. Lies felt like burns against my tongue, and I couldn't stand to play those types of games with people.

Something told me I'd have to get used to lying again if I wanted to survive the next few months, or however long I'd be a prisoner in this old home of mine.

The oldest girl, Presha, snapped her fingers and more than a dozen dresses floated into the room. She waved her hand and the large armoire in my dressing room opened up. The dresses arranged themselves according to color inside the wardrobe.

The other two girls went to work, pulling jewels and brushes from their bags. They dressed me from head to toe in amber-colored robes that slid across the stone floor when I walked. Margot stood on a stool and braided my hair, but it wasn't the simple long braid I'd been wearing for years. Instead, she created an intricate network of miniature braids, each one tied and twisted around the next until it was impossible to tell where one ended and another began.

I let them do what they wanted. I didn't care. This dress was never going to be as comfortable as my leather pants and t-shirts, but it didn't matter. If this was what it was going to take for them to see me as a princess again, then it was worth it.

They fussed for an hour, dragging brushes across my cheeks and placing gemstones in each braid. I had to resist the urge to pull it all out and scream at them to leave me the hell alone.

"You look beautiful," Presha said. She smiled at me, proud of her work. "You look like a real princess again."

She put her hands on my shoulders and spun me toward the mirror that lined the wall on one side of the dressing room.

I wasn't prepared for the way the transformation affected me.

I hardly recognized the woman in the mirror. This woman was soft and elegant.

I looked like my mother.

For all my talk of being strong and making them pay, I was nearly brought to my knees by the sight of my own face. Every painful memory and hope I used to carry inside myself pushed its way through the doors of my heart, demanding to be seen and heard and, worst of all, felt.

I nearly begged them to take me back to the dungeons.

"Are you okay, Princess?" Presha asked, placing her hand on my arm.

I closed my eyes and counted to five, inhaling the pain and breathing it back out again. By the time I opened my eyes, I was calm, the tears forced deep down inside.

"I'm fine," I said, giving her a smile I hoped looked sincere. "It's just been so long since I was home. It's a little over-whelming."

"I'm sure," she said. "I can't imagine what you've been through out there. I hear the lands outside the castle are very dangerous these days. You must be brave to have fought your way here to see your father."

So, it was definitely going to be a game of lies.

"Not so very brave," I said. "Just homesick and dying to see my father again."

The lie rolled off my tongue like honey, but it tasted like shit.

"He will call for you soon," she said. "I'm sure he is anxious to see you as well."

I stepped through the door of the dressing chamber and into the main room of suites.

I had no idea what Anastia had in store for me, but whatever it was, I'd rather stay in my room, thank you very much.

I was here to get information about the Council's plans, but if they wouldn't even let me talk to my own father, this was going to take a lot longer than I'd hoped.

"You look exceptional," Anastia said when she returned. "Your former schoolmates and friends will be so happy to see you looking well."

I nearly groaned. My only true friends from the time I lived here were long gone, which meant she was taking me to spend time with people I despised. Wouldn't this be fun?

For the second time that week, I was paraded through the halls of my father's castles, the eyes of the people of the court fastened to my face, some of them wide-eyed at my transformation.

I raised my chin and floated through the halls, careful to keep my expression serene and grateful. Gone was the defiant girl in leather who'd learned to shoot an arrow through the heart of any enemy. Gone was the broken girl who'd sat in the dungeons, almost wishing that life was over.

I was a princess.

God help me.

The next few weeks of my life were filled with mundane luncheons and lessons. All of my mother's friends wanted to welcome me home and take me to tea. I did my best to act interested in their lives and to answer questions about where I'd been, never telling them the truth.

Every chance I got, I told them I was thankful to be home and that I desperately missed my father. But still, he never called for me. He never came to see me, and neither did my mother. They were either avoiding me or punishing me, neither of which were particularly fun.

Finally, though, Anastia announced that it was time to see him. Presha and the other girls dressed me in the finest blue gown from my wardrobe. They fastened flowers in my hair— my father's favorite blue lilies from the valley near the frosted mountain.

My heart pounded as I walked toward the golden doors with their black obsidian handles. They swung open as the guards grew closer and we marched inside the king's chambers.

It had been a very long time since I'd set foot in this room. Not since I was a shadowling. I paused, nearly stumbling over my own feet as I stared at him. My father sat hunched behind his desk, his weight resting against a long, thin scepter made of gold and encrusted with stones of various colors, a large diamond resting on the top.

Without thinking, I raised my hand to my lips and drew in a breath. How was that demon my father? What had happened to him over the years?

I'd seen him briefly in the throne room when Aerden and I had first been brought here, but he looked even worse than I'd remembered. Weak and diminished. He was not at all the big, strong demon I'd looked up to as a shadowling. He was a ghost of himself, and the man I once admired was gone.

Behind me, one of the guards cleared his throat and nudged the back of my leg.

My instinct was to turn and wrap my hands around the guard's throat for even daring to touch me. Instead, I forced one foot in front of the other and dropped my hand to my side.

I kept my eyes on my father the rest of the way to his desk, trying to come to terms with what my eyes were seeing before I reached him. The degradation was startling. He looked physically smaller, hunched forward with a dingy white beard. The light in his deep-green eyes had dulled to an ugly gray.

As we drew closer, the guards at the front of our little parade peeled off and surrounded the king on all sides, as if he needed to be protected even from his own daughter.

I stopped a few feet in front of his large stone desk. I lowered my head, not daring to look him in the eyes. It wasn't that I was afraid of being disrespectful or breaking some type of custom. It was more that I simply couldn't bear seeing him this way.

Had I done this to him?

The thought nearly broke me, and my knees buckled slightly. Ezrah, who'd been standing to the side, rushed to me, gripping my arm and letting me rest my weight against him.

"Easy," he whispered. "Be strong."

I nodded and found my footing. Once I was sure of myself, I let my knees fall to the floor deliberately. Not out of sorrow or shock, but out of purposeful surrender.

I needed my father to believe that I was home and that I belonged to him once again.

"Father," I whispered. "I'm so sorry."

"You do not speak to the king unless you have been spoken to," his head guard said. He stepped toward me, his hand raised as if he actually meant to strike me.

If he'd dared to touch a hair on my head, this whole charade would have been over, and I'd have been thrown in the dungeons for killing a guard with my bare hands.

"Bartrem, stand down," my father said. The sound of his voice, still booming and strong and deep baritone after all these years, brought fresh tears to my eyes. There was still a part of him that was the same inside this shell of a demon. "Come to me, my sweet girl."

I lifted my eyes to him and he nodded, extending one hand toward me and motioning for me to join him.

I walked around the massive desk and fell again at his feet, my head bowed and my tears flowing freely.

To hear my father call me his sweet girl broke my heart in two. How could I viciously despise every choice he made and yet still love him with such fierceness? How could I yearn to throw my arms around him like a child and yet also want to pierce his heart with a dagger?

Maybe I was a traitor, after all.

A traitor to him, but a hero to my people. It wasn't an easy thing to understand, and I hated the feelings that battled inside of me.

I believed in the choices I'd made. I believed in the work I had done to save so many demons who'd been stolen from our lands. But there was a part of me that still felt ashamed for what I had done to my father. I was his only child and owed him my allegiance and my loyalty.

Instead, I'd abandoned him to follow after a demon who was never going to marry me or love me the way I once believed he did. I'd left my own family in order to help strangers. I had given up the part of myself that had once been sweet and soft and vulnerable to be a warrior instead. And as much as I believed I loved it, there was still a part of me that mourned the loss of this life. There was still a young girl inside me who missed her father desperately and wanted to go back to a time when things were much simpler, before I knew anything about the Order of Shadows and their intent to steal all strong demons for their own purposes.

It wasn't fair that I'd had to abandon it all. It wasn't fair that I was constantly being forced to choose.

"Why are you crying, my dear Lazalea?" he asked. My father touched my chin with his finger and lifted it upward. "If you have truly come home to us, this is a day for joy, not sorrow."

His demeanor was so different from the day Aerden and I were brought here. That day my father had barely even listened to what I had to say. He'd refused to let me speak. Why the sudden change of heart? Had my performance with Anastia really been so convincing?

"I cry for the things I have done," I said. "For the pain I've caused you."

"Do you know how many times I have dreamed of this moment?" he said softly. When I looked up at him, there were tears in his own dull gray eyes. "To see you here before me in your gowns again, looking like a true princess? It hurt me to put you in those dungeons, and I'm sorry it had to be done. But if it allowed you the time to reflect on what that demon, Denaer, forced you to do, then it was the best thing for all of us."

I studied him, surprised to hear him blame everything that happened on Jackson. Was that truly what he believed? That I had blindly followed my betrothed?

I could use this to my advantage. After all, wasn't that truly the reason I'd left the castle in the first place? If it hadn't been for Jackson, I never would have left my father's side.

Who cared that Jackson had begged me to stay home? He

had never forced me to join him, but my father didn't need to know that.

"I was blinded by what I believed was love. Duty," I said. "But now I see the truth. You are the only one I owe my loyalty to, my king. I will not leave you again."

"I knew it," he whispered, caressing my braids and touching my shoulder. "All this time I knew that you were not yourself when you were with him. You never meant to hurt me or your mother. You were simply lost, and now you have returned to us."

My gut twisted. Making him believe these things would only hurt him more, but what choice did I have? This was the path to life for me and for my people, no matter the cost.

I reached for his hand and met his eyes. "Yes, Father," I said, wiping a tear from his cheek. "I am home."

FAR AWAY

JACKSON

My sister sat on the steps leading up to the castle's entrance, her skirts billowing out across the stone.

I sat down next to her, wondering if she was still upset with me. We hadn't spoken in days.

"It's incredible, really," she said.

"What?"

"This place," she said, motioning in the air. "This city. I've been sitting out here nearly all day, just watching them. I never dreamed humans and demons could live together so peacefully. They seem happy."

"They are happy," I said. "I wish you could have known the king. He was truly a great demon, worthy of his station in life. The things we heard about the King of the South as shadowlings were all lies, meant to keep us away from this place so that we wouldn't see this for ourselves. So that we wouldn't know what kind of peace could come from living together like this."

"How did he die?" she asked.

"He died saving Harper's life," I said. "He didn't always approve of our war against the Order. He thought it was better to keep his people safe than to fight, but, unlike the King of the North, he didn't pick and choose who to save. He invited everyone to live here, and he wanted us to stay with him instead of fighting. But we had no choice. Not if we wanted Aerden to be free. I think the king finally understood that at the end. He brought his soldiers to our final battle against the sapphire priestess, arriving just as she struck Harper down and nearly killed her. The king sacrificed what was left of his life to save hers."

Illana was quiet, her eyes sweeping over the streets, watching the day-to-day life of the citizens living here in the domed city.

"I can't say that I understand love the way you do," she said. "But I do know what it's like to lose someone close to you. I know what it's like to wonder every single day if they are still alive or if they're ever coming home. I should have followed you and helped, but I was afraid. I'm sorry."

"And I'm sorry for what I said to you the other day. I didn't want to hurt you," I said. "I just need for you to understand what this is like for me. You may not agree with my methods, but I can't just sit around and wait for something to happen. I have to find her, Illana. Every minute she's gone, it's like a noose tightens around my heart."

"What if we went home?" she asked. "Lea and Aerden are already there. Maybe if we went together and talked to our parents—"

"I can't go back there," I said. "Not like that. Not to ask for their help again. You know how they were when Aerden was taken. They didn't so much as lift a finger to save him. Why would they help me rescue the heir to the Southern Kingdom? A girl who is half-human?"

"Maybe together we could convince them, Jackson. We should at least try."

"Right now, they have both Lea and Aerden locked away in the dungeons for treason," I said. "Do you really think we could just walk in there and ask for help fighting this war? Best-case scenario they throw us in the dungeons, too, instead of killing us on the spot."

"They would never do that," she said.

"How do you know what they would do?" I asked. "In their eyes, I'm a traitor, much worse than Lea or Aerden. Aerden was taken against his will, and Lea was only doing her duty by remaining with her betrothed. I'm the one who defied them. I'm the one who took her away and opened her eyes to the Order's evil. They won't welcome me home with open arms, and I think you know that. Besides, they don't know the first thing about fighting against the Order or finding the emerald priestess. The king has locked himself away so that he doesn't have to think about the Order of Shadows and what they've done to the Shadow World."

Illana wiped tears from her cheeks, but she didn't argue with me. It was the truth. No one in the castle was going to listen to me. If we went in there, it would be to rescue Lea and Aerden. And there would be bloodshed in the King's City just to get them free.

For now, they were safest where they were. I didn't want to jeopardize that.

"What else can we do, then?" Illana asked.

"I have a plan," I said. "And I'm going to need your help, if you're willing."

"Anything."

"I've told the others to meet us in the dining hall, so we can talk it over, but before we go, can I ask you something?"

"Of course."

"Before we even knew you had been taken by the emerald priestess, Harper had been dreaming of an old shack in the woods," I said. "When we rescued you, you told me you'd somehow been able to reach inside Harper's mind to show her those visions, hoping she would figure it out and come to rescue you."

"Yes," she said. "My powers were so weak inside the iron cage, but I was able to send some visions out to you both."

"Do you think you could do it again?" I asked. "Just to send her a message and let her know we're thinking of her. That we miss her, and we haven't forgotten her."

My heart tightened at the word forgotten. Did she even remember me at all?

"I've tried," she said. "When she first disappeared, I tried to reach out to her, but I didn't mention it to you, because I didn't want you to feel discouraged. You were already so sad, Jackson. I didn't want to make it worse."

I closed my eyes and lowered my head into my hands. "I don't understand," I said. "If you connected with her once, why wouldn't you be able to do it now?"

"I don't know," she said. "I can only tell you that she felt very far away, as if she'd been taken to another dimension. Another world."

I raised my head. "Another dimension? You mean she was removed from the human world?"

Illana shook her head. "I'm not sure," she said. "I wish I could tell you more, but it doesn't make any sense to me. She's alive, though, Jackson. I can feel her."

I paused, looking out at the people of her kingdom. She belonged here with us. It wasn't enough just to know that she was alive.

I stood and started back up the castle steps.

"Where are you going?" she asked.

"To the dining hall," I said. "We need to talk. All of us."

"Jackson, wait," she said.

I paused on the top step and waited for her. My sister placed her hand in mine.

"I really did miss you when you left," she said. "Just because I wasn't brave enough to come after you doesn't mean I wasn't thinking of you every day. I love you, brother."

I squeezed her hand. "I missed you, too."

"We'll find her," she said.

"I know we will." But as I walked through the throne room and down the hall to meet the others, I wondered if, when we found her, my Harper would be the same woman I fell in love with.

LIKE COMING HOME

HARPER

Days at the Evers Institute passed slowly, each one running into the next as if time were on an endless loop. Everything here was ruled by routine: Breakfast in the morning at seven sharp. Group therapy at eight. Art class from nine until eleven. Lunch and time in our rooms to properly digest, whatever that meant. If the weather was nice, we were allowed to go outdoors after lunch for an hour or two. If it was raining or too windy, we were allowed to either stay in our rooms or have social time in the recreation area indoors.

In the late afternoons, we worked. At the beginning of each quarter, every one of us was assigned a new job. For my first few weeks here, I'd been given the glamorous job of cleaning the bathrooms. From what I'd heard, it was a common assignment for new girls. Just my luck.

My only saving grace was that I enjoyed the company of the four girls I worked with. They were all younger than me, but we got along well and that helped to pass the time. We never talked about why we were here, but since I could hardly remember anything from before anyway, that was fine by me.

After our chores were done, we all cleaned up for dinner. And after dinner, we were sent to our rooms, where the nurses would come by and deliver our medicine, check our rooms, and finally turn off the lights and lock the doors.

They always locked us in, and as much as I hated having to clean toilets all afternoon, I hated the nights the most. Our room was small and cramped with four beds, and the second that lock clicked closed, I felt as if I couldn't breathe.

I'd met with Dr. Evers once a week since coming here, and she tried to assure me that locking the doors was for our own safety. But that was bullshit, wasn't it? What if a fire broke out? We would all be locked away in our rooms with no way to get outside.

When I told her that, she'd narrowed her eyes at me and asked if I'd remembered more about what happened before I came to the institute. She said my fear of fire was a rational response to having been through one and lost so many of the people I cared about most. Still, she didn't agree to stop locking the doors at night, telling me that there was little chance of a fire breaking out here.

Locking us away wasn't about our safety, though, and I knew it. It was about keeping us in line. Keeping us from seeing things the staff didn't want us to see. Or going places the staff didn't want us to go.

That's also the reason they gave us all little white pills to help us sleep.

The first night I'd spent in my new room, I'd taken their pills like the good girl they so wanted me to be. I'd felt groggy and tired about ten minutes later, and a minute after that, I was sound asleep.

But sleep was not a safe place for me these days.

The moment my eyes closed, the nightmares took over. Fire was the most common one: green flames the size of skyscrapers engulfing an old white house that looked like it had stood for over a hundred years.

But I also dreamed of other things. Things I didn't dare tell Dr. Evers or any of the nurses. I hadn't even told my roommates.

Sometimes I dreamed I was lying naked on a stone table, my body shivering from fever. A woman with dark-red hair spoke words of magic as she cut into the skin on my arms and legs with shards of emerald-colored glass. When I screamed in pain, the red-headed woman always smiled.

Other nights she tortured me by nearly drowning me in a black pool of water. It was too dark for me to see where we were. Inside somewhere. Maybe a basement. The pool was deep, though, and dark as night. She tied my hands and legs together and forced me under the water, holding me down until my breath was gone and my lungs begged for air.

At night, I was subjected to all kinds of torture in my dreams. Unimaginable things that felt more real to me than the times when I was awake. Things that couldn't possibly have been real, but that my mind had made up in order to deal with the pain of what I had lost.

So, I stopped taking the little white pills.

Instead, I kept my eyes open for as long as I could, listening to the soft sounds of my roommates' breathing. Sometimes I heard the echo of high heels against the floor and wondered who around here wore high heels. None of the nurses who I had seen. They all wore soft-soled white shoes that squeaked against the tiles.

It could have been the doctor, checking on us to make sure we were asleep, but I never dared keep my eyes open to look through the small window on our door. If I heard those shoes, I closed my eyes and turned away from the window, hoping whoever it was would simply pass us by.

Most nights, I spent the hours trying to remember.

Who was I? What was my life like before they brought me here?

I touched the raised scars that covered my arms and stomach and legs, begging my mind to break free of whatever was holding the memories inside. It was my only way out of this place. Maybe if I could remember what happened, Dr. Evers could help me figure out a way to deal with it. I could get better. Even if there was no one out there waiting to take me home, I could start a new life for myself somewhere.

But even after weeks of trying, my memories stubbornly remained trapped in my mind, refusing to come to the surface.

Other than the flames, there was only one thing that came back to me over and over. I closed my eyes and begged it to come, wanting to replay it in my head like a movie.

I was standing at a window, looking down on a garden that had seen better days. It was overgrown with flowers and weeds. A stone fountain in the center was covered in moss, but I knew it had the potential to be beautiful. There was a smaller house behind the garden, and to the right, a large shed.

I watched, waiting for the door of the shed to open, my heart always racing. When he walked out, my skin buzzed, and a smile played across my lips. He walked toward the smaller house and paused, stopping to look up at me through the glass that separated us. He raised a hand to shield his eyes from the sun.

It was my favorite moment. Seeing him was like coming home.

I waved, and his green eyes lit up, a touch of a smile lifting one corner of his mouth.

If I had the choice, I would spend my days trapped in that one moment with him. But no matter how hard I tried to hold onto it, the memory always faded, and the nightmares always returned.

Who was he? What did we once mean to each other?

And, most importantly, was he still out there somewhere waiting for me?

A MEMORY FROM MY PAST

HARPER

"**C**ome on, Harper, it's time to go outside for recreation time," Nora said, nudging my arm.

I sighed and got up from my bed, rubbing the sleep from my eyes.

I must have drifted off during our rest time after lunch.

"Hurry," Judith whispered. "She's coming."

I moved faster for her sake. Judith was always worried about getting in trouble. Always quiet and always following the rules to the letter.

I stood at the end of my bed and waited, hearing soft padded footsteps squeak against the tile floor. Nurse Melody walked into view, her ever-present clipboard pressed against her chest and her lips pursed into a straight, thin line.

None of the nurses here were pleasant, but Melody was the only one who was sometimes nice to me. Genuinely nice, not that fake crap most of them tried to pull until they got frustrated or I stepped out of line.

"Ladies," she said, quickly checking our names off her sheet. "Follow me."

We fell into line like little ducklings waddling down the hallway after her as she stopped at each room and marked each girl off her list. When we had all been properly collected, she led us through the institute's dated rec room with its faded couches, chess games missing a handful of pieces, and a single bookshelf full only of classic literature like *A Tale of Two Cities*. There was no TV, no magazines, no video games. It was as if this place had completely forgotten the modern world existed.

I followed the line out the French doors and into the chilly air of the afternoon.

The courtyard was bare and cold, everything made of cement except a stretch of brown grass past the concrete walkway. Cement benches. A cement bird-bath full of brown water and molding leaves. Many of the girls clustered in groups, sitting together to talk or play games, but I went to my favorite spot near the fence at the back of the property.

It was really more of a wall than a fence, made of sturdy red bricks stacked so high it was impossible for me to see out. Or for anyone else to see in, which was probably more the point. I had no idea where we were or what neighborhood the institute was in, but I could hear the sound of cars passing on a nearby street. I imagined wherever we were, the local residents wouldn't like to see the crazies hanging around outside.

I turned and pressed my back against the cold brick, pulling my sweater tighter as I slid down to sit on the grass. The brick tugged at the fabric as I moved, and I liked the feel of resistance. In some weird way, it spoke to my soul.

I hated this place, with its rules and our bland gray dresses and bare feet. I hated the way everyone else seemed to just accept this as reality without questioning why we'd all been locked away.

Or maybe it was fear that kept them quiet.

I closed my eyes, my body shivering against the cold winter air.

I wasn't sure what month it was, but if I had to guess, I'd say spring was just around the corner. The past few times we'd been outside, I'd heard birds chirping. The weather had gotten a few degrees warmer.

I'd been here at least three weeks and yet there had been no snow. When I looked up, I could see some trees on the other side of the brick fence, all of their leaves gone and no buds in sight. So, it was winter, but not somewhere cold enough for snow.

Was I still in Georgia? Close to home?

The nurses didn't know I'd remembered where I was from, and I wasn't about to tell them, but some of my memories had been coming back to me. Some of them in dreams and others when I least expected it, like small gifts dropping into my brain from some invisible benefactor.

I tried to remember my family. My life before Evers Institute. But no matter how hard I tried, I couldn't remember my mother and father. I couldn't remember a single thing about either of them, and it left a hollowness in my heart. Surely my mother and father were the people I'd spent most of my life with, so why couldn't I think of them? Why couldn't I picture them at all?

Instead, it was the green eyes of my mysterious man that kept coming back to me, over and over.

His dark hair was just long enough on top that it sometimes fell into his eyes. His deep-green eyes looked straight into my soul, and whenever I pictured him, I knew that he was mine. We belonged to each other.

I breathed in, willing the image of him to come to me now. I wanted to hear him speak and know that he had not given up on me. Wherever he was, I needed to know that he still loved me. That I wasn't all alone in this world.

But today he would not come.

I opened my eyes, tears pushing at the corners. I couldn't even remember his name or how we had met. I didn't even know if he was still alive.

I glanced around at the other girls, watching them talk and smile and laugh. But it was all fake. The laughter was joyless. Even with smiles on their faces, their eyes were empty.

Closer to the building, there was a row of girls sitting on cold cement benches, staring forward without moving. Some of them were in wheelchairs. Their mouths were turned down at the corners in permanent frowns. Their shoulders hunched slightly, and their hair was dirty and oily, as if they hadn't been bathed in weeks.

What had happened to them?

I shivered against the brick and turned away, my eyes drawn toward a girl standing in a group near the bird-bath. Her eyes were locked on mine.

I'd seen her before in the dining hall and for a moment, I'd thought I recognized her.

She was staring at me now, her gaze so intense I couldn't force myself to look away. Her hair was brown and fell just below her shoulders. Her face was beautiful and so familiar. Had we known each other before this place? If she remembered me, why didn't she just come talk to me?

I raised my hand in a wave and softly smiled at her, but her eyes darkened, and she looked away quickly, as if I'd offended her.

From the cement walkway, the sound of a bell rang out into the wind. "Let's go, ladies," Nurse Melody said. "It's time to get your chores done before dinner."

Awesome. Toilet-cleaning time.

Everyone moved quickly, heading toward the building, but I stayed, watching the girl with brown hair. Even her movements seemed strangely familiar, and I struggled to remember where I knew her from.

A headache ripped through me, as if everything in my body rebelled against the idea of a memory from my past. I brought a hand to my forehead, not wanting to take my eyes off the girl. Praying for something to push through, just once.

As she turned to walk toward the building, a faint shadow moved across the red brick wall behind her. My mouth turned dry, and I forced my eyes open against the sudden pain of the headache.

How was that possible?

The shadow seemed to follow the girl until she stepped onto the concrete walkway and followed the others into the building.

I knew what I had seen, but it didn't make any sense. There was nothing here that could have possibly created such a shadow, and the fence was too high for it to have come from beyond it.

"Harper, don't make me tell you again," Nurse Melody said, her voice stern.

I forced myself to stand and walk toward the house,

following the rules so that I didn't end up a drooling mess, sitting on a cement bench for the rest of my life.

But I dared one last glance at the brick wall, trying to make sense of what I had seen.

"What are you staring at?" the nurse asked. "What's back there?"

"Nothing," I said, almost convinced that I had imagined it.

Instead of a normal shadow—a human shadow—I could have sworn it had taken the shape of a horse.

FOLLOW THE SHADOWS

HARPER

The image of that shadow stayed with me for the rest of the day.

It had to mean something, but what?

It probably meant that I was losing my mind, and that I belonged here in this place

I laughed and shook my head.

"What are you smiling about?" Nora asked, taking a tray from the line.

"Nothing," I said.

"Oh, there was something going on in your head just now," she said. "I can tell."

She led us toward our normal table near the middle of the dining hall, her pigtails bouncing as she walked.

"Have you ever seen anything strange around here?" I asked, keeping my voice down and glancing around to make sure no one was paying me any attention. Judith was still in line, and I knew if I was going to talk about this, it needed to be before Little Miss Rules got here.

"Strange like what? Stranger than a bunch of crazy people?" she asked, tilting her head to the side and making a face.

"Very funny," I said, laughing and throwing a green bean at her. I had no real way of talking about this that didn't make me sound crazy myself. Still, I needed to know. "I mean, have you ever seen any strange shadows?"

Nora raised an eyebrow and took a bite of her mashed potatoes. "What in the world is going on with you?" she asked. "What kind of shadows?"

I shook my head and shrugged. "Never mind. It's nothing."

Nora twirled her finger next to her ear. "Cuckoo," she said, laughing. "You're losing it, Harper. Maybe you need a few extra therapy sessions."

"Therapy?" Judith asked, sitting down next to me, her eyebrows cinched together. "Why? What happened? Are you in some kind of trouble?"

I looked at Nora, begging her with my eyes to not say anything. But Nora says whatever she pleases.

"Harper thinks she saw some kind of weird shadow," Nora said. "I was just telling her she might want to ask for extra therapy to deal with that level of crazy."

"What kind of shadow?" Judith asked, her hand trembling. "Like a ghost or something?"

"Just drop it, okay?" I said. "I didn't see anything."

"Then why did you say you did?" Nora asked.

"I didn't," I said. "I asked if you had seen it."

"Well, you've been acting strange ever since we went outside today," Nora said. "And why are you always going off by yourself to sit against the wall, anyway? We had a lot of fun today playing cards. You should join us sometime."

I simply shrugged and looked down at my food.

I didn't want to make friends and become a part of this place like she had. I didn't want to accept it as my fate that I would spend the rest of my years here or in some other asylum. I didn't belong here, and as soon as I got my memories back, I would find a way to prove it. I would find a way to go home.

Images of a burning house pushed into my mind. I saw myself sitting on the ground, watching flames as green as emeralds tear through a beautiful old Southern home. In my arms, a girl with dark blonde hair lay limp against my body, the life gone from her eyes. I clutched her close, screaming as the fire raged on in front of me.

I closed my eyes and brought my hands up to my head, trying to shut the images out.

"Harper?" Judith touched my arm, and I shook her away.

"Don't touch me," I said, speaking more harshly than I'd intended.

Judith pulled back, tears in her eyes. She picked up her tray and ran, nearly knocking over her chair.

Shit. I hadn't meant to upset her. I grabbed my tray and followed her but tripped over something and fell hard against the floor. The tray flew forward, and I lifted my hands just in time to protect my head from hitting the ground.

Several of the girls sitting nearby laughed, but I didn't look at them. Instead, I looked for the nurses on duty. I didn't want to draw their attention, and I most certainly didn't want them asking why Judith was upset. If she told them anything about the shadows, it could get me into real trouble. I was trying to convince them I wasn't crazy and talking about shadows wasn't going to help my case.

But there was some kind of disturbance in the back of the room, and none of the nurses were paying any attention to me. I quickly scrambled to pick up the food that had fallen off of my tray, crawling on hands and knees on the floor.

I reached for a slice of bread, but someone's hand reached it just as I did, her skin touching mine for an instant and sending an electric shock through my body.

I pulled away and looked up, my breath catching in my throat.

It was her. The girl from outside.

"Thanks," I said, searching her face.

She smiled, and something tugged at my memories. Something about dropping a tray and being in a cafeteria very different from this one.

"Do I know you?" I whispered.

She handed me the bread, and when I took it, placed her hands around mine for a brief moment.

"Tonight," she whispered, so softly I almost couldn't hear her. "After lights-out. Follow the shadows."

She stood and walked away, her head down so that her hair hid most of her face.

"Wait," I said, nearly tripping over the food still piled on the floor at my feet.

When I looked up, she was gone.

DO YOU REMEMBER ME?

HARPER

I couldn't sleep.

I tossed and turned in my small bed, hearing those words over and over again, waiting for something to happen and having no idea how I would get out of this room even if it did.

Follow the shadows.

I hadn't been crazy. There was something going on with this girl, and even if I couldn't explain it, I needed to at least try to find out what it was.

What I didn't understand was how this girl expected me to get out of a locked room and follow her to wherever she was going.

I looked around, checking to see if my roommates were asleep. Judith was snoring louder than usual, which tomorrow she would blame on all the crying she'd done after I'd yelled at her at dinner. I'd tried to apologize, but she had refused to even talk to me. She'd come back to the room and covered her ears with her pillow, completely shutting me out.

It had been hours since lights-out, and the nurse had just made her second round of the night. That meant it was close to three in the morning, and no one would be by to check on us again until breakfast at seven.

So, I waited, staring up at the ceiling, waiting for something to happen. Anything.

My eyes began to close with sleep when a shadow passed in front of the door to my room.

There was only a small square window of light coming from the hallway, but my skin pricked when the light dimmed from movement just beyond. I sat up and stared at that window, listening for the nurse's footsteps or any way to explain that movement.

For a moment I just lay there, frozen. Unsure what to do. *Should I follow?*

It was crazy. I couldn't get out of here, and even if I could, there was no telling what kind of trouble I'd be in if anyone found me.

Taking a deep breath, I carefully slipped out of bed, my nightgown nothing more than a whisper against the sheets.

I lifted onto my toes and looked out the tiny window, watching for any sign of the nurses who roamed the halls during the night. Out of the corner of my eye, the shadow of a horse galloped along the wall and out of sight.

My heart pounded in my chest. I couldn't be imagining this.

The girl had said to follow the shadow, but we were under very strict orders not to leave our rooms. I'd seen girls come back from therapy sessions with lesions on their arms and bruises along their back. I'd heard rumors of shock treatments being handed down to anyone who broke the rules. Of course, those things had to be just rumors, right?

Still, my hand trembled as I reached for the doorknob. What if the rumors were true? What if there was something very wrong with this place? If they still practiced archaic forms of mental health therapies, who was going to complain to the authorities?

A criminally insane teenager who saw shadows of horses in a perfectly quiet building? I didn't think so.

I bit my lower lip and stared into the hallway, my hand gripping the cool knob of the door.

If I didn't at least try, I would regret it. There were so many things I didn't have an answer to, and if this strange shadow could lead me to even one of them, I had no choice but to follow it.

I took a deep breath and carefully turned the handle of the door. It was locked, just like I knew it would be.

So how was I supposed to leave?

I looked out the window again, searching for the shadow. It was long gone, and if I didn't go now, I would miss my chance.

What if that girl knew me? What if she could tell me something important about my past? About the guy with the green eyes?

I rested my head against the door, pushing back tears. I didn't want to be locked away like this, trapped here in this room.

Please open.

The moment I thought the words, something inside the door clicked.

I jumped back, gasping. What the hell was that?

I trembled as I walked back toward the door and searched the hallway. There was no one there. I tried the knob again, and this time it opened.

My lips parted, and I glanced around at my roommates, making sure I hadn't woken them up when I jumped. How was this possible? It was almost as if the lock had opened simply because I'd asked it to.

I pulled as gently as I could, wincing at the slight squeak the door made as it opened. I stopped and stood as still as a statue, waiting to see if anyone had noticed. None of my roommates moved, and there was no sign of anyone in the hall.

I pulled the door open just enough to squeeze through and stepped outside.

A dim light shone from the nurse's station at the other end, but there were no voices or sounds other than Judith's snoring. I closed the door and walked in the direction of the shadow, following the hallway all the way to the end.

When I reached a crossroads, a slight movement to my left drew my eye. The horse galloped along the wall, and I followed it, keeping my back against the concrete and ducking any time I passed the window of another room full of sleeping patients.

Barefoot, I followed the shadow through several turns and into corridors I'd never seen before, finally stopping in front of a solid metal door that read "Basement."

I looked both ways down the hall, my heart ticking like a bomb in my chest. This was stupid. I was going to get caught. I had no idea what I might find on the other side of that door, but I had not come this far and taken this big of a risk just to turn back now.

I turned the knob and pulled the door open, following the

shadow down the steps and into the freezing cold basement of the Evers Institute.

My lips parted as my breath quickened, turning to cool mist as it left my warm body. My feet froze with each step planted on the bare concrete floor. It was dusty and dirty down here, and the only light was coming from a room on the left just a few feet away.

I walked toward that light, praying I wouldn't find some nurse taking a break down here. Or worse. I took a deep breath and turned the corner, entering the room.

I stared, openmouthed, at the dark-haired girl sitting on the floor of the basement room. Her legs were crossed under her body. She held one hand out, palm-up, in front of her face. A glowing orb of light sat atop her hand, as if it had been created out of thin air. There was no flame, no candle. Just light.

"You made it," she said with a smile. "I wasn't sure you'd figure out the lock. Sit down. We don't have much time."

"How did you do that?" I asked, nodding toward the light in her hand. I sat down across from her on a small square of carpet, mimicking her by crossing my legs under my body.

"The light?" she asked. "You really don't remember anything, do you?"

"A few things," I said, not willing to trust her enough to give details.

"Do you remember me?" she asked.

I studied her face, her long, brown hair pulled back in the middle. I looked into her eyes, trying desperately to remember how I knew her.

A memory opened to me suddenly, like an envelope opening to reveal a photograph inside. I closed my eyes, trying to hold onto it. I could see her walking into a cafeteria, leading a group of girls through as everyone in the room turned to watch. She held her head high, looking down on the others as if she were royalty.

"I remember you walking through a room that looks like a high school lunchroom, maybe?"

She nodded, encouraging me to keep going.

"There are others with you," I said, closing my eyes again to grasp the memory more tightly. "A beautiful Asian girl with black hair and eyes. Two blondes. Everyone is watching you."

"That's the first time you ever saw me, I think," she says. "Do you remember anything else?"

I shake my head, the memory not going any further than that. "Not about you," I said. "Did we go to high school together?"

She smiled again. "Yes. For a little while," she said. "You came to my birthday party, too. Do you remember that night at all?"

I struggled to bring up any visions of a party, but only a fleeting image of a guy sitting on motorcycle in a field came to my mind. It was him, I just knew it.

"I remember a boy. A man," I said, correcting myself. Some part of me knew that even though he looked my age, he was much, much older. Could that be right? "He was on a motorcycle in the field."

"Across from my house," she said. "Watching you. Making sure you were okay."

"Who is he?" I asked, looking at her. "He's important to me. He's the only one I can remember, but I don't know his name. Do you know?"

"Jackson," she said, and the name pierced my heart like a dagger.

Tears flowed from my eyes, and I brought my hand to my mouth to stifle a sob.

"Yes. Jackson," I said, needing to hear the word on my tongue. To taste it. I'd been trying to remember for so long, and now that I knew his name, I wondered how I had ever forgotten.

I studied her, knowing now she was telling me the truth. How was it possible that someone I'd gone to high school with had ended up with me here in this place? It couldn't be coincidence. "Who are you? Why are you here?"

I had so many questions, but my mind couldn't put words to them all.

"That's not important," she said. "What's important is that you keep remembering. I can't stay much longer. If they find me here with you, they'll kill me."

I swallowed. "Kill you? Just for leaving your room?"

"No. There's a lot more on the line here than you realize, Harper," she said. She put her hand down, but the orb of light stayed in its place, hovering in the air between us. "And you are far more important than I am. The only reason they've allowed me to walk the same halls as you is because they think they have me under control. They believe they've successfully wiped my mind of everything that happened before they brought me here. And you should let them believe the same thing about you. It will be much easier for you if they think they've broken you, Harper. Don't tell them you remember anything."

"Why?" I asked. "Why am I important? I don't understand."

"You will," she said. "Keep pushing. Keep trying to remember but be careful. Stop taking your medicine."

"My medicine?"

"They're giving you pills, right?" she asked. "Small green pills?"

I nodded. "I stopped taking the sleeping pills, but they told me the green pills are supposed to help with memory loss."

"Make them believe you've swallowed them, and then when you have a moment to yourself spit them out and destroy them. They're poisoning your mind, holding your memories at bay. But don't let them find out or they'll start injections. And those are much worse," she said. "The injections are much harder to resist."

She held her arms out, and I gasped. She had bruises and track marks up her entire arm from where they had pierced her skin with hundreds of needles. Dear God, what torture had this girl been through?

"I have to go," she said. "But I'll try to meet you here again soon. If you see the shadow, that means it should be a safe night to find me here."

She stood, the light dimming as she walked toward the door.

"Wait," I cried out, standing and touching her arm.

She turned to me, her eyes searching mine. "There isn't time," she said. "I'm sorry."

"But I have so many questions," I said. "How did I open the lock on my door tonight? How did you create that light?"

She smiled, but I could see the tears gathering on her lashes. She swiped at them. "I think I know how you opened the lock," she said. "I used the same thing to create this orb of light. The answers you're looking for are all inside of you, locked away—just like you are locked away in your room every night. The doctors and nurses are doing everything they can to make sure you never unlock the doors to your mind, but you have the power to free yourself, Harper. I have to go now. Wait two minutes and then follow me out."

She walked away, but I stumbled forward, following her to the steps. I clutched her dress, forcing her to turn and look at me.

"The horse," I said. "How did you make that shadow? I need to know. I need to know who you are. Please, at least tell me your name."

The light went out, leaving us in complete darkness. At first, I thought she would walk away without another word, but before she disappeared through the next door, she grabbed my hand.

"Brooke," she said, squeezing once before letting go. There were tears in her voice as she spoke. "My name is Brooke."

THE WORST LIE OF ALL

HARPER

By the time I reached my room, I was out of breath from dashing under windows and into corners where there was less light. It took me awhile to remember the right turns, and I didn't have long before the nurses would start making their morning rounds. If Brooke was to be believed, the punishment for being discovered might be far worse than anything I'd imagined.

Were the doctors and nurses here really capable of murder? Would they kill a patient for simply not following the rules?

If so, there was a lot more on the line here than just my sanity.

I carefully opened the door to my room and slipped inside. I leaned against the wall, letting out a long sigh of relief.

I had made it.

But when I opened my eyes and started to walk toward my bed, I felt the hairs on the back of my neck prick up. I looked around, suddenly realizing that the room was silent. No snoring.

My eyes darted to Judith's bed. Her eyes were wide open, her covers tucked tight under her chin. She was staring right at me.

I stopped dead in my tracks, unable to move.

Of all the people to see me coming back to the room, Judith was the last one I would have chosen.

"I had to go to the bathroom," I said softly, my heart racing.

"How did you get the door open? You've been gone for a long time," she said. "I was scared."

I tried to relax my shoulders and act as if it was nothing important. Certainly nothing worth telling the nurses.

"I guess the nurse forgot to lock the door," I said. "I didn't mean to be gone so long, but it was dark out there. I couldn't find my way back."

"We're not supposed to leave the room," she said. Her hands gripped her sheets so tightly her knuckles turned white. "You could get us all in trouble for doing something like that. What if the nurse had come to check on us?"

"I really had to go," I said. The fact that we were shut in our rooms and not even allowed to go to the bathroom whenever we wanted was bad enough. Couldn't she see that?

"You shouldn't have done that, Harper," she said.

"You're not going to tell anyone, right?" I said, biting my lip. "No one saw me. I just had to go to the bathroom."

But I could see it written on her face. Her fear. Her anger. She wanted to get back at me for yelling at her earlier at dinner. She was going to tell someone, and I had no idea how to stop her.

"If you tell on me, it will get all of us in trouble," I said. "Even you. I won't do it again."

Even though I knew I would if I saw the shadow again. I had no choice. I needed answers and all the therapy in the world wasn't going to give them to me.

"Judith, don't tell anyone," I said. "Or I'll tell them you went with me."

I hated to threaten her like that, but I needed Judith to be scared. I needed her to keep her mouth shut. My life depended on it.

"You can't do that," she said. "It's not the truth."

I crawled under the covers on my bed, needing to warm myself. My feet were still ice-cold from the basement floors. I wanted to get some rest, so I could make sense of what happened tonight.

I rolled over, so I was facing Judith, our eyes meeting in the dark room.

"You've been here a lot longer than I have," I said. "I would have thought you'd have figured it out before me."

"Figured what out?" she asked. Her hands trembled.

I closed my eyes. I was on the edge of sleep, unable to worry about Judith or Brooke or anything else. I was so tired of it all. Tired of fighting to remember who I was. Tired of wanting to feel like the world made sense.

I pulled the blankets around my body and curled into a ball, shivering against the cold that still clung to my bones.

"Figured what out, Harper?" she asked again.

My eyes opened, and I looked at her. She seemed younger in the dark. Maybe only twelve or thirteen years old, if I had to guess. I wondered again what she must have done to get locked away like this.

"That the truth doesn't mean anything here," I said, thinking of Brooke and Jackson and how the doctor had told me that if I was a good girl, someday they would set me free. "Sometimes the truth is the worst lie of all."

DEFINITELY NOT THE LIBRARY

LEA

B eing in the castle again was harder than I expected it to be.

In the human world, I'd become used to spending my days however I damn well pleased. Here, though, even eating breakfast was an event. Every step I took was watched by at least five people who'd been told to either anticipate my needs or report my movements to the king.

If I so much as sneezed, three servants were there to hand me a tissue.

Anastia—who was still for some reason acting as my custodian—had told me to keep to my chambers as often as possible. She hadn't given me a reason why, but if I had to guess it was so I wouldn't have a chance to talk to the other demons I came across in the castle. They most certainly didn't want me wandering outside the castle gates and into the main city.

Maybe they were afraid I'd start telling people about what was really happening outside the walls. No one was allowed in, but no one was allowed out, either. None of the demons living here had seen the ruined and deserted villages that now made up the majority of the Northern Kingdom. There were rumors, sure, but until they'd seen it with their own eyes, they couldn't understand the destruction.

From the luncheons I'd been forced to attend, I'd noticed that most of the city's residents seemed to believe the rumors were a bunch of inflated nonsense. Talk about practicing holding my tongue.

So, I was told to stay in my room.

Which was exactly why I kept leaving it. I could play the part of the subservient loyal princess only so long before I started to lose my freaking mind.

Besides, as long as my father was on my side, Anastia couldn't touch me.

"I'm going to walk the halls," I announced to my room full of handmaidens. "I don't suppose you'll let me go alone this time?"

"My lady," Presha said with a curtsy. "We wouldn't dare leave your side."

"I figured as much," I muttered.

I spun on my heel and walked toward the doors of my outer rooms. Footsteps shuffled behind my back as the servants gathered into a group to follow me.

I sighed and pushed open the heavy double doors. I had no idea where I was going. I just wanted to walk. With no television or video game consoles, the Shadow World was not a fun place to be stuck in the same room for hours on end. Anything was better than the dungeons, but I'd spent enough time as a prisoner to last my whole life. I needed to move.

I walked quickly, making turns without a thought as to

where I was headed. I simply let my feet lead me. I remembered roaming these halls a lot as a shadowling, anxious to study the inner workings of the castle. I used to spend time visiting the kitchens and the laundry rooms with their warm air and sharp smells. I'd searched for hidden passageways and gardens. I used to know this place as well as I knew myself.

For the past several days, I'd been exploring again, rediscovering the beauty of this ancient place. I'd been trying to find the library, hoping maybe I could find something there that the Resistance didn't have in the Underground library. Something that could give us information about the Order of Shadows. If anyone asked, I'd say I was studying my family history or something.

I was pretty sure the library was down this hallway and to the left, but when I stepped through the door, sunlight fell across my face. I looked up, laughing. This was definitely not the library.

I closed my eyes and took a moment to enjoy the feeling of the suns on my skin. It was different than the sunlight in the human world where they only had one sun and one moon. Today there were four suns visible from where I stood in the small courtyard, each giving off a different sensation. All at once, it felt as if my skin was humming and sparkling, the light literally dancing across my skin.

"I almost forgot how beautiful you could be when you are happy."

My eyes snapped open and my knees buckled slightly. I played it off as a curtsy, lowering my head and placing my hand across my head. "My queen."

"You don't have to be so formal with me," she said. "Please, stand up straight and come walk with me."

I straightened and stared at her outstretched hand.

I hadn't spoken to my mother in a very long time, and yet she was acting like I'd just seen her yesterday. Truthfully, we'd never been close, even when I was younger. She'd always seemed disappointed that I was more interested in sparring with the twins than learning how to dance like a lady.

"Of course," I said, placing my hand in hers.

She led me around the edges of the courtyard while my handmaidens waited near the door like soldiers. For a long while she didn't say a word except to point out how nice the fire-blossoms were growing this year or how tall the spindle trees were getting.

After one full turn around the garden, she finally said something more personal.

"How have you been getting on?" she asked. "Do you have everything you need?"

I wanted to say that as long as Aerden was still locked away in the dungeons, I couldn't care less about what I needed.

"I'm happy to be home," I said, hoping my lie was convincing enough. "I have much more than I deserve."

"You deserve the world as long as you are here with us," she said. "As long as you are truly our daughter again."

As if it were something I could turn on and off like a light switch. I guessed I was only their daughter when I was doing what they wanted. Disobey and off goes the light.

"I am," I said. "It's good to see you again, Mother."

"When they brought you back to us, and I saw you dressed in those human clothes, it nearly broke my heart," she said. She lifted a hand to her chest and shook her head. "I was afraid you were truly lost to us forever."

"They were just clothes," I said.

"No." She stopped and faced me. "No, Lazalea, they were not just clothes. They were a symbol of everything you had become. A traitor, more worried about the welfare of humans than your own people."

"There are more than just humans trapped in that world, Mother. There are demons, too. Demons from the Northern Kingdom. Thousands of them, all prisoners of the Order of Shadows." I couldn't stop myself. I wasn't good at this subservient crap. It would be a miracle if I survived this whole thing.

"Shhh," she said. "Don't speak of those witches in my presence. I can't stomach the thought of them."

She talked about the Order as if they were a bad burrito she'd had once, rather than a coven of witches who'd stolen hundreds of thousands of innocent lives. Was she really this blind? Or was she just incredibly selfish?

"I'm sorry," I said, swallowing down the words I wanted to say. "What would you like to talk about?"

She smiled and looped her arm in mine. "Have you heard the good news?"

My eyes widened, and my heart flipped over. Were they going to free Aerden? Has Harper been found?

"Your father has decided to throw a festival in honor of your return," she said, her face beaming. "It will last an entire moon cycle."

"I hadn't heard," I said. "That will be lovely."

Inside, I cringed. Not just at the thought of the festival, but about the fact that I had actually just used the word lovely in a sentence.

"I've already talked to the seamstress, and she's preparing your gowns as we speak," she said. "We only have a few moons to prepare, but the king has appointed a special council to arrange the event. There will be dinners and performances here in the castle. A grand ball in the throne room, which we haven't had in ages. He's even decided to bring back the King's Games for the occasion."

My foot faltered, and I stumbled.

"Oh dear, are you alright?" she asked.

"I'm fine," I said, but I was scared and angry.

The games were barbaric and cruel, pitting prisoners against one another in a battle to the death in the arena while spectators watched and placed bets on who would win and who would die. Each round was over when one of the fighters had been brought to within an inch of his life. At that point, he was healed by the court shaman, only then to be asked to voluntarily pour his life-force into a stone in the king's crown.

Even though it was supposed to be a voluntary gift, the prisoner had no choice but to either sacrifice his life or be killed by the guards.

My father's grandfather had outlawed the games, declaring them a cruel and ancient tradition that had no place in the modern world. I, of course, had never been alive to witness them, but I'd heard and read about them many times when I was younger.

"I thought the King's Games were outlawed three generations ago," I said, trying to somehow sound cheery about the whole thing.

"It's something Kael suggested." She kept walking forward, and I had to force my feet forward, taking care with each step. "I think it's a wonderful idea, don't you? We can truly celebrate the return of our princess."

I paused at the sound of a foreign name. "Who is Kael?"

She smiled. "You'll meet him soon," she said. "He's a member of the Council, and he's become one of your father's most trusted advisors over the past few decades."

My heartbeat quickened. A new advisor? Was he the one turning my father's mind to evil? If he'd suggested the King's Games, this Kael had to be trouble.

The idea of a huge crowd cheering as two demon prisoners fought to the death as a form of entertainment turned my stomach. He was doing this in my honor? Or to test my loyalty to the crown above all others?

And then I remembered just who was being held prisoner in the king's dungeons.

My knees buckled, and I reached out to the stone wall to steady myself, letting go of my mother's hand.

"Lazalea, what's wrong?" she asked, touching my forehead. "Presha, call for the shaman."

"I'm sorry," I said. "I think I've done too much walking for one afternoon. I'm still weak from my time in the dungeons, and I shouldn't have pushed myself so hard."

I didn't want to admit why I'd really collapsed, but my mind was spinning at the thought. I had to get Aerden out of there. If they'd set me free, why were they still holding him prisoner? Of all of us, he was the one who deserved freedom and respect the most.

"Here, sit down," my mother said, leading me to one of the benches near a mossberry bush. "You look pale, sweetheart. Take a deep breath."

"I think I should get back to my chambers," I said. "I just need to rest for a while."

"Of course," she said. When the shaman appeared a minute later, my mother whispered something in her ear and the woman nodded. "Lisette will take you back to your room and give you some healing herbs to help you sleep. If I had realized you weren't feeling well, I would have never walked you around this courtyard for so long."

"It was nice to spend time with you," I said. "Hopefully we can do it again when I'm rested."

My mother patted my arm and left me alone with the shaman.

"Drink this," Lisette said. "It will help to calm your nerves."

"I'm fine," I said, waving away the small glass bottle in her hand. "Really, I just need to rest."

"Drink," she said, tipping the bottle toward my mouth.

Reluctantly, I opened my lips and drank the sweet potion. Instantly, my eyelids felt heavy, and I wasn't sure I could stand even if I tried.

I had the sensation of being weightless as Lisette took my hand and shifted to shadow, carrying me through the castle to my chambers. She placed me on my bed and pulled the curtains around it so that almost no light shone through.

When she returned a few minutes later, I could barely hold my eyes open. She placed a soft cloth across my forehead that smelled of herbs and flowers. It cooled my skin and tingled a little, and I remembered the sensation from when I was small.

"Thank you," I said.

"Anything for the demon who helped to set my daughter free," she whispered. "I owe you my life, warrior."

I stared up at her, surprised to see tears shining in her lavender eyes.

I wanted to ask her more about her daughter, but sleep tugged on me, drawing me down into its darkness.

"Sleep," she said softly, caressing my hand. "I will stay by your side until you wake."

I couldn't resist it any longer, and my last thought before I passed out was of the cold, dark dungeons and the demon who had been a prisoner for far too long.

NOT ALONE

AERDEN

Trention kept my secret, and in return, I helped him in the sapphire fields when the guards weren't looking. In the evenings, when most of the other demons had gone to sleep, he often came to sit by my side.

At first, we talked about the stories I remembered from my childhood and shared the things we missed most about our lives when we had been free. Lately, though, he'd been asking a lot of questions about my time in the human world.

As I grew to trust the old demon, I told him everything I knew about the Order and how Harper and the others had defeated the sapphire priestess.

"For ages, we have been told there was no way to stop what the Order was doing here," he said when he came to sit down late one night. "How did a human girl figure it out? It's remarkable."

"She's half-demon, too," I said, smiling.

"Yes, yes, of course," he said. "But still, she's so young compared to most. Barely more than a child, really."

"She is remarkable," I said, my voice tinged with sadness. The last I'd heard of Harper was that she'd been taken by the emerald priestess. She'd managed to save my brother and sister but had somehow been captured in the process. Ezrah told me that no one knew where she was or if she was still alive.

But I knew she was alive. The bond that had held me to her family for so long still lingered somewhere inside me, and I could feel the beating of her heart. It was faint, but clear. She'd been through something terrible recently. Torture so horrific it was amazing she'd survived. But Harper was stronger than most people gave her credit for.

She was fighting, and I wanted to be out there looking for her. I knew that Jackson would do everything he could to find her, but she was far away. I couldn't explain it, but it was more than just the distance between the Shadow World and the human world. There was some other magic at play.

"You care for the girl," Trention said.

"I was bound to protect her," I said. "And without her, I would still be a slave to the Order, along with thousands of other demons."

"You said she stole the heart of the priestess?" he asked.

I nodded. "For centuries, everyone believed that the priestess controlling each of the five colors of gates lived a normal human life-span of no more than seventy or eighty years at most," I said. "When she died, we believed her demon passed to her eldest daughter, who then became Prima. That's the way it works with all the gates, so it seemed logical that it was the same with the priestesses. But Harper discovered that each of the five priestesses had never died. They were the same exact witches who had first opened the original gates almost two hundred years ago."

"But how is that possible? Humans don't normally live so long," he said.

"It's not possible," I said. "Not without the use of dark magic. In essence, when her eldest daughter came of age and had three daughters of her own, the priestess sacrificed that daughter, stealing her life and glamouring herself to become her. She also consumed the lives of many witches along the way. Those who betrayed her or no longer served her purpose. The priestesses stay alive by killing others and consuming their power."

Trention closed his eyes and leaned back against the stone wall. "It's horrifying what they've done," he said. "To demons and humans."

"The sapphire priestess kept a large stone inside her body. She called it the master stone, and it was one of the original stones from the first sapphire gate that was opened," I explained. "In the final battle, when Harper ripped the stone from the witch's chest, it broke the spell that kept the priestess alive. Whenever she consumed a life, she stored that power in the stone, and was using it as some type of life support. Without it, she couldn't survive."

"And they used that stone to free you?" he asked.

I nodded. I'd told him this story a handful of times already, but he wanted to hear it over and over again, each time asking new questions. As if it could make any difference to us down here in the dungeons.

"As long as they have all of the original items used to first open a gate, they can reverse the spell and close the gate forever, freeing all of the demons still bound to that gate," I said. "That's how they set me free."

"It seems so simple," Trention said. "Yet who would have ever believed the witch could have lived so long and done such horrible things?"

"I wish the king would have listened to us when we tried to tell him the truth," I said. "When the guards brought us here, the king barely let us speak. He labeled us traitors and threw us both in the dungeons, refusing to even let us speak about the war against the Order. I don't understand why he doesn't march his army through a portal and kill them all. It doesn't make any sense. If a seventeen-year-old girl could raise an army large enough to defeat one priestess, the King of the North could destroy the entire Order in a matter of weeks."

Trention sighed. "I'm afraid the king is not himself these days," he said. "He hides away, hardly ever making an appearance in court. Your mother and father handle most of the king's day-to-day duties now."

"They do?" I asked. This was a surprise. I knew my father was a high member of the Council, but hearing that they'd moved up to nearly take over the king's duties was shocking. Especially since my own mother had all but told me there was nothing she could do to get me out of the dungeon.

"Oh, yes," he said. "The rumors were that the king and queen were so grateful for their loyalty after you and your brother both disappeared that he gave them free rein over many of the decisions that are made in the King's City. Even your mother has a seat now on the Council."

I shook my head, trying to make sense of it. Was this why my parents had refused to help free me or even to come look for me at all? Had they basically traded my life for power? Bile rose in my throat, and I had to force it back down.

I would never forgive them for what they had done. Even now they were happy to let me rot down here while they practically ruled the kingdom.

"Can I ask you a question?" I wanted to change the subject. I didn't even want to think about my parents again tonight. Being taken by the Order had been difficult, but being betrayed by my own parents had nearly broken me forever.

"Of course," Trention said.

"Why are you here?" I asked. "When I lived in the castle, you were the headmaster of the school. You were a leader, well respected by everyone."

He rubbed his face where a thick beard had grown in. "I made a mistake," he said. "I was well aware the Council had no desire to join the fight against the Order, but I found a piece of information during some research that gave me hope. I should have kept it to myself or found someone who could get word to the Resistance, but instead, I took the information to the Council. To your mother, in fact."

"My mother?" It seemed I couldn't get away from the thought of her, after all. "What information?"

"In my spare time some evenings, I used to like to go to the royal library and make my way through the books there," he said. "You've seen it?"

"The library?" I asked. When he nodded, I smiled, remembering how many times I'd gone there searching for Lea, usually finding her with her nose in a book. She loved to read about magical creatures who'd long since gone extinct and the warriors who'd fought them.

"There must be a hundred thousand books in that library,"

he said. "Maybe more. Even in a few hundred years, I'd only managed to get through about five thousand of them."

My eyes widened. "You've read five thousand books?"

"I've read more than that," he said with a laugh. "But only five thousand of the ones in the royal library. There are many books there that can't be found in bookshops or apprentice libraries. Tomes as old as the castle itself. Some of them truly ancient, written in dead languages."

"How can you read them if the languages are dead?" I asked.

"It's one of my gifts," he said. "And the reason I became a scholar in the first place. I have the ability to decipher any language as if it were written in my native tongue."

"That's quite a gift," I said, thinking of the ancient tomes Andros had mentioned. The Resistance Army lived in a secret hideout they called the Underground. It had been built by trolls, a race believed to be nothing more than legend. They'd been extinct in these lands for thousands of years, but Andros had found proof of their existence in the Underground and had built a home for refugees among the ruins. Jackson and the others had hidden down there for a while, but I'd never been there myself.

Andros said he had a library there of old troll manuscripts, most of them written in the troll's language. He had a group of scholars working to decipher those manuscripts, but it was taking them years. If Trention and I ever found our way out of here, I would have to take him to the Underground. It would probably only take him a few minutes to read what it had been taking those other scholars years to figure out.

"It's been a blessing and a curse," he said. "Many of the books in the library are simple spell books or recounts of historical events from various points of view. Some of them are fantasy tales written by bards or traveling storytellers. But a few years ago, I found something special."

The way he said it made my skin tingle. I leaned forward, listening.

"It was a history book unlike any I had ever read before," he said. "It was a language I didn't recognize, and the pages were decorated with the dust of diamonds."

"Diamonds?" I whispered. Diamonds were rare in the Shadow World. There were several mines of sapphires, emeralds, rubies, and a few other precious stones, but there were no diamond mines anywhere in the north or the south. A few diamonds had been found here and there, but no huge deposits like the sapphires we mined every day outside the walls of the King's City.

"I had the alchemist test it to be sure," he said. "At first, I thought it must be another fantasy tale, made up hundreds or maybe even thousands of years ago. But as I read, I started to believe it could be true."

"What did it say?" I asked.

He leaned close, glancing around before he continued.

"It said that we are not alone."

I blinked, not understanding.

"As far as we have always known, the Shadow World is made up of a single kingdom, once split into north and south," he said. "There are a few small islands scattered off the coast of the Sea of Glass, but nothing substantial."

I nodded, anxious to hear where he was going with this.

"This book described another kingdom far to the west," he said. "An entire land even larger than the entire north and south combined."

My mouth fell open, hardly believing what he was saying. "It can't be true," I said. "Demons have been fishing the Black Sea for ages. If there was another kingdom out there larger than our own, they would have found it by now."

"I thought the same thing," he said. "But then I discovered the map."

I stopped breathing, hanging on his every word. "The map?"

"Hidden in the binding of the book was a map of the Shadow World," he said. "It was old. Perhaps older than me, even. I can't be sure. It was unlike any map I had ever seen, clearly showing our kingdom in perfect ratio with a much larger kingdom to the west across the Black Sea."

"That's impossible."

"Think of what it could mean if it were true," he said. "Another kingdom of demons, untouched by the Order of Shadows."

"An entire army who might be able to save us all," I whispered.

"Exactly," he said. He frowned, touching his shoulder.

"Are you still hurting?" I asked, moving to examine his shoulder.

He waved me away. "I'm fine," he said. "I'm healing, thanks to you, and may yet live to see the day when we defeat the Order for good."

I smiled at that, proud that I was able to help him when I'd been helped by so many others.

"You told my mother about the map," I said. "That's why you're here, isn't it?"

His eyes slowly lifted to mine, and he nodded. "I was going to bring the book to the attention of the entire Council, but she intercepted me before the meeting and asked what I planned to discuss with them," he said. "I showed her the book and explained what it might mean for our kingdom. She told me it was obviously nonsense, written by someone who was either insane or indulging in their own fantasies. She took the book from my hands and when I protested, promised she would tell the king what I had discovered. Next thing I knew, a set of guards stormed into my study and threw me into the dungeons, declaring that the king had called me a traitor to the crown. They didn't even let me say good-bye to my family."

I looked away, not wanting to believe him, but knowing he had no reason to lie.

What was my mother's part in this? Had she even shown the book to the king at all?

"Why would they want to keep this information hidden?" I asked.

"I've had a lot of time to think about it in my years down here," he said. "The only thing I can imagine is that your mother saw the map as a potential threat to the Council's power. If the kingdom to the west is larger, they could have a very powerful ruler and a much stronger army than the dwindling one your father now controls."

"Why wouldn't they at least try to contact them? Send a group of spies to look into it? Something?"

"I can't answer that question," he said. "For all I know, the Council has done just that and discovered that the book was full of lies. It's not as though the guards here keep me up to date on the king's business."

He winked at me, and I smiled. How the old demon was able to make a joke at a time like this was beyond me, but I admired him for his good humor and true heart.

"Sounds as though we've both been betrayed by my mother," I said. "I don't understand how she can continue to be so loyal to a king who seems to be growing weak."

"I hope you'll excuse me for saying this, but her loyalty makes perfect sense," he said. "The weaker he grows, the more powerful she and your father become. Without an heir, the throne will go to the highest member of the Council when he passes from this world. The way the Council now stands, that would be your father, or a demon named Kael."

I took a deep breath and held it in my lungs until it burned. I tried to calm my anger, but it blew through me like a fierce wind.

"Now that the rightful heir has returned, I can only wonder what your parents plan to do," he said.

My eyes snapped open and fear swirled around my heart like a flame. "Lea," I whispered. "Do you think she's in danger?"

I couldn't believe my parents would hurt her, but I never would have believed they'd abandon me, either.

"As long as she's trapped in the dungeons, she doesn't pose any threat to their power," he said. "But if her father lets her go, I imagine it will upset the plans your parents have for themselves and their daughters."

"Daughter," I said absently. "My sister Illana fled the King's City a few months ago to come looking for me after she'd heard I'd been set free. She's with my brother now in the Southern Kingdom."

Trention frowned and shook his head. "Illana?" he asked. "That's strange."

"Why?" I asked.

"She seemed absolutely devoted to your mother," he said.

"I hope you'll forgive me for saying so, but I once overheard her telling one of her handmaidens that she was glad you and your brother had both left. That it gave her a chance to be closer to her mother."

Tears stung my eyes. I knew the old demon wouldn't lie to me about something like that, but it still hurt to hear it.

"Well, she must have had a change of heart," I said. "I didn't get a chance to see her myself, but a friend told me she'd crossed over to the human world and gotten captured by the emerald priestess. Jackson and Harper saved her, but that's when Harper was taken prisoner."

"Jackson?" he asked.

I smiled. "Denaer, my brother. Jackson is the name he took when he crossed into the human world. He prefers it now."

"A strange name for a demon," Trention said. "And I'm sorry about your sister. That means the only child left in the castle is your sister Orian."

"If the king passes his crown to my parents, she would someday become the Queen of the North?" I asked.

"As long as none of your other siblings return and manage to get back into their good graces," he said. "Orian is the youngest, isn't she?"

I nodded. She'd been a shadowling when I'd left the castle. I bet I would hardly recognize her now.

"Queen," he said softly. "That's a very powerful temptation. Enough to want to keep another kingdom hidden at all costs. Enough to make sure the king's daughter doesn't come back to claim her throne."

The thought turned my stomach, and I closed my eyes, picturing Lea in the dungeons of her father's castle.

Under normal circumstances, Lea was fully capable of

protecting herself. But this was not a normal circumstance. Just like mine, her powers were off-limits inside the dungeons. Anyone could slit her throat and she would be almost helpless to defend herself.

A smile tugged at the corners of my mouth. Well, not exactly helpless. That woman could fight with the best of them, and I had no doubt she would fight like hell against anyone who dared to cross her. Magic or not.

But a powerful member of the Council with an entire army at her disposal?

Even Lea could be outnumbered beyond hope.

What exactly was my mother capable of in the name of power?

The thought chilled my bones, and I wrapped a tattered blanket around my shoulders.

"You best get to sleep, old man," I said with a laugh. "Or it will be a rough day for you in the quarries tomorrow."

Trention braced his hand against the wall and pushed himself to a standing position. Even that small effort brought a hint of perspiration to his forehead.

"I suppose you're right," he said. "Though I could sit here talking to you all night if I were young again."

"I'm sorry for what my mother did to you," I said softly. "I don't even know who she is anymore."

"It's not your fault," he said. "We can't be held responsible for the sins of our parents."

"Maybe not, but we can do what we can to make it right," I said, standing to show my respect to this honored demon who'd been imprisoned for simply telling the truth and trying to save the lost. "I will make it right, Trention. That or die trying."

He smiled and clasped my hand. "Your life is not yet half

lived," he said. "Don't waste it worrying over an old relic like me. Save as many as you can. Get out of this place and keep fighting against the Order of Shadows until every last one of those witches' hearts has been ripped from her chest. That will honor me enough."

I smiled and watched as he made his way back to his corner of the dungeon, but as I sat back down and leaned against the wall, my smile faded. Lea was in danger, and I was helpless to do anything about it.

I had to find a way out of these dungeons. Ezrah had said to keep my head down, but I didn't have time for patience. I didn't have time to wait down here until someone else came to rescue me.

This time, I would have to find a way to save myself.

IT WILL ALL BE OVER SOON

HARPER

For two days I believed that my threat to Judith had worked. She hadn't spoken to me much since that night, but at least no one had come to punish me or confront me about leaving my room.

I looked for Brooke, too. Not to talk to her, but just to know that she was real and that she was okay.

I didn't see a single glimpse of her anywhere. I knew that they had several wards here in the institute, and from the looks of it, a lot more patients than I had ever seen in the dining room or the courtyard at one time. Either that or there were a lot of empty rooms. This place must have held hundreds of beds, and I had no way of knowing whether they were all full or if many of them were empty and waiting for more girls to come in.

Brooke was on a different ward, which meant she was normally on a different schedule from me.

"Harper, could you come with me, please?" Nurse Melody asked. She said it so sweetly, as if I had a choice.

"Where are we going?" I asked. There were no clocks on the walls, so I had no idea what time it was, but it was easy to fall into a routine here. And easy to tell when something was off.

By my calculations, it was Friday around one in the afternoon, and I wasn't scheduled for anything exciting today except a shower, which I'd already had.

My stomach knotted as I rose from the rec room couch. Several girls around me quieted, their lips falling open as they watched.

Nurse Melody didn't answer me, which didn't help the worried feeling in my gut.

I searched the rec room for Judith, but she wasn't there. *Crap.* The little rat had told on me. I knew it in my bones. Normally she spent our rec room hours sitting by an old record player, listening to albums no one had cared about for sixty years.

But she wasn't there now, and I couldn't believe I'd missed that detail earlier. She must have gone to the nurses when I'd come out here.

I followed behind Nurse Melody as she led me down the familiar path to Dr. Evers' office, my body tensing with each step. What would they do to me? And more importantly, how much did they know?

The nurse knocked on Dr. Evers' door and waited, not looking at me. I wanted to run but knew I wouldn't get very far. Not in this place. I didn't even know where the front door was in this maze of a building, not that it would be open for me to run right through anyway.

"Come in," Dr. Evers said.

Nurse Melody opened the door and stood there, waiting for me to go inside. My feet didn't want to move, but after a long moment, I forced them forward into the office.

"Harper, have a seat. Melody, you may wait outside."

Dr. Evers stood by the window that faced out toward the courtyard. Usually when I came to her, she was sitting at her desk, but today she was in a different place. I didn't think that was an accident. She wanted me to sit down so that she would have the upper hand, where usually she wanted me to feel that we were on equal footing. Friends. The psychology of her stance was not lost on me.

I had no choice but to sit in the hard leather chair across from her desk. I sat up straight, my legs crossed at the ankle and my hands in my lap, just like a lady. I had broken their rules, but I would not let them break me.

"One of your bedmates has told me something I find very disturbing," she said. "Do you know what it is?"

I breathed in through my nose, letting the air into my lungs until they burned. I held it there, waiting for my heart to calm before I spoke.

"I don't know," I said.

"Oh, I think you do." She looked at me and pulled her glasses off. She rubbed her eyes as if she was tired of me already. "This will all go much smoother for you if you would simply tell me the truth."

There was that word again. She taunted me with it, as if she had ever spoken any truth to me since I'd arrived here.

"I can't imagine what you're talking about," I said.

"Harper, some of the girls who come here are deeply troubled when they arrive," she said. "We do what we can to help them adjust to their new life here at Evers Institute. We try to rehabilitate and get to the root of the problem so that one day they might have hope of rejoining society. Some girls do very well, but others cause nothing but problems."

She walked away from the window to stand beside her desk. She leaned against it, standing closer to me than she ever had before.

"You don't want to be the kind of girl who causes problems, do you?" she asked.

I almost laughed. Whether the urge came from fear or irony, I wasn't sure, but I pushed it deep down so that the good doctor wouldn't see me smile. But she had to see the irony in her question. She was, after all, talking to someone who she claimed burned down her own house and killed her entire family. I was the poster child for the kind of girl who causes problems.

"Of course not," I said.

"Good. So, will you please tell me why you broke one of our most sacred rules and left your room without permission the other night?"

I shook my head. "I didn't," I said.

She slammed her hand down on the desk, making me jump. "I don't tolerate lies in this office," she said. "I want to know where you went. According to this young lady, you were gone for at least an hour in the middle of the night. We both know it doesn't take an hour to find the bathroom and relieve yourself, now does it?"

"I can't imagine it would," I said.

"What, then, were you doing all that time?" she asked. "And if you tell me another lie, I can promise you that you will regret it."

I held my tongue. I knew that denying it again would only make her angrier, but I couldn't tell her the truth. Not without risking Brooke's life in the process. There was nothing I could say to her that wouldn't carry some level of danger, so I chose silence.

"I believed that your treatment was going well," she said, moving back to the window. "But it's not uncommon for a patient to regress, especially when she is dealing with depression and memory loss. Perhaps when you broke this rule, you were not in your right mind, which leads me to believe that our planned treatment has not been as effective as I'd hoped."

I clasped my hands tighter, weaving my fingers together and holding onto myself. I did not like the way this conversation was going, and I had a feeling it was about to get a lot worse.

"Perhaps I will have to adjust this plan so that you can get the treatment you need," she said. "Sometimes drastic cases call for drastic measures."

She looked at me, a fire in her eyes telling me just how much she enjoyed this. She was glad I had broken a rule, because it gave her some excuse to torture me. And I knew it was going to be bad, just from the look on her face.

I held my head high, knowing I had no choice but to face whatever she was going to throw at me. I had no power over her. No power over my own fate or what they did to me. The only power I had was my own reaction to it.

And I wasn't going to let her know she scared me.

"I will give you one last chance to tell me what you were doing during that hour you were out of your room," she said. "I want to know where you went and exactly what you saw."

Her words brought my eyes to her face. What I saw?

Now why would she be so concerned with information like that? Unless there was something going on here she most definitely did not want me to see.

My skin broke out in goosebumps.

"I went to the bathroom," I said. "I knew it was wrong to leave the room, but I had to go. My stomach was upset from dinner."

"The bathrooms are only a few steps away from your room, Harper. You want me to believe that you were gone for an hour to use the restroom?"

"I was ill," I said. "I looked for a nurse, but no one was at the desk at the time. I went to the bathroom and sat there for a long time, hoping I would feel better. When I did, I went back to the room. I'm not sure how long I was gone, but I didn't go anywhere, and I didn't see anything."

"I want to believe you, Harper, but I have been a doctor at this institute for a good many years, and I have learned when a patient is lying and when a patient is telling the truth," she said. "And you are lying to me."

I shook my head, but before I could protest, she came around her desk, barreling toward me like a bull. She grabbed my arm and yanked me up, her fingernails digging into me like daggers.

"You obviously don't care how much work and effort we have put into your rehabilitation," she said. "You deny me the respect I deserve, and I will not stand for it."

I tried to pull away, but she had a death grip on my arm. She pulled me toward the door, my feet sliding against the rug. She was so much stronger than I expected her to be, and no matter how hard I pulled against her, she held tight.

"You're hurting me," I shouted.

She stopped and looked into my eyes, an evil smile playing on her lips. "I haven't even begun to hurt you," she said. "Yet."

The way she spoke took my breath away. She wanted to hurt me. It burned inside her like a flame.

She opened the door, and Nurse Melody ran toward us.

"What's happening?" she asked, taking my other arm in her hands and pulling me farther down the hallway.

"This patient is suffering from delusions and severe depression," Dr. Evers said. "She needs immediate treatment, and I'd like to see to it myself that she gets the full dosage."

"Yes, Doctor," Nurse Melody said, but her lip trembled.

Both women held onto me as I dug my heels in and tried to pull against them. The slick tile floor wasn't helping, and I slid across it with almost no resistance. I had no idea what treatment they had in mind for me, but I didn't want to go through it.

I dropped my weight, going limp and heavy in their grasp. The nurse faltered for a moment, but Dr. Evers didn't flinch. She continued to drag me down the hallway with only one hand clasped around my arm, as if I weighed nothing.

They led me to a hallway I'd never seen, through silver double doors that led to a set of stairs leading down to the basement.

Neither of them spoke as they rushed me down these stairs. I continued to fight against them, but I couldn't break free. And even if I did, I wasn't sure where I would go. I was a prisoner here, not a patient. They could do whatever they wanted to me and no one would have anything to say about it.

Dr. Evers kicked open a door in the basement and dragged me inside, only letting go of my arm when the heavy door closed behind us. Nurse Melody locked it with a key and tucked the keyring back into her pocket. Her eyes were wide and nervous as she looked at me, which only made me more afraid.

If the nurse was scared of what was about to happen to me, it had to be bad.

I moved into the corner, taking the arrangement of the room into view. It looked like some kind of operating room, with surgical equipment and machines lined up on one side and a narrow hospital bed in the center of the room.

A single light hung from the ceiling directly over the bed, and unlike the pristine white of the sheets and rooms on my wing of the institute, there were bloodstains on the floor in this room. The sheets were dingy and leather straps on the rail of the bed were worn and dirty, spots of red staining them in several places.

I shook my head as the doctor wheeled a machine toward the bed.

"Get her into the straps," she said.

"No," I protested. "I didn't see anything, I swear. I'll never leave my room again. Please, don't hurt me."

Nurse Melody looked to me and then back at Dr. Evers. "Are you sure you—"

"Don't question me unless you want to be strapped in next," Dr. Evers said, her normally sweet voice now bitter and poisonous.

Nurse Melody walked over to me, reaching her hand out as if she actually expected me to take it and walk peacefully to my own torture. I squeezed into the corner of the room, but with the door locked, there was no hope of escape.

"You're only going to make it worse for yourself," the nurse whispered. "Come on. It will all be over soon."

"What is she going to do to me?" I asked, looking at the machine and the various instruments Dr. Evers was preparing next to the bed.

"It's better if you don't speak," she said. "Come on, Harper. The more you resist, the worse it will be. Please."

There was fear and disgust in the nurse's eyes. She didn't like this at all, and yet I saw that she was powerless to stop it.

And so was I.

Nurse Melody reached for my arm, and I let her lead me. Tears sprang to my eyes as she gently pushed me down onto the bed. She worked to secure the leather straps to my ankles and wrists, adding another around my neck. It was so tight, I had to struggle for each breath.

With my movement limited, I couldn't see everything the two women were doing, but I did see when Nurse Melody held up a long needle and began to fill it from a small glass bottle. But Dr. Evers shook her head.

"No sedation," she said. "She's going to feel this."

"But Doctor, you can't—"

"I can, and I will," she said. "Don't forget your place here, Melody. Or where you could end up if I feel you are not performing your duties as requested."

Nurse Melody shuddered and dropped the needle and medicine to the metal tray with a clang. "Yes, Doctor. I'm sorry."

"Open her mouth," Dr. Evers said.

On instinct, I clenched my teeth together, my jaw locking down tight. I could hardly move my head, but I cut my eyes to the side, trying to see what Dr. Evers was doing.

Nurse Melody leaned over me, placing her hands on either side of my face. "Just relax," she said. "It will all be over soon."

A tear slid down my face, and I tried to shake my head. What were they going to do to me?

I refused to open my mouth, but Nurse Melody pushed on a place high up on my cheeks and forced my jaw open. Before I could clamp it shut again, Dr. Evers shoved a piece of cloth with something hard wrapped inside between my teeth. I screamed, my mouth watering around the cloth and nearly choking me as I tried to swallow and catch my breath at the same time.

I swore I wouldn't let them break me, but I had no idea what they were capable of until that moment.

If this was what they did to someone on a first offense, how much worse would it be if I messed up again?

Dr. Evers moved behind me and placed something against my temples. I couldn't see what it was, but anything that close to my head was not a good sign. She twisted a knob and it made a clicking sound.

I struggled against my restraints, but it was no use. I was going to have to endure whatever she had planned for me, and I was helpless to stop her.

The nurse backed away and suddenly pain exploded through me. Every muscle tensed and seized, my body jerking violently. I wanted to scream, but I couldn't move my jaw. I couldn't control anything or think beyond the brilliant light that kept erupting behind my eyelids.

It seemed to go on forever, and just when I thought my heart might stop beating, it finally ceased.

I shuddered against the table, trembling uncontrollably as tears leaked from my eyes.

I heard the clicking of the knob again and Nurse Melody drew in a sharp breath and looked away.

No. I wanted to beg and plead for her not to do it again, but I had no voice.

I tried to brace myself against it, but the pain came again, electricity blasting through my brain and taking control of me. I couldn't breathe as my body seized again, every single muscle tense to the point of excruciating agony.

The last thing I saw before I blacked out was the smiling face of Dr. Evers as she leaned over me and whispered, "I only wish my mother could have been here to see this."

THIS IS OLD SCHOOL

JACKSON

I woke up in a sweat and ran to the desk in the corner of the room. I opened my drawing pad to the first empty page and began to draw as fast as my hand would move.

I had felt her pain in my dream, and it ripped through me like a blade.

I sketched furiously with my pencil, breaking the point several times before the image showed itself. Tears stung my eyes, and I pulled at my hair, crying out as I stared down at the drawing.

Harper was strapped to some kind of metal table, her arms and legs bound with leather. A woman hovered over her, some device pressed to Harper's temples.

What were they doing to her?

Where was she?

I wiped the tears from my eyes and studied the drawing, trying to make sense of it. It looked like some kind of medical procedure, but nothing like I'd ever seen in any hospital. I ripped the page from the book and flew down the hallway toward Mary Anne's door.

She was human, and even though she was younger than I was by many years, she might recognize it.

I pounded on her door until a sleepy Essex opened it, his eyes darkened with worry.

"What is it that has happened?" he asked.

Mary Anne came up behind him, rubbing her eyes. "Jackson, it's late," she said. "What's going on?"

I pushed through the door and entered the room, turning on the lights and slapping the drawing down on a table in the center of the outer room.

"I dreamed of her," I said. I paced the floor, running a hand through my hair. "I felt her, Mary Anne. She's in pain. They're torturing her."

"Harper?" she asked. She walked over to the drawing and picked it up, her eyes widening. "Oh my God."

"What is it?" I asked. "Have you ever seen anything like it before?"

"Only in movies," she said. "It looks like shock treatments, but not the kind they do now. This is old school."

"Shock treatments?" I asked, shaking my head. Dammit, this was all my fault. I couldn't stand this anymore. I had to find her, or I would lose my mind.

"It's something they used to do in mental asylums," she said. "I think it was used to treat depression."

"Depression?" I asked, pacing faster. "This isn't treatment —it's a horror show. They were hurting her."

She sat down at the table, studying the image I'd drawn. "What's this in the corner?" she asked. "Is that a nurse?"

I leaned over her, trying to decipher the scribblings of my

hand. "It could be," I said. "Sometimes I can't see the entire picture, only pieces of it."

"Jackson, this looks like a nurse's hat to me," she said. "What if they've got her locked away in a hospital somewhere? We could start searching the mental institutions. Questioning nurses when they change shifts. Maybe someone will recognize her."

"Even if they did, do you really think they'd talk to us?"

I walked over to the archway that led to the balcony and slammed my hand against the stone, pieces of it breaking off and falling to the floor.

Essex put a hand on my shoulder. "Jackson, please have a seat," he said. "I will make you some tea. It will be helping to calm your nerves."

"I don't need to calm my nerves," I shouted. "I need to find my fiancée."

"Yes, but what good will you be to her if you are angry and confused with such rage?" he asked, his accent heavy and his voice calm. "I will be helping you. Please, sit down and let us talk this over."

"I'm sick and tired of talking," I said. "I'm tired of sleeping in her bed alone while she's out there somewhere being put through hell. I can't take it anymore."

Mary Anne stood and put her hand on my arm. "I know how hard this is," she said. "But Essex is right. We need to sit down and figure this out. This drawing could be a valuable clue, Jackson. I can send a message to Joost and Cristo and the others. Have them start searching every mental institution they can find that's close to an emerald gate. It's a place to start at least."

I shook my head. They wouldn't find her. The emerald

priestess wasn't dumb enough to have her in some place that anyone could just walk into. She was hidden somewhere out of our reach, and until I found someone who was willing to betray the priestess, Harper was lost to me.

"We need to move the schedule up," I said. "We need to execute the plan tonight."

"We're not ready," Mary Anne said. "What you're asking is going to take weeks to plan. We'd be walking into a nightmare if we tried to do it now. We need more resources. More people helping."

"Then get Andros," I said. "Get the Resistance involved. Rend. John Pierce. Whoever we can find. Tell them to be here tonight."

Mary Anne touched my arm. "I know you want to do something, but if we rush into this right now, someone is going to end up getting killed," she said.

I groaned and paced the floor.

Dammit, why does everything have to be so difficult? I wanted to just get it done without all the careful planning.

But Mary Anne was right.

We needed more time.

"Contact the others," I said. "Tell them to start searching every mental institution and hospital within a fifty-mile radius of every emerald demon gate. If they don't find anything, tell them to go a hundred miles."

I grabbed the drawing.

"Where are you going?" she asked.

"I need to kill something," I said, opening the door. "I'm going hunting."

A DESERTED WING

LEA

As soon as I had the opportunity, I shifted and soared through the castle. It was nearly impossible to ditch my handmaidens, but I'd caught them all looking at something out on the balcony.

They weren't fast enough to keep up with me, but I knew I didn't have long before one of them found me. I needed to find Ezrah quickly, so we could talk in private.

I flew toward the guards' quarters, hoping he might still be there this early in the morning. But somehow, I got turned around and ended up in a deserted wing of the castle. A storm had destroyed part of this wing decades ago, and from the looks of it, my father still hadn't ordered any repairs on what used to be the main quarters for the maids and cooks.

How many more demons from the Outerlands could have lived here in the King's City if this wing was renovated? Fifty? Maybe more.

I shook my head and turned around, trying to reorient

myself when I heard voices coming from one of the old chamber rooms.

The tiny hairs on my arms stood up as I heard my name. I quietly inched toward the room to listen more closely. It was a risk to be here alone when my loyalty was still in question, but I wanted to know who was talking about me.

"Let me deal with the princess," a woman said.

"Her reappearance here in the castle couldn't have come at a worse time, Mother. We were so close this time, and we can't afford any more setbacks right now."

It took me a moment to place the voices, but when I did, I had to stifle a gasp. It was Tatjana and Orian—Aerden's mother and sister. What were they doing here away from the main part of the castle? And why would my presence put their plans in danger?

"She's nothing but an annoyance," his mother said. "Sooner or later we'll find a way to prove she isn't loyal to the crown, and that will be the end of her. Besides, she could be very useful to us."

"How?" Orian asked.

"She knows things we don't know," his mother, Tatjana, said. "Like the location of the Resistance forces. Information about the domed city in the Southern Kingdom. I'll convince the king that these are resources we must have, and that in order to prove her loyalty, she'll need to give the information willingly."

"And what if she doesn't?"

"Then she'll be labeled a traitor and the king will get rid of her himself," his mother said. There was a smile in her voice that made my heart tighten in my chest. "I've got everything under control, so stop worrying. It won't be long now. You have to trust me."

"I do trust you," Orian said. "It's her I don't trust."

The voices grew closer and footsteps sounded against the old white stone that paved the floor in this ancient section of the castle. I wanted to hear more of what they were discussing, but I couldn't afford to be caught listening in.

Reluctantly, I shifted and flew through the corridor and turned down another hallway. I found my way to the guards' quarters and slowed.

I took a deep breath to calm my heart and smoothed my dress and hair. I needed to look presentable, like a princess who didn't have a care in the world except serving her kingdom. The thought alone made me want to gag, but desperate times called for desperate measures.

When I found him, Ezrah was preparing for a patrol outside the gates of the King's City. His eyes widened when he saw me approach, but he forced a smile and stood.

"Princess Lazalea," he said. "To what do we owe this honor?"

"My mother has just informed me that preparations have begun for a festival in my honor," I said, chin tilted upward, as if he was nothing more to me than a nameless guard. "I need to speak with you about my security at the event."

"Of course," he said. He cleared his throat and excused himself from the room.

As soon as we were around the corner and out of sight, he grabbed my arm. "What were you thinking, coming here? It's too dangerous for us to be seen together like this," he said. "You have to stop thinking of yourself and start thinking of what it would mean to the Resistance if my true identity was discovered."

"If you expect me to be your leader someday, you won't ever speak to me in that way again," I said. I ran a hand across my braid. I hadn't meant to snap at him, but if he realized just how much I'd been sacrificing of myself to be here, he wouldn't accuse me of being selfish. Not now. "I had to speak to you. Did you hear about the games?"

"Of course," he said, glancing around to make sure no one else was in the hallway with us. "I probably knew about it before you did."

"Aerden's going to enter," I said. "He'll volunteer. You have to stop him. He isn't ready."

"He won't," Ezrah said. "I've told him to keep his head down. I've told him to wait for us to make a move before he does anything."

"And how's that been working out?" I asked, an eyebrow raised. He'd told me about Aerden's run-in with the guards. How he'd stood up for the older prisoner and risked his own safety to save someone else. "Look, I know him better than you do. He's not going to stay in that dungeon if he thinks he can fight his way to freedom. He was powerless for years, unable to do anything to earn his own freedom. He thinks he has something to prove."

"I'll talk to him," he said. "But if he decides to enter, there's nothing I can do to stop him."

"Find a way," I said.

"I need to go. We shouldn't be talking like this."

"Wait." I grabbed his arm and he paused, shifting his weight. "There's something else I need to tell you. Something about Aerden's mother."

"It will have to wait," he said, motioning toward the approaching footsteps of his fellow guards. "We're out of time. I'll come to you when I can get away."

I clenched my jaw and took in a deep breath. I hated not having more control than this. I hated having to constantly wait and see what would happen next. I wanted action, not waiting.

"Dammit, Ezrah, you said you wanted information. I'm offering it to you. This is important," I said.

He sighed and glanced behind him. "Speak quickly."

"When I was searching for you, I ended up in the deserted wing near the old church," I said. "I overheard Tatjana and her daughter talking about me. I didn't hear the entire conversation, but it sounded like they were plotting against me. Trying to get rid of me for some reason. They said I could be useful because I know information about their enemies like the Resistance and the Southern Kingdom, but other than that, they wanted me gone."

"I had a feeling something like this would happen," he said. "Since you've been gone, a lot of demons have been making strategic political moves to try to position themselves as the next heirs to the throne."

I sucked in a breath. "They want to take the throne for themselves?"

"Yes," he said. "And it doesn't surprise me that Tatjana and her husband are making moves to see that happen. There are others, too."

"Like Kael?" I asked.

"What do you know of him?" he asked.

"Only that he's become a trusted friend and advisor of the

king," I said. "Mother mentioned him the other day in the courtyard."

"Lea, there's something you need to know," he said, his face dark with worry. "I heard a rumor that your parents are planning to make an announcement at the festival. You're to be betrothed to Kael."

I fell against the wall, my mouth open in horror. "You can't be serious."

"I'm afraid it's very serious," he said. "They're planning for a very rapid courtship and engagement. The wedding is scheduled for the end of the third moon cycle."

I shook my head. "That's only a few months away," I said. "I've never even met this man. How can they expect me to marry him?"

"Because a married princess is much easier to keep in line," he said. "And Kael has been angling for the throne. Now that you're home, this is the best way for him to get it."

I forced back tears. It was all starting to make sense. "Kael was the one who suggested the King's Games to my father," I said. "He must know Aerden will fight."

His head flinched back slightly. "Why would that have anything to do with Kael?" he asked.

I didn't know how to answer that question. It was Jackson, not Aerden, who had been chosen as my mate from the day I was born. And yet, ever since he'd been freed from the Order, there had been something growing between us.

I'd been denying it, because I didn't want to risk my heart again. But sometimes the heart has a mind of its own.

"Just make sure he doesn't enter those games," I said. "I don't care what you have to do."

Ezrah nodded. "I have to go," he said. "I'll come find you when I have the opportunity."

He bowed and started to walk away.

"Ezrah," I called.

He turned, frustration pinching his features. "Yes, Princess?"

I met his eyes, pleading. "Don't tell him about the engagement," I said. For reasons I wasn't quite ready to admit to myself, I knew it would hurt Aerden to hear that I'd been promised to someone else. "He doesn't need to know."

"I won't tell him," he said. "But news like this travels through the dungeons quickly. I can't control what he hears from someone else. Why? Do you think it will matter?"

I shook my head but didn't offer an answer.

Ezrah bowed again and hurried toward the other guards leaving for patrol.

A few younger trainees passed by me and bowed their heads, but I could see the question in their eyes: *What was the princess doing here in the guards' quarters?*

Ezrah was right. It had been risky to come here.

I walked back to my room in a daze. I hadn't been living in the castle for a whole month yet and they'd already found me a husband.

What they'd done was put a time limit on my residency here. I would die before I married a demon like Kael. Someone who was willing to put another man in a fight to the death just to open up a slot for himself in the arms of the princess.

If he thought he could win my heart by killing someone I loved, he had no idea who he was dealing with.

There was more going on here than I could explain, and Aerden getting mixed up in the King's Games was only going to complicate everything. I was already at war with my own heart here, having to face old memories for the first time in decades. The last thing I needed was a set of new worries to occupy my every waking hour.

Tatjana and her daughter were plotting against me to take over the kingdom. Kael had arranged the games just to get rid of Aerden. My parents had promised me to a demon I'd never even met and already despised.

How could things possibly get worse?

But that was a foolish question. Things could always get worse.

If Aerden fought in those games, he'd be risking his life. He was an amazing warrior, but his powers were blocked. He'd be at a major disadvantage against every single opponent he faced.

But if I knew Aerden, nothing Ezrah could say would stop him from entering the games. He would fight, and I had to do everything in my power to make damn sure he would win.

THE ONE WHO RETURNED

AERDEN

Three suns warmed the skin on my shoulders as I threw the pickaxe over my head and down into the sapphires. I pretended to be completely immersed in the work, but I was watching the guards.

They had moved Trention to another section of the group, far away from me where I couldn't help him if they wanted to punish him for not working hard enough. But I always had the old demon in my sights. Only cowards and bullies picked on the oldest and weakest, and someday I would find a way to make the worst of these guards pay for their treatment of my friend.

Things had been quiet the past few weeks, and it had me on edge.

I'd expected the guards—especially Reynar and Karn—to torture me any time they saw the opportunity, but they avoided me instead. I suppressed a laugh. I think they were afraid of me. Reynar had poured every last drop of his power into the lightning spell he'd cast on me that day, and I had not so much as fallen to my knees.

But their fear had unexpected consequences.

My days of anonymity were over the second I grabbed Karn's whip. The prisoners still didn't know my name, but they watched my every move. They looked at me as if they weren't quite sure whether I was a hero or a ticking time bomb.

Except for Trention, they kept their distance, but they noticed me now. I heard them whispering about me at night in the cell when they thought I was sleeping. They told elaborate made-up stories of my life before I'd been sentenced to the dungeons, each prisoner guessing at what I'd done to get here or where I'd come from.

Some of them made me laugh, like the one who was sure I'd come from a small mountain village where I'd grown up battling rock golems for sport. Others hit closer to the truth, guessing I'd been a member of the Resistance, caught while trying to assassinate the king.

I let them tell their stories. They were much more interesting than the truth. I was a coward who had abandoned his kingdom and gotten kidnapped by the Order of Shadows. I'd been a slave for a hundred years, saved by a human teenager.

My story was not a heroic one. Not yet.

But I'd been spending my days and nights thinking of the best plan to rescue Lea.

Ezrah told me she'd been brought up from the dungeons weeks ago and had rejoined the other royals in the castle. She'd somehow convinced her father that she was truly home and that she would be loyal to him, no matter what.

I smiled at that as I mined the gemstones. It was hard to

imagine Lea playing the role of the obedient daughter. She must have been biting her tongue so much these days it was probably swollen and bruised. What I would have paid to be a fly on the wall for just an hour in that castle.

But I also knew that her presence in the castle put her in danger. Anyone who'd had their eye on her father's throne would want her dead or exiled. Including my own parents.

Everyone knew her father was in terrible shape. He may not willingly pass on, but the Council had the power to remove him from the throne if they agreed he was not fit to rule.

If the king had not named a successor, the Council also had the power to elect the next king or queen. Since my parents now held two spots on the Council, they also held two votes in all the decisions being made.

Lea showing up again had likely messed up everyone's plans. My guess was that no one on that Council wanted to see her as their queen.

She was a survivor, and she would find a way to fight. But other than Ezrah, she had an entire castle full of demons who desperately wanted her gone. One way or another.

I swung my pickaxe harder, the tip smashing through nearly a foot of raw sapphire. The prisoner next to me paused and stared at the stones, his eyes wide. I ignored him and turned my thoughts back to Lea.

Was she thinking of me at all? Or did she roam the halls of her father's castle thinking of my brother and what she thought she'd lost?

I swung my axe again, determined to make it right. Even if she could never love me, she deserved to know the truth. I was done with the lies and the fear.

I was done being a coward.

Just as my axe hit the ground, a commotion broke out near the front of the line. I pulled back and stepped to the side, trying to see what was happening.

Reynar had pulled a younger demon to the side and pushed him to the ground. He'd removed the boy's shackles, which was never a good sign.

I couldn't hear what he was yelling about, but Reynar had his whip in his hand, and the boy was trembling.

"What's going on?" I asked the demon in front of me. He was a tall man named Perrick. We'd only spoken a handful of times in passing, but he seemed to be honorable.

Perrick held up his hand to me and leaned forward as the prisoners in front of him whispered something in his ear.

"News just passed down from the front," Perrick said. "They're saying the young one was spreading rumors about a festival at the castle. Something to honor the return of the princess and her new engagement."

The pickaxe fell from my hand, and my heart stopped beating.

She was engaged?

This couldn't be happening. Not again.

Fear and anger warred within me. Part of me wanted to drop to my knees in tears, and the other part wanted to rip these chains from my body and kill every guard in sight.

"It's a shame, really," Perrick said. He'd been talking, but I hadn't heard anything past the word engagement.

"What?"

"The boy," he said. "He's been in trouble for spreading rumors before, and Reynar warned him just last week that if he was caught talking about news of the castle or the outside world, he would beat him within an inch of his life unless he confessed where the information was coming from."

"They think he has some kind of source?" I asked.

"He has to be getting information from somewhere," he said. "Prisoners are forbidden to communicate with anyone outside of these dungeons, so either a guard is passing information or that boy has a dormant ability that isn't controlled by these chains. Either way, unless he confesses, I'm afraid he won't survive another beating. The last one nearly killed him."

Why would this boy risk talking out here if he knew his life was in danger? Why wouldn't he whisper it to the others inside the darkness of the dungeons late at night? It didn't make sense, except that he was young and didn't know any better.

We all made foolish decisions when we were young.

Reynar tore the young demon's shirt from his back and lashed his whip across the bare skin. I winced and took a step forward, but Perrick grabbed my arm.

"Don't," he said in a low voice. "Ezrah told me to look after you. There's a plan in place, Aerden. The Resistance is working to get us both out of here. Lay low and be patient."

I narrowed my eyes and stepped back. "You belong to the Resistance?"

"Quiet," he said, glancing around. "You'll get us both killed."

"I don't care what Andros is planning," I said. "I can't stand here and watch that young demon be tortured to death."

"One boy is nothing compared to the suffering out there," he said. "You of all demons should know that."

I clenched my jaw and stepped back, my heart thundering

in my chest as Reynar whipped the boy again. One more blow would end him.

"Let's bring them all up to hear the news," Reynar shouted. "If you're so eager to share gossip like a pretty maiden, maybe you can tell them all what the king has in store for you."

The guards moved quickly, drawing the entire group of prisoners into a tight circle around Reynar and the boy, who was bent over, blood dripping from the gashes on his back.

I tightened my hands into fists as I stood there in the front of the group.

"Tell them, boy—go on."

The boy looked up at the menacing guard, his body trembling in fear.

Reynar raised his whip as a threat, and I took another step forward. Again, Perrick pushed his arm in front of mine to block my way.

"The king's daughter, Princess Lazalea, has returned to the castle, and there is to be a great festival in her honor," the boy said, his voice choked by sobs. "To celebrate her expected engagement to Kael, son of Reagan, there will be a tournament."

The boy cowered, his body bent, and his head lowered toward the ground.

"And what kind of tournament will it be, since you're dying to tell everyone who will listen?" Reynar asked, holding up the whip again.

"The return of the King's Games," the boy said.

A ripple went through the crowd of prisoners. The King's Games had been outlawed generations ago. I knew of them from my history lessons as a shadowling, but where everyone around me saw this as a death sentence, I saw it as the first shimmering light of hope.

"The king wants volunteers," Reynar said. "Five demons from every dungeon in the city to fight to the death in hopes of getting a chance to beg for their freedom. I think we'll start choosing those volunteers right now. What do you think, boy?"

The young demon shook his head and collapsed onto the ground at Reynar's feet. He'd taken a harsh beating, and it would take him a long time to recover from the lashings. I was amazed he'd stayed upright as long as he had.

"I'll assume by your lack of response that you would happily volunteer your life in service to the king's entertainment," Reynar said. An evil smile spread across his lips, revealing yellowed teeth. "Karn, why don't you choose the next volunteer."

My head snapped toward the other side of the circle as Karn walked toward Trention. My friend's eyes met mine as Karn unlocked the chains around his wrists and ankles and shoved him forward. Trention fell on his knees next to the boy.

I drew an angry breath. He wouldn't dare put a young boy and the oldest, weakest demon in the dungeon on the battlefield of the arena. They'd be dead in seconds against a mediocre opponent. They were not fighters.

Historically, the first round of the King's Games was a group round. Five on five. If the others in their group were good enough, these two might survive round one, but when the battles whittled down to smaller and smaller groups, they would surely lose their lives.

"Yes, I think these two will make a good start," Reynar said, laughing. "Who else is willing to volunteer their life in exchange for an audience with the king? If we have five worthy volunteers, perhaps I will let these two weaklings live another day."

I stepped forward, but Perrick gripped my arm tightly.

"This is not the way, friend," he said. "You're in no shape to fight, and even if you were to win, there's no guarantee the king would set you free. Ezrah told me that Lea begged him to make sure you didn't enter these games. It would destroy her if anything happened to you."

His words knocked me back. Lea had begged him?

No one believed I could win on my own. And maybe they were right. I didn't even have control over my magical powers. I was good with a weapon, but the demons in the arena would be strong in every way. They would be well-trained and determined to win their freedom.

In the history of the games, there were always surprises, too. Monsters brought in from the wilds to wow the crowds. Conjured abominations that appeared out of nowhere in the middle of a battle. Only a fool would volunteer when he couldn't so much as cast the simplest spell.

If I was smart, I would wait here in the dungeons until the Resistance came to rescue me. Deviating from whatever plan Andros had so carefully laid out might put the entire operation in danger. But this was the chance I'd been waiting for. A real chance to prove myself in battle and face my darkest fears. A chance to show Lea that I was ready to fight for her.

Reynar lifted his whip. "No one will volunteer? Are you a bunch of cowards who would send your weakest off to die?" he asked. "Or perhaps you need some extra motivation?"

He brought the whip down hard against Trention's back, and the old demon screamed in pain. Tears stung my eyes and my jaw tensed as I watched my friend be beaten.

Trention's eyes met mine across the circle and he shook his head, warning me not to intervene. But I was done following anyone else's orders. I was done waiting for someone else to rescue me while I stood by and watched the fight from the sidelines.

I brought my hands together and drew what power I could find into my veins as Reynar's whip hit my friend again. In one swift motion, I pulled my hands outward, snapping the iron chain between my shackles. I reached down and ripped the chains from my ankles, feeling the surge of power run through me as the spell that contained my magic broke free.

I shifted to smoke, ignoring the gasps of surprise that rippled through the prisoners. I swirled around Reynar's body and grabbed his whip with one hand and the dagger at his belt with the other. Before he even realized what was happening, I had the dagger pressed against his throat.

"You are the only coward here," I whispered in his ear. "Touch him again and die."

The other guards raced forward, taking my arms and pulling them behind my back. They yanked me away and pushed me to my knees, and I dropped the dagger to the ground.

Reynar stretched his neck forward and readjusted the collar of his uniform. "Well, lads, it seems we have our first volunteer," he said. He spit on the ground and then turned to face me. "Aerden, son of Walther, it will be a pleasure to watch you die."

"Aerden?" someone shouted.

"It's him."

Voices joined in, questioning my identity.

"But you were dead," someone else said. "Taken by the Order. How can it be?"

Reynar crouched in front of me and pulled my long hair back from my face. "Have you really not recognized him all this time? The son of the king's top advisor shared a dungeon with you for months, and none of you realized?" He laughed. "You are all much bigger fools than I thought."

But Reynar was the fool. Calling me out for who I really was did nothing but bring the entire crowd of prisoners to my side.

"Is the Order defeated?"

"Have our demons returned?"

"If you're alive, there is hope."

Everyone spoke at once, their eyes never leaving my face. I studied the crowd, recognizing hope and admiration in their eyes. I could see in them the desperate need to believe that the world was not over. To believe that if we fought together, we could defeat even the most impossible enemy.

"I volunteer," a demon said, stepping forward. I didn't know his name, but he looked me right in the eyes as he said it. "If Aerden fights, so do I."

"I volunteer," two others said, joining the first demon.

"I will fight with the one who returned," another demon said, nodding at me as my eyes met his. "I volunteer to fight with this warrior."

One by one, every demon along the line stepped forward, volunteering their life to fight at my side.

My heart opened in that moment, kneeling there beneath the pure demon sky. This was the Shadow World I remembered. Not the run-down villages or the war-torn cities. At its core, this was a place of great strength and beauty, where demons willingly gave their lives to protect their own. It was a place where honor and justice once meant something.

Despite their situation and all the wrongs that had been done to them, these demons still believed in something great. They refused to give up on hope and the idea that if we stood together, we could do impossible things.

There are few moments that change you. That make you who you are. That inspire you to be the person you always knew you could be. But this was one of those moments for me.

Kneeling there, I realized that everything I wanted was within my grasp. All I had to do was find the courage within myself to reach for it.

These demons believed in me because I had stood in the face of evil and survived. It didn't matter that I'd been saved by the persistence and strength of my closest friends. What mattered was that I was here. I was proof that evil could be defeated, and that love was stronger than any other force in this world or the next.

I had no idea what the future would hold, but I did know this: I would fight with all of my soul and strength. I would stand until they forced me to my knees for the last time.

Sapphires gleamed in the sunlight, the pure blue color of the stones reminding me that I was once as hopeless and afraid as the demons in this ravaged land. I was as broken as the abandoned ships that lined the shore like wooden skeletons.

All it took was a handful of people who believed in the impossible and refused to give up. I had been resurrected by their love and their willingness to give themselves wholly to the fight.

Up until now, I'd carried my freedom like a burden. But as

I knelt under the expansive sky with the suns warming my face, I saw it for the first time as the gift it truly was.

We would win this war, or we would die fighting.

And when the time came, I would stand in the arena of the King's City, and I would honor those who had given me back my life. I would prove to everyone that as long as you believed in something so much you were willing to die for it, anything was possible.

THE KEY

AERDEN

After the guards brought us all back down to the dungeons, Reynar grabbed my new chains and led me to the solitary cell on the other side of the cave. He locked me inside and spit on the floor at my feet.

"You think you're above me because of what you've overcome, but I know the truth," he said. "You're nothing but a deserter. You abandoned your king and your people when they needed you most, and you should have paid for that crime with your life. Maybe now you finally will."

He left me to the darkness, but for the first time in ages, there was a light of hope in my heart. Yes, Lea was engaged, but I knew her well enough to know that she would not go through with a wedding to someone her father had chosen for her. She would fight before she agreed to marry Kael.

I finally had a way to prove to her that I was in this fight, too.

Hours later, when sleep had started to drag me down into

its depths, a door opened at the end of the hall and light fell across the stone floor.

I stood, expecting to see Ezrah again. I expected to have to explain my decision and to stand up for what I'd done, but it wasn't Ezrah who walked into the room. It was my mother.

I hadn't seen her since my first nights in the castle's holding cells when she had come to me and refused to set me free. I didn't want to see her now, and I most certainly didn't want to hear her beg me to step down from my decision to fight in the games.

"Oh, Aerden, look at you," she said, running forward and clutching the steel bars between us. "What have they done to you in this place?"

"That's a fine question to ask when you're the one who left me here to rot in the name of my own safety," I said.

"Don't speak to me like that," she said. "You have no idea how much it hurts me to know you're here."

"I'm sure," I muttered. I had nothing nice to say to her. It was her fault I was still down here instead of up at the castle with Lea. And it was her fault my friend Trention, a great scholar, had been doomed to death down here with me. I wasn't exactly in a forgiving mood.

"Aerden, you cannot fight in these games," she said. "It's too dangerous. You're putting your entire life on the line, and for what? It's madness."

"Madness?" I asked, stepping closer to her. "Do you know what madness is? It's having to live inside the body of a witch for an entire century, hearing her voice in your head and obeying her every command. Madness is not having any control over your own body or your own power for what felt like a lifetime. Madness is being abandoned by the parents you believed loved you more than anything. You know nothing of madness, Mother."

She turned her head away, as if the sight of me sickened her.

"I told you, if we'd had any reason to believe that you could be saved, we would have moved heaven and hell to get you out of there," she said. "How could we have known?"

"A sixteen-year-old human girl believed in me," I said. "My brother believed in me. Why couldn't you?"

"I tried to protect you," she said.

The key. I suddenly remembered the diamond key she had given me. Was that what she meant now? Was that how she'd meant to protect me?

A chill ran through my body, and I touched her hand to force her to look at me.

"How did you try to protect me, Mother?" I asked, my voice softer. I needed to know. "Is that why you gave me the key?"

When she looked at me, there were tears in her eyes. "If you'd had the key with you, they couldn't have taken you through that portal, Aerden. I don't understand."

"I don't either," I said.

She shook her head. "What?"

"Where did you get the key, Mother? How could you have known it would protect me from the Order?" I asked.

"That's not important," she said, taking a deep breath and stepping back from the cell. "What's important is that you're safe now. You can't put your life in jeopardy again just to...what? Prove something to yourself?"

"What kind of life is this?" I asked, motioning to the tiny cell that held me. "Being stuck in here is no better than living in the human world and serving the Order. I'm still not free, can't you see that?"

She closed her eyes and ran a fingertip across her cheek. "I just want my children home with me and safe," she said. "Once things have calmed down and your sister and brother have come home, I'll make sure the king sets you free. I promise."

In other words, she didn't want me free now. She didn't trust me.

And more importantly, she didn't want me fighting against the Order. Any of us. She wanted us home where she could control us.

"Where did you get the key?" I asked again. "What are you hiding?"

Her eyes widened, and she stepped back until her shoe touched the stone wall across from my cell. I wanted her to tell me that she'd found the key somewhere on accident and had learned it would protect its wearer from the Order. I wanted her to tell me that she had no ulterior motives in keeping me locked away.

But when she didn't speak, I knew. There was a reason my mother didn't come looking for me when I disappeared. There was a reason she locked me away as soon as she had the opportunity. Something more was going on with her than I had ever realized.

She was hiding something. Something big. Something she didn't want anyone—especially her own children—to know.

"I'm going to fight in the King's Games," I said. "I'm going to win my freedom and go back to where I belong, Mother. And there's nothing you or anyone else can do to stop me."

Tears fell across her cheek and she stared at me, a mixture

of anger and disbelief in her eyes. She was hiding something from me, and she would let me die before she would allow me to figure it out. I could see that now.

She squared her shoulders and lifted her chin. She smoothed out her white dress and wiped the tears from her eyes.

"I don't know what I did to raise such disobedient children," she said. "Fight in your games, but I'm telling you, you will do nothing more than learn your own fatal weaknesses, Aerden. Remember that when you're dying on the battlefield of the arena. I tried to save you twice, and you wouldn't let me help you. I won't intervene again."

She took a shuddering breath and turned her back on me one last time.

SOME THINGS ARE WORTH DYING FOR

HARPER

I lay dying on the battlefield, the sound of war echoing in my ears. Bright lights blossomed into fireworks all around me, but I couldn't seem to find the energy to lift my head. We had fought with all our hearts and souls, but it was too hard. They were too strong.

A tear slipped down my cheek as I realized this was the end. I had failed them all.

My eyes began to close, sorrow weighing heavily on my heart. But a warm breeze caressed my skin, and a glowing figure leaned over my broken body. I forced my eyes open, squinting against the light that surrounded him. I could just make out the white of his hair and the deep silver of his eyes.

"Dad?"

I called his name and reached up to touch his face, but the dream slipped from my grasp and his image wavered.

"Some things are worth dying for," he whispered. He placed an emerald stone in my hand and pressed it hard against my palm. "You are a true warrior, Harper. Set them free."

I tried to tell him that I didn't understand, but before I could say another word, the dream disappeared. The light was replaced by pain as I woke.

Every muscle in my body ached, and the moment my eyes opened, a headache began to pound against my skull.

I groaned and tried to roll over, but my arms wouldn't move. I forced my eyes open, wincing at the light, and saw that my wrists were bound by leather straps. I wasn't in my normal room. They'd moved me to a small room with white walls and a white ceiling, much like the one I remembered from my first day here at the institute.

The light was blinding, and I closed my eyes against it, wishing I could fall back into my dream. The man with the impossibly silver eyes had been trying to tell me something. Was he really my father? Or had my brain simply made him up?

At first, I couldn't remember how I'd even gotten here. I remembered being in the rec room when Nurse Melody asked me to follow her, but everything after that was gone, as if it had been erased from my mind.

Slowly, though, the memory of the basement came back to me. I could see Dr. Evers smiling over me, so proud of her torture.

In that moment, I knew with sharp clarity that this was no normal mental institution. Shock therapies may still exist in some extreme cases, but there was no way it was still allowed to be so barbaric. There was nothing medical or safe about what had been done to me. Even the nurse knew that.

And yet, somehow, this institute was still functioning. They were allowed to do whatever they wanted to their patients, and Dr. Evers hadn't seemed the least bit concerned about some government official shutting them down for what she'd done. Which meant that Brooke had been right.

Brooke had been real. I hadn't made her up. There was more going on in this place than anyone was telling me.

I swallowed, my throat dry and aching. There was no IV attached to my arm, and I had no idea how long I'd gone without food or water. I lifted my head to try to find the door, but pain shot down my spine.

I let my head fall back against the bed, too exhausted to keep fighting. It was pointless, anyway. I was strapped down to a bed in a locked room with no one I could trust to help me.

How had I gotten here?

Not just to this room, but to this place? The nurses and the doctor kept telling me I had burned down my own house and killed my family. They said no one could be sure if I had done it on purpose, or if it had been an accident.

If that was true, wouldn't I have been questioned by the police? Thrown in jail or brought to trial? Wouldn't I have some memory of what happened to me after the fire?

Instead of a trial, I remembered the pain.

I remembered glass cutting into my skin, blood trickling down my arms and my face. I remembered a dark room and the chanting of voices. I remembered being immersed in scalding hot water, emeralds draped around my neck and tied to my arms.

No court would have sanctioned something like that.

So why was I here?

What was this place, really?

Whatever it was, it most certainly was not a rehabilitation center for the emotionally challenged or the temporarily insane. There was more going on here than that, and none of these treatments had ever been meant to rehabilitate.

No, this was about control and manipulation. It was about punishment.

I left my room for one hour and was subjected to torture in the name of making me better. But Dr. Evers had smiled. She was a sadist, taking joy from the pain of others.

I closed my eyes and heard her voice in my head.

I only wish my mother could have been here to see this.

She probably thought I would be too messed-up to remember her words, or she never would have dared to speak them, but where my memory had failed me before, it was crystal-clear now.

This wasn't about a fire or any crime I had committed. This was personal, and as I lay there for the next several hours waiting for someone to realize I was finally awake, I vowed one thing over and over in my head.

I would fight them. I would find out what this place was, and I would do everything in my power to remember my past and why I was important to them. I didn't care if I had to go through a thousand shock treatments, injections, or other tortures. I would find the truth, and I would make them pay for all the things they had taken from me.

TRUSTING MY OWN INSTINCTS

HARPER

I don't know how many days passed before they moved me back to my room. With no windows and a light that stayed on around the clock, there was no way for me to tell if it was day or night.

Every once in a while, a nurse I didn't know came in to inject me with vial of green liquid that put me to sleep for a very long time. When I woke up afterward, I always felt clouded and confused. But the memory of what they had done and the determination to find the truth always returned to me. The man with the silver eyes stayed with me as I slept, encouraging me to never give up.

None of my roommates spoke to me when I entered our room, but I made a point to look at Judith until she found the courage to look back.

I wanted her to know that I understood our relationship a lot better now. She was not to be trusted.

She looked away, huddling against the wall with her legs pulled tightly against her chest. Her eyes were ringed with dark circles, as if she'd hardly been sleeping. I wanted to tell her I'd slept enough for the both of us.

Nora sat on her bed, reading a book, but didn't dare glance up at me as I passed her.

The room was silent and still, Mary Ellen as quiet as ever with her back turned away from the door and her black hair hanging over her face. I was unsteady on my legs, but I managed to walk on my own from the door to the bed. I sat down, out of breath even from those few steps. Recovery would take a while.

I had lost a significant amount of weight, which told me I'd been locked away for days without much food. Maybe even a full week.

I needed to talk to Brooke, but I had no way to get in touch with her. I needed answers, and she was my only hope of finding them. Did she know that I'd been taken away? Had she tried to contact me while I was gone?

In my current condition, I wasn't sure I'd be able to follow the shadow back down to the basement even if she did send a message to meet her there. I'd barely been able to walk twelve steps without help.

But I was strong, and I was going to get through this. All I needed was time, and here in this place, that was the one thing I had plenty of.

I rested as much as I could when we were confined to our room. I ate everything on my plate at meals, though I noticed that ever since I had gotten back, my portions were smaller than everyone else's.

When we were allowed to go outside, I walked around the edge of the courtyard the entire time, not even taking a break when I was tired and thought my legs might give out. I kept moving, determined to regain my strength.

Instead of pills, the nurses now injected me with the same green fluid every night at bedtime. Brooke had been right about that, too. The injections were much harder to resist. They confused me and made the memories harder to grasp, but somehow, I managed to always fight against the medicine. It shouldn't have worked that way, but by sheer force of will, I refused to let my memories fade.

I practiced fighting against it. When the drug threatened to close my eyes against the truth, I forced them to stay open, allowing myself sleep only after hours of careful practice resisting its magic.

Because that's what it was, right? Magic?

Nothing else could explain all of the strange things happening here: Brooke's shadow. Her light. The emeralds all the nurses and doctors wore. The green poison they forced into my veins every night.

It all tied together, along with the emerald flames that consumed my family's home.

It was all connected, and even if it killed me, I was going to find out how.

Spring came while I wasn't paying attention, and it brought rain. I stared out the window in the rec room, studying the courtyard. The grass was no longer brown and withered, but instead had become lush and green.

I was growing stronger, too, as if a new season had arrived in my life. I kept my head down during group therapy, pretending to listen but never offering to speak unless I was forced to. In my private sessions with Dr. Evers, I barely said a word. I pretended that I had no clear memory of what she'd done to me. I played her game, saying the things I knew she wanted to hear. I followed her rules, and she seemed to believe that her therapy had worked wonders.

Wouldn't her mother be proud?

I spent a lot of my time trying to piece together the puzzle of my memories, wondering how in the world my doctor's mother could have any part of this. But between the injections and the endless, mind-numbing routine, I hadn't gotten any closer to finding the truth.

Just when I thought I couldn't take it any longer, the shadow of a horse passed by the window one day when we were playing cards in the rec room. It took me by surprise, and I gasped.

Beside me, Nora jumped. "Jeez, Harper, what in the world is your problem?"

"I'm sorry," I said. "I thought I saw lightning."

"So? Is that any reason to scare us all to death?"

"I'm terrified of storms," I said, laughing and trying to play it off.

"There's no lightning. It's just a little bit of rain," she said. "Get it together."

"Sorry," I mumbled again.

I glanced back up at the window, hoping to see the shadow again, but it never reappeared. It was enough to see it once, though.

Sneaking out again would be tougher this time. Between the nightly injections that made me sleepy and confused and the fact that I had a tattletale roommate to worry about, I wasn't looking forward to risking everything for a few minutes in the basement with a stranger. But I needed to see her.

When Nurse Melody came to mark us off her list for lights-out, though, she skipped my injection. I watched her check it off her list, but she never gave it to me. Instead, she held my gaze for a few seconds and nodded slightly. Her eyes dropped to her tray with its white paper cups full of pills.

I glanced at them, at first not noticing anything out of the ordinary. But as she handed one to Judith, I saw that one of her normal green pills had been switched for a white one.

A sleeping pill.

It was the closest thing to an apology I'd gotten in the weeks since the incident in the basement.

I nodded back and crawled into bed, praying Judith hadn't noticed the change in routine.

I wasn't sure why Nurse Melody had decided to help me, but the fact that one of the nurses knew what I was planning to do tonight scared me to death. I hoped she wasn't setting up some kind of trap, and that she genuinely was trying to help me get to Brooke.

I lay awake, listening to the rhythms of the girls' breathing. I could tell when each one of them finally drifted off to sleep. Judith snored, which made it easy to tell when she was out. Nora's breathing simply slowed and calmed. She hardly moved at all when she slept. And Mary Ellen, who was always quiet, grew as still as death itself.

When the nurse came in to check on us at three in the morning, I pretended to be asleep. And as soon as I could no longer hear her footsteps in the hallway, I carefully slipped out of bed. I rearranged my sheets and pillow as best I could to make it look as though I were still in bed, asleep.

I stared at the lock on the door, my skin prickling with excitement and fear. Brooke told me I knew exactly how I had opened the lock last time, but I hadn't wanted to believe it. It was easier to believe that it was some kind of trick.

If it worked again this time, though, I would know.

I placed my hand on the lock and closed my eyes. I took a deep breath and pictured the mechanism inside the lock turning. A light click sounded and when I turned the knob, it opened with ease. Somehow, I had just opened a lock with my mind.

I quietly made my way down the hall, through the corridors, and down to the cold basement room.

Brooke was waiting for me.

"I'm glad you made it," she said. "Are you okay? God, I'm so sorry about last time. What happened?"

"My roommate woke up while I was gone," I said. "She told Dr. Evers I broke the rules."

"I heard you were gone for a while," she said. "Did they hurt you?"

I rolled up the sleeves of my plain gray dress and showed her the needle marks. "Dr. Evers gave me shock therapy, and then they started injections," I said. "You were right about this place. It isn't a normal mental institution, is it?"

"Not by any stretch of the imagination," Brooke said. "Have you remembered anything new?"

I shook my head. We didn't have much time, and I needed answers. "No. I think the injections are keeping my memories locked away," I said. "I need your help. I know that there's more going on here than just treatment for mental illness. Dr.

Evers thinks I don't remember the shock therapy, but she let something slip that's been on my mind ever since."

"What?" Brooke asked. The same glowing orb of light rose from her hand. It flickered slightly, casting shadows around the small room.

"She told me she wished her mother could have been there to see it," I said. "Do you know what that means? Why would her mother have anything to do with this place?"

"Her mother has everything to do with this place," Brooke said, but didn't offer more of an explanation.

I was tired of cryptic messages and half-truths. I wanted to know what the hell was going on and how I was going to get out of here.

"I know you said you need for me to remember on my own, but nothing is happening. After what they did to me when I met you last time, I realized there has to be more to this place, but I'm powerless to find the answers on my own. Not with them injecting that poison into my veins every night," I said. "You remember, don't you? All of it? I need you to tell me. I can't keep going like this."

"You can't give up, Harper," she said. "I understand how frustrating this must be for you, but handing you all of the answers isn't going to do you any good. You'd just forget them again with the next injection. You have to remember so that you can reconnect with your magic."

I stared at the glowing orb. "So, it's real?" I asked. "Magic is real?"

"Very real," she said. "Every girl in this place has some control over magic. That's why they keep us drugged and locked away."

It sounded crazy, but I knew she was telling the truth.

"Try it," she said, nodding toward the orb of light.

"I don't know how," I said.

"Yes, you do."

I swallowed and lifted my hand. I had no idea what to do, but at some point, I was going to have to start trusting my own instincts. I was going to have to admit that something was different about this place and about me. I couldn't fight back against the doctor if I had no idea who I was or why I was really here.

It was time to start remembering.

I stared down at my palm, waiting for something magical to happen.

"Breathe deeply," Brooke said, her voice calm and soothing. "Imagine there is a well of energy deep inside of you like a bubbling spring. Reach into it and connect with it. Let it flow through you until your skin is buzzing with its energy."

I listened, slowly taking deep breaths into my lungs. I closed my eyes and imagined that deep wellspring of power. At first, I thought it was useless. I didn't feel anything at all. But then it happened. A tiny tingle of energy prickling at my senses. I latched onto it, going deeper toward that power.

I imagined it flowing through my veins and traveling to every part of my body. I imagined a bright light forming in my hand.

"That's it," she said. "Harper, open your eyes."

Slowly, I opened my eyes and gasped at the brilliance of the light sitting on my palm. I dropped my hand and slid back on the floor, hardly able to believe what I was seeing.

The light hovered in the air, much brighter than Brooke's small orb, and as my heart began to race, the light grew even more intense, flickering across the walls around us.

"How is this possible?" I asked.

"You are incredibly special, Harper," she said. "You're capable of so much more than you realize. I know it's hard to understand after what they've done to you, but the world needs you to get better. The world needs you to reclaim your powers and fight against this place."

"Everyone keeps saying that, but I don't feel special," I said. "I feel lost."

"Everyone?" she asked.

"There was a girl my first night at dinner," I said. "Robin. She knew my name. She said that if I was here, the whole world was lost. And then there was a man. In my dreams, after the shock treatments. He had the most beautiful silver eyes."

"Your father," she said.

My gaze snapped to hers. "He's real?" I asked, my lip quivering. "Did I... Did I kill him? In the fire? They told me I killed my family in that fire."

Her expression softened, and she shook her head. "You should know better than to believe anything they say as truth."

"But I remember the fire," I said. "A beautiful white house burned to the ground. I think it was my home."

"Harper, your father died on the battlefield," she said. "That was the last time I saw you, actually. You were dying, and he saved you. He sacrificed his own life to heal your wounds, long before your house burned down."

I closed my eyes, tears streaming down my cheeks. "My life for yours," I whispered, remembering. "He told me to set them free. What does that mean?"

Brooke glanced toward the door of the basement room. "We're almost out of time," she said. "It may be awhile before we can meet again, but if you find the opportunity, you should keep coming down here. Practice your magic. It will help you remember."

"Don't go," I said as she stood. "I need you."

She turned and smiled. "No, Harper. That's what you still haven't understood," she said. "The truth is, I need you."

EVERY DETAIL

HARPER

I didn't see Brooke again for weeks, and I didn't dare ask anyone about her. What we shared was our little secret, and I understood now the consequences of breaking the rules of this place.

Instead, I did what she suggested and found ways to sneak down to the basement to practice.

I wasn't sure what she'd said to Nurse Melody or why the woman was helping me, but the injections had stopped. Every night, she marked it off her list, but she never used it. And every night, she gave Judith the same white pill that helped her sleep, giving me the opportunity to sneak away.

I started with simple things: Orbs of light. Picking up objects with my mind and moving them around the room. The more I practiced, the easier it got.

And then one night when I came down, there was a bag of items sitting in the corner: Candles. Gemstones. Stacks of paper. A mirror.

I practiced creating flames out of nothing more than the power that lived within me. I floated multiple pieces of paper around the room, strengthening my ability to move more than one object at a time. I wasn't sure what the gemstones were supposed to do, but when I focused on them, they began to glow and pulse with light.

A week later, I found a book of spells inside the bag. I hugged it close to my chest and laughed as I flipped through the pages. There were so many possibilities, and I wished I could stay down in that basement all day practicing and testing my abilities.

By the time three weeks had passed, I could easily create flame and light. I learned to create glamours, making one object look like something else entirely. I sometimes held the mirror in front of my face and practiced changing my hair color from blonde to purple or blue. My eyes changed from brown to green.

As I grew better at it, I was able to make myself look exactly like one of the nurses or one of my roommates.

When I wasn't in the basement, it was hard to keep from using my magic. If I dropped my napkin on the floor at dinner, I was tempted to use magic to float it up to my hand, rather than bending down to pick it up. I had to stay alert, remembering that any use of my new abilities would be deadly for me at this point. I needed to get stronger.

In my therapy sessions, I was quiet. I told Dr. Evers that I couldn't remember anything about my life before this place. She asked if I remembered the fire, and I told her that sometimes I thought I did remember what I had done, and that I was sorry for it. I told her I wanted to get well, and that seemed to make her happy.

In the mornings when they gave me my green pills, I tucked them into my gums at the top near my teeth, opened my mouth and lifted my tongue to show that I had swallowed them. Then, when I was alone in the bathroom, I spit them into my hand and wrapped them in toilet paper. I washed them down the drain and watched to make sure they didn't get caught or come back up.

At night, when everyone else was asleep and I couldn't get away, I whispered what I knew to myself, urging more memories to come forward.

"Jackson," I whispered, not giving any sound to the name. Only air and breath, wishing with all my heart that he could hear me.

I pictured him there in that field, the light of the full moon shining down on him. Brooke had said he was there watching out for me. He wanted to make sure I was safe. But safe from what? Or who?

I spoke to no one about my meetings with Brooke in the basement, and my loneliness wore on me like a heavy weight strapped to my shoulders.

What was going on while I was locked away inside this place? If Brooke was right and I was important in some way, then the girl who'd recognized me my first day here had also been right. She'd known who I was, and she'd said the world was lost without me in it.

I'd spent so many late nights thinking about her words and trying to figure out what she'd meant. What she'd known.

If I really was important, did that mean there were others on the outside trying to find me? Did I have any hope of them rescuing me someday?

Other nights, I wondered if I had imagined all of it.

Brooke. The magic. Everything. What if I was crazy and suffering from delusions? I mean, it's not like crazy people knew they were crazy. They believed it, which was kind of the point. Maybe I belonged here, and my brain had just created these other things to make it seem more bearable. Maybe I was simply holding onto a hope that didn't exist.

When you're locked away and told you're insane, how could you trust yourself and your own mind ever again?

"Harper, did you hear me?" Dr. Evers said, tapping on her clipboard.

I looked up, taking in a sharp breath. It was our weekly Tuesday appointment, and I'd barely said two words to her.

"No, I'm sorry," I said. "I must have drifted off."

She leaned forward against her desk, setting her clipboard and pen down. "Harper, these sessions are an extremely important part of your recovery," she said. "What could you possibly be thinking about that would distract you from this important work?"

I searched for some excuse that would sound real, but I couldn't think of a good enough lie. I was so tired of these fake therapy sessions where she pretended to listen to me and I pretended to care.

"I'm sorry," I said, not giving an excuse or answer.

She sighed and leaned back. "I asked if you had remembered anything new since we last spoke," she said. "I want to help you work through what happened, but in order to do that, you need to accept your role in the fire. I need you to remember what you did."

I glanced up at her, trying to hide my emotions so that she couldn't see just how much I despised her. The truth was that she didn't want me to remember anything except her version of events. She wanted me to remember her lie and call it truth. To give up on myself and accept that I belonged here.

I wondered what would happen if I played her game. What if I fed her lies of my own?

"I was angry," I said, not meeting her eyes. I looked down at my hands, instead. "I started the fire to get back at them for something, I think. I didn't mean for anyone to get hurt."

"So, you do remember?" she asked, her eyes widening as she gripped her pen. "Tell me every detail."

"I think I must have used a lighter and some loose paper from one of my notebooks," I said. "I don't remember exactly what happened, but I do remember being so angry that I wanted them to pay for what they had done."

"And what did they do?"

I shook my head. "I don't know," I said. "I'm trying to remember, but it's all still so unclear. I think my parents wouldn't let me do something I wanted to do?"

I said it as a question, wanting her to fill in the rest of this fake story. They had told me snippets of what they wanted me to believe, but if I was going to convince them that I had fallen for their lies, I needed to get this right.

"Yes," she said. "Your parents. Do you remember them?"

"A little," I said. "When I think of them, I feel regret and pain. I can't see their faces, but I feel like I did something bad to them."

"You did," she said. "You did a very bad thing, Harper. That's why you're here."

"I know," I said softly. When I looked up at her, I had tears in my eyes. Fake tears, maybe, but hopefully convincing. "Can you help me? I just want to get past this and show that I'm sorry for what I did. I want to get better."

Dr. Evers raised an eyebrow as she continued to write on her notepad. There was a hint of a smile on her lips, and I knew that she was excited. I could feel it in the air.

I drew in a breath, filling myself with this new energy in the room. I let it flow into me. I let it fuel my anger and my desire to know the truth.

Something deep inside me woke up, and I could almost feel it there, like a beast waking from a long slumber. My hands tingled, and my skin felt alive. At first, I tried to push against it, scared I would accidentally cast a spell and she would know the truth.

But something felt different this time. A new ability was trying to get out or reveal itself to me.

Should I trust myself? Or make it stop?

I tapped into it. I pushed this new energy out along my veins, letting the warmth of it flow into my blood and become a part of me.

"I can help you," she said. "That's all I've ever been here to do, Harper. I hope you know that. I'm on your side."

I heard her words, but it was difficult to fully concentrate. Energy flowed through me so intensely that it buzzed in my ears, my pulse pounding. I looked at the folder on top of her desk and watched her scratching away at her notepad, and all I could think about was how much I wanted to know what was in those notes. I wanted to look over her shoulder and see them for myself.

I'd been searching my own mind for answers, but like Brooke said, they were carefully locked away by something far more powerful than I could comprehend.

But I knew in my soul that some answers were just a few steps away, written in that folder.

If I saw it and it truly said that I had murdered my own family in a fire and was suffering from severe delusions, then I would know that I'd officially lost my mind and was in denial.

But if the file told a different story, then I would know that Brooke was real. Jackson was real. And that I did not belong here.

Staring at that folder, I felt such anger rush through me. This doctor had all the answers right there at her fingertips and she was keeping them from me. She played this game with me, ordering pills that messed with my mind and asking me to admit to a truth that was never real.

Instead of pushing against it, I gave in to that anger. I plunged into it, losing myself inside it. I imagined myself standing up and grabbing the folder off her desk. I needed to know what was there. My life depended on it.

And suddenly, a heat flowed into me. A power unlocked, and in an instant, I was standing outside my own body, looking back at myself.

I looked down at my hands, and I was nothing more than a ghost of myself, my body invisible and not even there. But I was also still sitting in that chair, my face calm as I stared down at the hands cradled in my lap.

How was this possible? How could I be in two places at once?

Dr. Evers kept talking, telling me about how she was going to help rehabilitate me. She said that if I could learn to take responsibility for what I had done, there was hope I could someday leave this place.

She was talking to me, looking directly at my body sitting in the chair across from her. She didn't seem to notice the ghostly me standing at her side.

I had no idea how I'd done this or how long I could keep it up, but this was my chance to see those files. I moved around the desk and leaned over Dr. Evers's shoulder.

My folder was open on her desk. Some of the pages were fanned out, and even though I couldn't read everything included there, it only took three lines to convince me I had found the truth.

A highlighted passage on the first page burned into my memory, giving fuel to my anger and pain.

Harper Brighton, murderer of Priestess Eloisa Winter and traitor of the Order of Shadows, must be purged of all memories.

Do whatever must be done to convince her she has lost everyone she ever loved and that we are her only family now.

Do whatever it takes to break her.

I stared at Dr. Evers, seeing her for the evil she truly was. As I returned to my body, I had one thought. It was going to take a lot more than she was capable of to break me.

Do your best, witch.

A DOLL OR A DAUGHTER

JACKSON

I waited until shadows fell upon the house of the town's Prima. She'd come home at five, just as Kristie had said she would. Her youngest daughter played on the living room floor as I'd watched them from my perch in a treetop just outside her home.

The Prima's two teenage daughters had come home just before dinner, and the family sat down to a healthy meal, discussing their day as if they were a normal family instead of servants of one of the most evil witches to have ever lived. I wondered if her daughters understood what was in store for them when they came of age. As daughters of the Prima, they would not be forced to enslave a demon until their mother died, and even then, it would only be the eldest of the three who would take over as Prima.

Once she had a daughter of her own, her younger sisters would be released from the duty of the Prima, but their lives would never truly belong to them. They'd been slaves of the

Order from the moment their mother brought them into this world.

I didn't want to hurt them, but I would do whatever I had to do to get the information I needed.

We'd been waiting for this night for nearly a month, laying out our plans with acute attention to detail. I hadn't wanted to waste valuable time, but Mary Anne had been right. With the plan we now had in place, we would catch them all off-guard. One night and everything would change.

Once the three girls had gone up to bed and their lights had gone out, I flew down from the tree and entered the house through a small crack in a second-story window. I kept to my demon form, hiding in the shadows of the home. I stopped by each of the daughters' rooms, knowing they were the key to this whole thing.

I found the Prima sitting at her desk, alone in her bedroom. Her husband was still downstairs watching TV, although I was pretty sure he'd fallen asleep.

It would be better for him if he stayed that way.

I entered the room silently, but the Prima's hand stopped moving across the page of her journal the moment I came inside.

"What are you doing here, demon?" she asked. She turned calmly in her chair and searched the dark places in her room. "Show yourself."

I shifted to human form and stepped forward.

"I need information," I said. "If you give it to me willingly, I promise no harm will come to you or your family."

The woman was beautiful and young on the outside, but I could see through glamours and illusions. I could see the wrinkles on her aging face even though she hid them from the rest of the world. I guessed she was nearly fifty years old and carried herself as though she had been in control of this coven for many years.

"What kind of information?" she asked. She set her hands calmly in her lap, making no move to grab a weapon or stir her powers.

"Your emerald priestess has taken something valuable from me," I said. "I need to find her. Tell me where she lives or how I can find her, and I will spare your life."

The woman smiled and stood, placing her hand on the back of her chair to steady herself. "And what makes you think I will simply betray my priestess to help you out?" she asked. "As if my own life matters more than hers?"

"Doesn't it?" I asked.

"I would sacrifice everything in service to my priestess, or don't you know how this works?"

"Not every Prima feels that way anymore," I said. "A lot of them are tired of being controlled and manipulated by the Order. Many Primas don't want to see their daughters' lives controlled by the Order."

She flinched at that.

"Not every Prima is worthy of her title," she said. She walked to the window and pushed it open, drawing a cigarette from her pocket and lighting it as she leaned against the window frame.

"Do you know who I am?" I asked.

"I have an idea," she said. "And I know who you're looking for."

"Then you know that I will stop at nothing to find her," I said.

She took a long drag of her cigarette and leaned toward the

open window, blowing the smoke through the screen and out into the night.

"I also know how much my priestess would love to capture you for herself," she said.

I smiled. "You're welcome to try if you think you can survive it," I said.

She laughed and crushed her cigarette against a glass vase on top of her dresser. "I don't want to fight any more than you do," she said. "But I won't betray my priestess. I'll give you the opportunity to leave now before things get messy between us."

A spark of energy lit on her fingertips. The sheer power of that single spark spread throughout the room, sending chills down my spine. This Prima was from one of the oldest covens of the Order, and her power was no joke.

But I hadn't come this far just to turn around and go home. She already knew that.

"I'm afraid it's too late for that," I said.

"What do you mean?"

"As we speak, your daughters are asleep in their beds down the hall," I said. "I know this because I stopped at their rooms first before coming to yours."

Her lips parted, and she swallowed a lump of fear. "You better not have hurt them, demon, or I will kill you where you stand."

"They aren't injured," I said. "Yet."

I lifted my hand, revealing three dark ropes of energy that led into the hallway.

"If you don't give me the information I want, I will snap their pretty necks with one flick of my wrist."

I hated the words even as I spoke them. These girls were still innocents. It wasn't their fault they were born into this family. But I had no choice. Harper was in trouble, and I was running out of time. Tonight was our best hope, and it had to go perfectly.

The Prima straightened, her eyes darting from mine to the three ropes of shadow in my hand.

"Please," she said, blinking back tears. "Don't hurt them."

"No matter what your priestess has told you, I'm not a monster," I said. "I don't want to hurt your innocent daughters, believe me. But I have to find Harper. I'm willing to do what must be done. It's your choice."

She closed her eyes and leaned against the side of her bed. "I can't tell you where to find her," she said. "Priestess Evers never tells any of us where she lives, and she always comes to visit us through the Hall of Doorways. I don't know anything more than that."

"I don't believe you," I said.

The Prima looked away, lighting another cigarette. Her hand trembled slightly.

"You realize that if I tell you anything important, the emerald priestess will punish me and my daughters beyond anything you can imagine," she said.

"I know that her evil has no boundaries," I said.

She tilted her head. "My mother wouldn't have hesitated to let you strangle me in my sleep," she said. "She was fiercely loyal to her coven and her duties."

"And you?"

She looked away, her eyes landing on a photo of her with her daughters when they were younger.

"I love my children more than my mother loved me," she said.

I studied her. Was she going to talk to me?

"You have to understand the situation you're putting me in here," she said. "If I don't give you what you want, you'll kill my daughters and fight me as well. If I do talk to you, the emerald priestess will find me and punish me, likely taking my daughters away from me to—"

"To make them part of her collection?" I asked.

Her head snapped toward me. "Yes," she said. The Prima's eyes flashed for a moment in the half-darkness of the room. "Who told you that?"

"A hunter confessed it to me with her dying breath," I said. "A young woman from your coven who used to be called Juliana when she was still human. Did you know her?"

Her hand fluttered near her heart. "Juliana," she whispered. "She had so much potential."

"So, you remember her?" I asked.

"I remember everything," she said. "The women in the Prima family aren't given the luxury of forgetting. We have to rule the coven and keep things in order, which means that we know all of the horrible things that go on. Juliana was a sweet girl, but she wouldn't listen to reason. Her coven needed her, and she turned her back on us. I'm sorry to hear she's dead."

"Did you know she'd been turned into a hunter?" I asked.

The Prima shook her head. "I only knew Priestess Evers had taken her. I assumed she had either been turned into a doll or a daughter. That's usually the way of things."

"Doll?" I asked.

"If I tell you what I know, you have to make me a promise," she said.

I waited, not agreeing to anything until I knew what she was asking of me. I'd been making a lot of promises lately, and I didn't have time to mess around. Right now, all over the world, my friends were standing in similar houses, having similar conversations.

In and out, that was the plan. I needed to get whatever information I could and leave.

"What do you want?" I asked.

"Promise me you'll take us someplace safe until this is all over," she said.

I stepped back, surprised at her words. "You want to leave your coven?"

She closed her eyes for a brief moment and shook her head. "I don't want to leave, but I don't want to lose my daughters, either. If you're as powerful and determined as I have heard, you're going to find her one way or another," she said. "And when you do, I want to be sure that my daughters are safe from her anger."

I didn't tell her that I was taking her to the Southern Kingdom tonight, anyway. By morning, our dungeon would be filled with emerald gate Primas and their daughters. In a single night, we will have crippled the emerald priestess's covens and put every single emerald witch in danger. Kill the Prima and her daughters, and the entire coven dies in an instant.

The emerald priestess wouldn't be able to ignore that the way she'd ignored the deaths of her hunters.

"I promise to take you somewhere the emerald priestess can't get to you," I said. "I can't promise it will be very comfortable, though."

She let out a breath of smoke. "Comfort is the least of my concerns," she said. "I have your word?"

"As long as I have your word that you won't fight or harm anyone when we get to this place," I said.

She nodded and put out her cigarette, closing the window.

She laughed softly. "A demon and a Prima trusting each other," she said. "I never thought I would see the day. But then, it's a Prima you're looking for, isn't it?"

"She was," I said. "But now she is free. Just as you will be soon."

"We'll see about that," she said. "Now, release my daughters so that I can think straight."

I shook my head. "I don't trust you that much," I said.

She sat back down in the chair by her desk. "Okay, then," she said. "I'll tell you what I know. Then will you release them?"

"I will."

"Like I said, Priestess Evers has never invited me or any of my family to her home. I have no idea where it is, except that it lies beyond a door engraved with an emerald scarab beetle," she said.

That much, I already knew. I waited for her to say more.

"I can tell you something about her collection, though," she said. "I'm not sure how it might help you, but it could give you some clue as to what she's done with your Prima."

"I'm listening."

"The priestesses of the Order pride themselves on their ability to continue their family line and name," she said. "As I'm sure you already know, most of them have a particular cycle of birth and rebirth."

"I know how it worked with Priestess Winter," I said. "She had three daughters of her own. When her eldest came of age and had given birth to three daughters of her own, Priestess Winter would consume her power and her life-force, taking on the woman's identity and essentially pretending to become her through the use of glamours. The second would become permanently glamoured through sacrificial magic and sent out to a strategic location where she would become a spy for her mother. The third was trained in defensive magic and stayed on to protect the priestess until the day she died. Then the cycle would repeat."

"That is true for all of the priestesses," she said. "Except Priestess Evers."

I stared, confused.

"Priestess Evers is infertile," she said. "She can't have children of her own, and to this day it is the single most devastating truth of her life."

I drew in a breath. No wonder the emerald priestess was so determined to gain power over her sisters by reopening the sapphire gates. She felt she had something to prove.

"How does she continue her line?" I asked.

"She steals from her faithful covens," she said. "Whenever a young girl catches her eye or shows a display of power that Priestess Evers likes or thinks is unusual, she takes that young girl for herself. She wipes the memory of the mother and everyone in town besides the Prima. She wipes the memory of the girl through a series of spells and rituals, and then she refills her with memories of their life together. The girls, for the most part, come to believe they are her daughters, as if they'd been born of her, just as my daughters were born of me."

"That's horrifying," I said.

"You don't know the half of it," she said. "Sometimes the mothers of these girls are hard to keep in line. Their memories come back, or they refuse to let go of this emptiness inside of them. Some of them lose their minds with grief. In those cases,

Priestess Evers captures the mothers before they can cause too much trouble."

"What does she do with them?"

"Sometimes they become hunters," she said. "Other times they become fuel for the priestess's darkest spells. And, of course, both mothers and daughters sometimes become fuel for her life-force. Since she doesn't have daughters of her own to consume, she eats the power of those who disobey her. Those who serve her but have grown older and less beautiful. She takes what she wants and does as she pleases."

"How many?" I asked. "How many girls do you think she's taken over the years?"

"I couldn't even begin to guess," the Prima said. "From my records, she's taken fifteen girls from our coven in the past century. Some of them were just babies at the time. Others were like Juliana, already initiated into the Order and paired with a demon spirit."

I gasped. "Fifteen from this coven alone? But there are hundreds of emerald gates around the world."

"I imagine she has quite the collection by now, don't you?" she asked.

"And she keeps them all with her?" I asked. "In her home?"

"From what I've guessed, she has a place near her house where the girls are…let's call it rehabilitated," she said. "If I had to guess, that's where she's put your Prima. Your Harper."

"What does she do to them there?" I asked, unable to mask the trembling in my voice.

"Essentially, she brainwashes them," she said. "I don't know her exact process, but she works to wipe their memories and then she tells them lies until they believe them to be the truth. I can't tell you anything more than that, because I've never seen it for myself."

I thought of the emerald shards of glass found on the floor at Winterhaven. Rend's tests had shown the shards were infused with pieces of Harper's memories. She was planning to add Harper to her collection, stripping her of her memories of me and her life before she was taken. She was planning to make Harper her daughter.

I shook my head, not wanting to believe it could be true.

"You said something earlier about dolls," I said.

The Prima sighed. "Sometimes, if the girls can't be convinced to leave their past behind them, she turns them into living dolls," she said. "She showed me a picture once, bragging about how beautiful a collection she'd managed to put together over the years. I'll spare you the details, but it was arguably one of the most sickening things I've ever seen in my life."

My jaw fell open, and I shook my head back and forth.

"I know this isn't what you wanted to hear," the Prima said. "But it's been months since Harper disappeared. If you saved her now, she would probably fight you to the death. She likely has no memory you ever existed, and if she's been obedient to the priestess and believed her lies, Harper may even be calling Priestess Evers her mother by now. Either that or she's sitting in a room, all dressed up and posed at a tea party."

"You don't know her," I said. "She's not exactly the obedient type."

The Prima sighed. "Then things could be much worse for her than that," she said. "Priestess Evers does not forgive easily when she doesn't get what she wants. And if she's taken

Harper, there is only one thing she wants from her. The lucky, obedient girls are turned into daughters. The less obedient are turned into dolls. The really naughty girls are turned into hunters or consumed for their power."

"Harper is a fighter," I said. "She won't let go of her memories easily. And even without her memories, she won't follow the rules blindly. She'll question them at every turn."

"Then I can only pray, for your sake, you find her before it's too late," she said. "A girl like that, half-demon, half-human, with such remarkable power? She could extend the priestess's life by another fifty years. Maybe longer."

"I'll find her," I said through clenched teeth. "All I need to know is where she is."

The Prima smiled. "It's not where you find her," she said. "It's when you find her."

"Thanks for the vote of confidence," I muttered. "Is there anything more you can tell me before we go?"

She shook her head. "Give me a moment to pack a small bag, and I'll walk with you to wake my daughters."

"What about your husband?" I asked.

"He can fend for himself," she said. "The less he knows about who I truly am, the better. I'll whisper a spell into his ear as he sleeps. Make him think we've gone south to visit my aunt for a few weeks. She's been ill."

I nodded and waited as she packed. When she finished, we walked downstairs so she could whisper in her husband's ear. The man nodded his head and turned on his side, his eyes never opening. She led me back up the stairs and down the hall where she woke her older daughters one at a time, telling them to quickly pack a bag of their own and come with us.

At her youngest daughter's bedside, she paused, taking a

moment to smooth the wild hair of her sleeping child. "Would you really have killed them?" she asked, tears glistening in her eyes.

"Would you ever have let me?" I asked.

I reached for her hand as her two older daughters entered the room, their eyes filled with fear and confusion. The Prima grabbed my hand, and then placed her other one on her youngest daughter's, gripping it tightly. She motioned for the others to follow suit, and her oldest daughter carefully took my free hand and grabbed her sister's. Once we were all linked together, I shifted to smoke and carried them through the house, out the crack in the window, and into the night toward home.

THE HORROR OF IT

HARPER

From the spell book in the basement, I learned that my new ability was called astral projection. According to the book, it was a rare ability, but extremely useful. If practiced, a strong witch could extend her consciousness miles away from her own body.

On nights that I wasn't able to go down to the basement to practice magic there, I strengthened my astral projection instead, pushing myself farther and farther into the asylum, exploring every corner I could find.

I had no problem walking through doors or walls, and each night I was able to go a little farther before I tired and had to return.

Tonight, exactly a week after the first time I'd used the ability, I decided to explore the doctor's office a little more thoroughly.

The biggest downside to astral projection was that since I wasn't in my physical body, I also couldn't seem to physically move anything. I couldn't open the doctor's files or search through her desk, so I had to settle for whatever she'd carelessly left out at the end of the day, which wasn't much.

All of her files seemed to be safely locked away. Her desk had been cleared completely, and the only thing that caught my eye was a picture sitting on top of her desk. I hadn't paid much attention to it before since I could usually only see the back of the frame from my seat in the chair. But tonight, I stared at it, the woman in the photo incredibly familiar to me.

The sight of her red hair and green eyes put a bad taste in my mouth and every scar on my body seemed to burn with flame.

I reached out to touch the photo, forgetting for a moment that I couldn't actually touch it until my hand passed right through it like a ghost.

The door to the office swung open, and I jumped, scared I had just been caught snooping.

Dr. Evers entered the room with a sigh, walking straight through me to stand behind her desk. She had no idea I was even here.

She opened the smaller drawer in the middle of her desk and retrieved a large brass key that had a small emerald embedded in a swirling design at the top.

"I swear, if that woman didn't have her head screwed on, she'd forget it," she mumbled. She tucked the key into her pocket and left the room, locking the door behind her.

I followed, wondering if the doctor lived here at the hospital. Why else would she still be here this late at night?

She took a familiar path toward the main entrance of the hospital. I'd never actually left the confines of the asylum. I usually tired out when I got close to the front door, but tonight I pushed forward, determined to see where she was headed.

Dr. Evers pushed the front door open and stepped out into the near-total darkness of the night. She crossed the front lawn and opened the gate of a tall wrought-iron fence that surrounded the property. She stepped toward the quiet street separating the asylum from a large Victorian home.

Was that where she lived?

I paused near the street as she crossed, my head feeling dizzy for a moment. I wasn't sure I'd be able to keep following, but I had to at least try. I needed to know if the woman in the picture lived in that house.

I needed to remember how I knew her. The woman had done something horrible to me, I could feel it.

As the doctor opened the door to the Victorian and disappeared inside, I pushed deeper into the well of power at my core and forced my feet across the paved road and up the stairs of the old house. Before I stepped inside, I glanced back at the asylum, curious to know what the building looked like from the outside.

It wasn't at all what I'd expected. I guess I had thought it would look more like a hospital, but it was a beautiful building with dark-red brick and tall windows. The roof was decorated with cross gables that rose into the sky and mimicked the shape of the Victorian home across the street. White stone archways over the windows made it almost look more like a church than an asylum.

A sign across the gate read "Evers Institute for Troubled Girls," the only indication that it was an asylum. It didn't look like the kind of place that tortured its patients. Which I guessed was exactly the point. Who would ever think to question it?

I looked away, not wanting to lose the doctor inside the large house. I passed through the front door without a sound and listened for footsteps. Somewhere upstairs, the familiar clack of high heels against the hardwoods echoed through the house.

It sounded just like the heels I'd heard roaming the halls of the asylum late at night.

I made my way up the stairs and followed the light. Most of the house was dark, but a room at the end of the hall glowed brightly, light spilling out across a faded green rug that ran the length of the hallway.

As I got closer, I heard them talking. Two women, maybe three.

"It's not working," one woman said. "The demon should have been caught by now and exterminated in the most painful way possible. Instead, he's gotten to each of my most loyal Primas and locked them away in the dungeon of that demon castle, where I can't reach them. I want to know why he isn't dead yet."

"I'm working on it, Mother," another, younger, voice said. "I promise. I have the perfect trap set up for him. Jackson won't even know what hit him. I'll have him here to you by tomorrow night. Two days at the latest. You can kill him yourself."

I stopped at the sound of his name. They were talking about Jackson. They'd called him a demon, and yet the word didn't frighten me. It was as if I'd known all along that he was different. Older and more powerful than a normal human guy could be.

It wasn't the demon part that had sent my heart racing. It was the trap part. They were going to kill him.

I nearly lost my concentration and had to push harder to stay present, so I could hear the rest of their conversation.

"Good," the first woman said. "I want her to know he's dead. I want to break her poor little heart and break her spirit for good. Without him, she'll be nothing."

Anger pulsed through me as I reached the doorway and turned the corner into the room. If I'd had a voice, I would have screamed.

Three women stood in the center of a large bedroom. All three of them had red hair to match. Dr. Evers, a woman I'd never seen who looked to be no more than twenty-years-old, and her—the woman from the photograph. I recognized her suddenly. She'd tortured me, and as I stared at her, I could see an image in my head of her standing over me and smiling as she cut into my arms with shards of broken glass.

Who was she?

And more importantly, what the hell was going on in this room?

All around the space, there were girls dressed up as dolls. Life-sized dolls, positioned just so with their frilly dresses and bonnets. Four of them were positioned around a small round table, china tea-cups in their hands, as if they were frozen in a perpetual child's tea party.

Two small children were laid out on the bed with their eyes closed and their hands clasped. They didn't move at all, and I wondered for a moment if they were dead or alive. I wondered if when they sat up, their eyes popped open like little dolls.

Three more girls sat in a window seat, fake smiles plastered on their faces.

They were all arranged as toys, but they were girls. Real girls.

The horror of it nearly caused me to drop the spell and return to my body. Who would do such a thing?

I forced myself further into the room, studying their faces. Were they still alive?

"What about Harper?" the older woman asked. "How are her sessions coming along?"

"Wonderfully," Dr. Evers said, beaming. "She's finally starting to fall in line, parroting back memories we've fed to her. I think she's finally believing them to be true. I can tell her spirit is weakening. She hardly even glances up at me anymore during sessions. She's close to breaking, Mother. I can feel it."

Mother. This woman was her mother. What did she have to do with all of this? Why was she torturing me?

Brooke had said Dr. Evers' mother had everything to do with this place. Did she own the asylum? Bring girls here to torture them and distort their memories?

But why?

"I knew you were the right person for this job," the mother said, taking Dr. Evers's chin in her hands. It might have been a loving gesture if she hadn't been gripping her so hard. "You are by far my favorite daughter. I hope you know how proud I am of you and how much I love you."

"Thank you, Mother." Dr. Evers had tears in her eyes, and I wasn't sure if it was from pain or joy. "You're my whole world. I'd do anything for you."

"I know you would, Monica," the mother said. She

released the doctor's chin and placed her palm against the woman's chest instead. "After all, you have my heart."

I struggled to hold onto the magic, but it was too much. I'd been gone too long, and I wasn't strong enough yet to keep it going. Dizziness washed through me, and I struggled to breathe.

I needed to get back to my body.

I turned and headed for the door, but one last doll caught my eye on the way out.

A rocking chair nestled in the corner by the door held a single girl, and this time I knew her face. It was the girl who had recognized me that first night at dinner. *Robin.*

In her hand, she held a small red carousel, as if she were a child with her most treasured toy.

I brought a hand to my mouth, stifling a scream that would not come.

Is this what they did to some of the girls who disobeyed them? They turned them into some kind of creepy doll collection in this woman's home?

I reached out with my ghostly hand, wanting to touch Robin and let her know that she wasn't alone. I wanted to let her know that I was going to figure a way out of this place, and that I would take as many girls with me as I could.

I knew she couldn't feel me, and she shouldn't have been able to see me, but just as my spectral hand touched hers, her eyes flicked to mine.

YOU CAN'T AFFORD NOT TO

JACKSON

"Green Monster," I said, taking a seat at the bar.

Franki grabbed a rocks glass from the shelf. She poured clear liquid from a bottle beneath the bar. It was a busy night and she'd barely looked up at me, but when she slid the glass toward me, her eyes widened.

"Jackson, is that you?" she asked.

I pulled my hood down and nodded, grabbing the shot and downing it in a single gulp. I usually didn't partake of Rend's various concoctions here at Venom, but tonight I needed all the courage I could get.

So, Green Monster it was.

She placed her hand on top of mine and squeezed. "Why didn't you tell us you were coming?" she asked. "I could have arranged a private room or something. Who all is here with you? Do you want me to find a spot for you?"

I shook my head and waved my hand. "I'm here alone," I said. I didn't want any special treatment, and I definitely didn't want to disappear into some back room. I just wanted to sit at the bar and drink for a while. I wanted to wait for the spider to try to draw me into her web.

Or the beetle. But that didn't make as good of a metaphor.

A dark look crossed Franki's clear blue eyes. She reminded me so much of Mary Anne. The two of them were cousins and both had the signature blue eyes and shiny black hair of their crow coven heritage.

"How are you holding up?" she asked. When I didn't respond, she gave me a sad smile. "I guess that's a stupid question, huh?"

I shrugged and slid my glass toward her. She refilled it without hesitating.

"We're slammed tonight, but if you need anything at all, just let me know," she said.

"I need to talk to Rend," I said. "Is he around?"

She stood on her toes and glanced around the dark interior of the club. She lifted her chin toward the back corner. "He's talking to a few demons up there on the balcony that overlooks the dance floor," she said. "If I can catch his attention, I'll signal for him to come down here as soon as he can. Do you have a few minutes to stick around?"

"I've got time," I said. "I'm waiting for someone."

"Who?" she asked.

"I don't know yet."

Time was a funny thing these days. It moved so slowly, stretching out in front of me like a black hole, empty and meaningless. But I also had the constant feeling that I was racing against it, never doing enough to save her. I had no idea how Harper was holding up against the emerald priestess's spells. Had she already become a part of that witch's collection?

I shuddered.

"Okay," Franki said, smart enough not to ask more questions. "I'll make sure Rend stops by soon."

She filled my glass a third time, and I thanked her before she walked away to deal with a group of young fairies who appeared to be celebrating an engagement. Their tinkling laughter grated on my last nerve. No one deserved to be that happy when there was such evil and sorrow all around us.

I hunched over my drink, taking a deep breath and letting the potion work its magic. I glanced around the bar, looking for faces I recognized from my years here in the human world. I knew several of the vampires and demons, a few of the witches who had escaped the clutches of the Order. I saw a few others I knew by face, if not by name. Fae, gnomes, werewolves. A few of them met my gaze and raised a glass, but without fail, every smile soon dropped from their faces, and their eyes filled with pity as they whispered something to their companions.

Everyone knew what had happened to Harper. She was famous in this community for having killed one of the five main priestess sisters of the Order of Shadows. Demons and witches alike practically worshiped her, and everyone had believed that together we were invincible. They had foolishly believed that our group, the Demon Liberation Movement, would be the ones to bring down the entire evil organization that kept so many demons enslaved in this world.

But we had failed.

We'd had the emerald priestess right there and we let her slip away. Harper was the only one who'd gone after her, and somehow, the priestess had defeated her. I still didn't know the details of the fight, but there had been enough blood from both of them in the hallway at Winterhaven to mean they'd both walked away hurting.

Or been dragged away.

I closed my eyes, my jaw tightening. I downed the rest of my drink and waited. Enough people had noticed me. Word was probably spreading from group to group right now, everyone talking about how lonely and dejected I looked. How vulnerable I seemed.

It was only a matter of time before someone was sent to talk to me.

So, I waited. Hours passed and Franki never questioned or judged the number of drinks I requested throughout the night. She just kept filling them up. They weren't the kind of drinks that made you drunk. Not exactly. Green Monster made you feel brave. It helped keep your worst fears at bay. I should ask Rend for a damn case of the stuff.

By the time the crowd started to slim, I worried I'd been wrong about coming here. But just as I stood to excuse myself and head home, a young demon named Riley caught my eye. He was heading straight toward me, a confident smile on his face as he said hello to everyone he passed.

I sat back down.

"Riley," I said, nodding as he sat down next to me.

"Jackson," he said. He lifted a hand toward Franki and she came over a few seconds later.

"What can I get you?" she asked.

"The usual," he said. It wasn't lost on me that he refused to name his poison in front of me. Since the drinks were clear, there was no way for me to know which concoction he'd chosen. Judging from the confident smile on his face, I'd say he was drinking Lady Luck.

He swallowed it in one gulp and threw a twenty on the counter.

"Thanks," he said.

"No problem," she said. She glanced from Riley to me and when I nodded once to let her know I was fine, she nodded back and walked away to give us some privacy.

Riley was well known in some circles for being the messenger dog of a big bad wolf of a demon named Jereth. Everyone knew of Jereth, though not many people lived to tell stories of him. Especially not if they'd gotten on his bad side. He was an old demon, much older than myself, and had been here in the human world since before the Order of Shadows was even created.

He had a following, if that's what it was called. A devoted group of demons who did his dirty work and cleaned up after his messes.

I hated the guy. He was everything that was wrong with most free demons in this world. He used his powers to take advantage of humans, bleeding them of money and information before he killed them or betrayed them. He had no honor, and I despised him almost as much as I despised the Order.

"What do you want, Riley?" I asked.

He fidgeted and glanced around before he sat down on the barstool next to mine. He faced backward toward the club, as if he meant to keep his eye on everyone just in case someone more important came along.

"I heard about what happened to Harper," he said.

"You and everyone else in two worlds," I said.

"Yeah, that's a tough break," he said. "I know you've been looking for information on where they're holding her."

I glanced up. I hadn't been expecting him to be the one to come to me with this tonight. I thought the news would come from a witch or a vampire, but never from someone like Riley. What exactly did he have up his sleeve?

"Do you know something?" I asked.

"Jereth found something he thinks you might be very interested in," he said. He licked his lips and ran a hand through his hair. "He wanted to get this information to you sooner, but you haven't exactly been an easy demon to find these days."

"I've been busy," I said. "What kind of information?"

"He wouldn't tell me, but he said it could be the key to finding Harper," he said. "He wants you to come by the bar. Tomorrow night. Bring payment and come alone."

"How do I know I can trust him?" I asked, which was a stupid question. No one could trust Jereth.

"You can't afford not to," he said. He downed another drink and tossed a ten-dollar tip on the bar. He walked away without saying another word. I stared after him, knowing that this was the message I'd been waiting for.

I wasn't sure how Jereth had gotten mixed up with the emerald priestess, but I guess I shouldn't have been that surprised. Jereth had a history of not caring which side he was working for as long as he was getting paid. The demon had no loyalties except to his own crew.

Hell, he had fought in the First World War, posing as a soldier from Great Britain. At the same time his crew was providing weapons to the German army. He was definitely not to be trusted, but this was my best chance at finding Harper.

If Jereth was looking for me, he was doing it because the

emerald priestess had asked him to. And if he was working for her, he would be in close contact with her or one of her many daughters.

"Jackson," Rend said, reaching his hand out to me as he crossed the dance floor and approached the bar. He was dressed in an expensive, tailored black suit with a white button-down shirt that probably cost more than most people's cars. Business seemed to be booming these days. Everyone needed a safe place to trade information without fear of being killed, and Venom was the only place like it. Needless to say, I wasn't surprised Jereth hadn't met me here instead of asking me to join him in his lair.

"I'm sorry I kept you waiting so long," he said. "I had some political bullshit to deal with, and I couldn't walk away. How are you doing? Any news?"

"Maybe," I said. "I need a favor."

"Anything," he said. "Want to come to my office?"

I shook my head. "Not the office."

Rend raised an eyebrow as I downed the last of my drink and stood up.

If Jereth was the one I was going to have to get through, I was going to need all the help I could get. It wasn't going to be an easy fight, but if he was the last one standing between me and the emerald priestess, I would kill him twice if I had to.

"The lab," I said. "I'm going to need some new potions."

THE LOVE THAT SURROUNDED ME

LEA

The festival began just as the leaves on the winterberry trees had fallen and the spring blooms had finally burst forth to bring their cheery color to the King's City.

It was normally such a dark place with its black towers and stone streets, but this had always been my favorite time of year. I still wasn't allowed to leave the castle, but I liked to stand on my balcony and look out over the city. Demons rushed to prepare, decorating their shops with aster blossoms and strands of fairy lights.

It was late afternoon and the suns were slowly being replaced by the colorful moons of spring when Presha came to stand at my side to watch as the streets filled with families on their way to the castle for the opening feast.

"They seem happy," I said.

"They're excited to see their princess," she said. "It's been a long time since there was something to celebrate within these walls."

A young shadowling dropped her flower on the street and tugged on her mother's hand, begging to go back to pick it up. Her mother leaned down and gently touched her daughter's face, wiping the tears from her eyes as the father went back for the flower. The little girl's eyes lit up as he handed it to her and kissed her forehead.

I wanted to look away, knowing that would never be my life. But I couldn't force my eyes away from the happy family. It didn't matter that I would never have a true husband or that I would probably never have shadowlings of my own. It was no longer about me and what I wanted in my deepest heart.

It was about them. These demons here in the castle and all those who were still unprotected by any walls. It was about the demons in the villages who struggled to survive. All of them had lost someone they loved. I was not unique in that manner.

We had all lost something in this war.

We had all sacrificed our dreams in some way, but as I watched the pretty shadowling girl disappear into the crowd surrounding the castle, I realized that she was the one I did this for. Those of us old enough to understand the Order's evil would never be the same, even after the war was over. But if we won and the Order ceased to exist, there was hope for that little one. Hope that she would someday be free to marry the love of her life and start a family of her own. Hope that her children would never know the suffering we had known.

The Shadow World was weakened, but it was not dead. As long as we kept fighting, there was the chance of a better future for my people. I would not let them down.

"It's time to get dressed for the banquet," Presha said. "Come inside, Princess."

I nodded but lingered on the balcony for a few minutes. Tonight, they would reintroduce me to the demons of the King's City as their long-lost princess, returned from the war unharmed and ready to take my place at the king's side. Ready to become engaged to a demon I'd never met in the name of duty and loyalty.

I thought of the axe I'd hidden under my bed this morning. I'd had it secretly commissioned from the royal weaponsmith, and although it wasn't a perfect replica of Aerden's original axe, it was a weapon worthy of his strength.

I thought of the battles ahead, longing for my bow.

It wouldn't be long now.

"Why isn't she ready?" Anastia's voice rose from the other room, and I sighed. "The doors have opened downstairs, and she isn't even dressed."

"Princess?" Presha asked.

"I'm coming," I said.

Tonight would be my greatest test so far, and in two days the King's Games would begin.

Aerden's test. He'd volunteered, like I knew he would. He was strong enough to win, but only if he believed it. I refused to watch him die.

The future was so uncertain for both of us.

For all of us.

I missed the days when we were a group. I think I had taken it for granted those months we lived together at Brighton Manor. I had allowed my own pain and the bitterness I felt at Jackson and Harper's relationship to blind me to the love that surrounded me when I was there. Here in the castle, I was the loneliest I had ever been in my life, and I missed them.

Even Harper, though I'd never admit it to her face.

Where was she? Was she still alive?

I'd always been so hard on her, but the truth was that she had united us all. This half-human teenager had forced us all to set aside our differences and work together. She was the princess I had failed to be.

I wouldn't fail again.

Someday soon, I would get the chance to be the leader everyone expected me to be. I hoped I was half the leader she'd been.

We were scattered now, all on our own individual journeys, facing our own nightmares. But we'd be together again. I was connected to them even though we were apart. They were a piece of me, and I drew strength from their love.

Someday, Harper would bring us all together again, and we'd be a family.

"Wherever you are," I whispered into the night, "come back to us. We need you."

TO SAVE US ALL

HARPER

I walked around in a fog the next day, images of the house across the street creeping into my nightmares and making it impossible for me to get any sleep.

What kind of demented person kept girls frozen and dressed like little dolls in her bedroom?

Someone evil.

There was no doubt that the woman who owned that house—Dr. Evers's mother—was the one behind this place. She was responsible for every girl here, and everything that had happened to us.

Had she even set that fire at my house?

Had she killed someone close to me?

I knew from talking to Brooke that my father had died before the fire at my home. And deep inside of me, I knew that I had never met my own mother. I couldn't explain how I knew, but as my powers grew, some of the truth came with it.

Who was the girl I cradled in my arms when I dreamed of

the fire? I could almost feel her long blonde hair draped across my arm, her body ice-cold despite the flames that raged around us.

She had meant something important to me, and whoever this woman was, she had taken her from me.

I was going to get my memories back. I was going to find my way out of this place someday and make her pay for what she had stolen.

But how? I was running out of time.

She'd set a trap for Jackson, which meant he'd been searching for me. If she hurt him in any way, the witch would live only to regret it for a moment before I ended her life.

He had been my solace in this place. My memories of him were the only ones strong enough to resist any torture they'd performed on me before they brought me here, which meant that he was a part of me. What we had was stronger than magic.

"Harper, are you coming?" Nora asked. She'd been quiet lately, at least around me. The first few weeks I was here, she'd hardly shut her mouth, but even Nora seemed to understand that things were getting dangerous around here.

"Sorry," I mumbled. I stood and straightened the sheets on my bed before I joined her in the doorway of our room. I noticed we were one person short, though. "Where's Mary Ellen?"

"I don't know," Nora said. "She never came back from breakfast."

She was so quiet, I had completely missed the fact that Mary Ellen hadn't been around this afternoon or at lunch. I'd been so wrapped up in my own thoughts, it hadn't even dawned on me.

Was she in some kind of trouble?

It was hard to imagine since she was always docile. She never stepped out of line or talked back to anyone. Maybe she wasn't feeling well.

I shuddered at the image of her dressed in a frilly child's gown with a bonnet on her head.

One of the nurses led us outside. It was fully spring now, with birds chirping all around and the sun warm on our faces as we stepped into the light. Someone had already wheeled the girls in wheelchairs out into their row near the cement benches. They stared ahead, their eyes blank, as if they weren't even aware of their surroundings.

"What happened to those girls?" I asked Nora.

"Which girls?" she asked, looking around.

"The ones in wheelchairs and up there sitting on the benches?" I asked. "I only see them out here and in the rec room. They don't even talk to each other. What happened to them?"

She shook her head and looked away. "Those are the girls who have been taken in for the procedure."

"What procedure?" I touched her arm as she started to walk away.

"I don't want to talk about this," she said. "Can't we just enjoy the sun for a little while?"

"I need to know, Nora," I said softly. "I need to understand what's going on in this place."

"No, you don't," she said, yanking her arm away from me. "That's your problem, Harper. You can't just let things be, and it's going to get you into trouble."

"You seriously don't care that they're holding us here for no real reason?" I asked. "That they torture us if we break the rules and no one seems to care or stand up for us? None of that matters to you?"

"What matters to me is staying alive," she said. "You've already gotten into trouble once. If they catch you again..."

Her voice drifted off and she looked away, hugging her arms close to her body.

"What?" I asked. "If they catch me, what?"

"They won't settle for shock therapy or injections," she said. "They'll take you straight to the procedure, and you'll end up just like those other girls. You think it's bad to lose your memories? What if you lost everything? Your mind. Your ability to walk or talk. It isn't worth it."

"We're prisoners in here," I said. "How could it not be worth it to try to fight them?"

Tears welled up in her eyes and she moved to stand beside me. "Do you see that girl on the far right? The one with the pink ribbon in her hair?"

I nodded.

"That's Jessica. She was my best friend my whole life, even before we got thrown in here," she said. "The nurses and Dr. Evers don't know that I remember her, but after a few months here, we both realized how we knew each other. We used to sit and talk about what we remembered, trying to piece it all together. But then Jessica went too far. She got angry during a group therapy session and accused the nurses of trying to hold us hostage. She accused them of trying to manipulate our memories."

"And they did this to her?" I asked.

"They tortured her first. Shock therapy. Injections. Maybe more that she didn't tell me about," she said. "She had cuts on her arms when she came back, just like you. For a while she didn't even speak to me. She acted like she had never seen me before in her life. Then one day during dinner, she pulled me to the side. She told me if I ever got out of this place to promise to find her family and tell them she loved them."

Nora started to cry, and I touched her arm, but she pulled away.

"I never spoke to her again. After dinner, she pulled a knife on one of the nurses. I don't even know where she got it," she said. "But she cut the woman pretty badly before they were able to drag her away. A few weeks later, she returned in a wheelchair, drooling all over herself. There's nothing left of my best friend in there, anymore. I think she wanted to die, to be honest. I think she thought if she did something terrible, they would just kill her for it. I can't imagine she wanted to end up like this. And neither do you."

I stared at the girls in the perfect row near the door. "They've been lobotomized, haven't they?"

It was a procedure everyone knew about, but no one actually performed anymore. Why wasn't the government stepping in to intervene here?

"Just be careful," Nora said. "Follow their rules. Tell them what they want to hear. Maybe someday, if we're lucky, someone will come to save us. Until then, don't let them take away what little of you there is left."

She walked away, and my stomach twisted inside. Was that what everyone else here was doing? Waiting for someone on the outside to save us all?

And why did I suddenly feel like that someone was supposed to be me?

YOU CAN FLY

HARPER

Near the end of our rec time, the French doors swung open, and Mary Ellen stepped out onto the concrete patio. Her eyes were puffy and red from crying, and she squinted against the sunlight.

I sat near the brick fence and watched as she made her way to a secluded spot next to the bird-bath and sat down. Her black hair hung around her face, hiding her from the rest of the girls in the courtyard.

I stood and walked over to her.

"Hey," I said, sitting across from her.

She didn't respond.

"Is everything okay?" I asked. "We were worried about you."

She shook her head and began rocking back and forth, her arms clutched tightly to her body.

"Mary Ellen," I said, touching her knee.

She stopped and looked up at me, her eyes wide. I'd never

actually gotten a good look in her eyes before. She kept them hidden behind her hair and lowered to the floor most of the time, but the crystal-clear blue of them shook me to my core.

A memory flashed in my mind of a girl with pale skin, and I smiled. Mary Anne. The name came to me in an instant, and I knew her as though she had whispered it in my ear. Could this girl be related to her?

They had the same pale skin and striking blue eyes. The same raven-colored hair.

"Want to see something cool?" I asked.

Mary Ellen nodded, a light in her eyes that looked so innocent and scared. Childlike, though she must have been at least my age.

I searched the ground around us for a flower or leaf or something I could use. A clump of tall weeds grew around the base of the bird-bath, and I reached over and plucked them out at their roots.

I placed the grass in my palms, hiding them for a moment inside my hands. I brought them to my heart and closed my eyes, imagining the wings of tiny black birds flapping against my skin. I blew into a hole between my thumbs, pushing a piece of my magic into them.

I smiled at Mary Ellen and glanced around quickly to make sure we weren't being watched. I opened my palms and a small cluster of black crows flew off my palms and into the air around her. She laughed and tried to catch them.

It was the first time I had ever seen her smile.

The birds faded a moment later, turning to grass again and falling across Mary Ellen's legs and hands. She touched the green tip of one and looked up at me.

"How did you do that?" she asked.

I smiled. "Ah, so you can speak," I said, an eyebrow raised.

A pink blush colored her cheeks and she looked down.

"It's called a glamour," I said. "Where you make one thing look like something else for a while. This one is kind of advanced, because I wanted to make them move like birds. It takes a lot of practice, but I bet you could learn to do it, too."

"They were beautiful," she said. She placed her hand on top of mine. "Thank you."

"It's worth it to see you smile," I said. "What happened to you earlier? What did they do to you?"

She shook her head. "It's just something they do sometimes," she said softly. She held her arm out to me. Fresh pinpricks of red dotted the skin on her forearm.

"They injected you with something?"

"No," she said, pulling her sleeve down. "They drew blood. I don't know why. They say I'm special."

"You can fly," I said. The memories were right there on the edge of my consciousness. I could almost piece together the puzzle, but something was missing.

"What?" she asked.

I shook my head. "I don't know," I said with a half-smile. "Forget it. I'm crazy, remember?"

We laughed, and as I glanced around, the smile quickly faded from my face.

Judith was standing by the door, staring right at us.

DARKNESS PERSONIFIED

JACKSON

I sped through the night, the motorcycle's engine grumbling back at me from the tree line as it sliced through the darkness. I revved the engine, pushing harder. Faster.

It had been a long trip from Chicago to this small town in Tennessee, but I was almost there, and I was anxious now, adrenaline racing through my veins.

I itched to shift to shadow and fly to my destination, but where I was going I didn't want to be followed. Using my demon magic would leave a trail, and I didn't want to leave any sign that I had been there.

So I raced faster, the cold wind whipping at my face. The hood of my sweatshirt blew off my head, and my hair flew wildly against my skin, stinging me like a dozen tiny ropes whipping at my forehead.

It was quiet here on the back roads of Tennessee. I hadn't seen a car in hours. There were only trees, and as I passed, I gathered tiny amounts of their power, sucking it in through my nose as I breathed. I didn't take enough for it to be noticeable. Not enough for someone to track me. Just enough to fill me up so that when I needed it later, I would be able to cast and kill.

The people I was going to see were not known for their hospitality, and they were most certainly working with the emerald priestess. Lose-lose. Plus, I hadn't seen Jereth in more than twenty years, and we hadn't parted on good terms. To say the least.

But I had to try.

Even if I was walking straight into a trap, I had to go. If there was any hope of finding her, I couldn't just walk away.

I saw her face in front of me at each mile, knowing this was for her. It was all for her. I couldn't live without her, and I couldn't feel anything but the distance between us.

I didn't care what I had to do or who I had to face. If my actions had drawn the emerald priestess herself to Tennessee, then either she would die tonight, or I would.

I pulled into the parking lot of a shady honky-tonk, its neon lights the only thing visible for half a mile in either direction. A few pickup trucks with rusted beds were parked in the front spaces, but the place seemed mostly deserted.

Good.

The fewer humans here to witness whatever was about to go down, the better.

I pulled around back and parked my bike next to a pristine Harley-Davidson that probably cost ten times what mine had even when it was new. There was a row of hogs, each one bigger than the next. I guessed some demons really liked their bikes.

This crew especially.

My heart pounded as I stepped into a puddle of mud left from an early afternoon rain. What if this was the key? What if this was the last step to finding her?

I'd spent so much time searching when maybe the only thing I'd ever had to do was make a mess and wait for the witch to come to me.

I secured my hood over my head and pushed my sunglasses back up the bridge of my nose. I was in all black tonight: Black jeans, boots, jacket, hoodie. Black soul. All of it. Without her, I was darkness personified, and I knew there would be no more light until she was safe in my arms.

The back door of the bar didn't look like much. There was a dirty trash can outside of it and a stray cat that hissed as I approached. I reached down to offer my hand to the mangy thing, wishing I had a little food to offer her. She hissed again, but finally found the courage to sniff my hand. She rubbed against my knuckles, and her small body vibrated as I tickled behind her ears.

"Shhh," I whispered to her. "Go on, now. You might want to be clear of this place before I go in."

The cat meowed in protest and rubbed against my leg before trotting off toward the dumpster and the dark tree line beyond.

I straightened and cleared my throat. This was it.

I knocked once on the rickety wooden door and waited.

A minute later, a big, burly man about six inches taller than me answered. His face was covered in a thick red beard, and he looked down at me with eyes as black as night.

"I think you knocked on the wrong door, brother," the man said. "You want a drink, you go around front."

I shook my head once. "I need to talk to Jereth."

The man snorted and rubbed his thumb under his nose. "Yeah, good luck with that," he said. "Jereth don't see no one without an invitation, and so far as I know, he hasn't invited anyone out here tonight. Why don't you just turn back around and head back to whatever hole it is you crawled out of."

"I'm not leaving until I talk to him," I said. The power I'd stolen from the trees pulsed through my veins like a drug, pumping me up and winding me so tight, I wasn't sure how long I could hold that energy inside.

I was ready to mess something up, and this guy looked to be as good a place to start as any.

"Don't make me ask again," I said. Ice formed on my fingertips, spreading quickly up my hand and arm with a crackling that was noticeable even with the loud music pouring from inside.

The bouncer narrowed his eyes, glancing toward my icy gloves and back up at my face. "I think you're out of your league here, demon," he said. He spit tobacco juice to the ground, a long string of it getting caught in his beard before he wiped it away. "Now, get your—"

I got tired of waiting to hear what he was going to threaten me with next.

I flicked my index finger forward, sending a thread of blue ice across the pavement between us. The ice grabbed onto his boots and spread quickly all the way up his body, encasing him in a dim blue light. I paused the ice when it got to his neck.

He struggled against the frozen prison, his lips shivering and turning blue.

"What the hell, man?" he asked.

"Still think I'm out of my league?" I asked.

"S-s-screw you," he said.

I shook my head. That was the thing about rogue demons who got involved with people like Jereth. They took whatever they wanted from this world and met little resistance along the way. It went to their heads, and they got power hungry, forgetting that there were still things that went bump in the night. Things they would have been afraid of if they were smarter.

"I don't have time for this," I said. I lifted my finger and the demon screamed as the ice crept up his neck and surrounded his face. His eyes were frozen in a look of sheer terror.

I stepped around him and opened the back door of the honky-tonk, giving the block of ice a hard kick as I passed.

The demon fell onto the pavement, the ice shattering into a million tiny pieces, what was left of his power dissipating into the air as the ice began to melt.

I shook my head and sighed. One hell of a start to the evening, and I had a feeling things were about to get a whole lot worse.

WHATEVER CAME NEXT

JACKSON

I walked down the steps leading to Jereth's lair. Call it a bar or a gang or a club, but in the end, it was just a lair. The kind of dark, desperate place demons like Jereth hid themselves in when they wanted to make deals with the devil.

The air was filled with smoke and loud music, and the only lights in the place were coming from the huge TV screens and a single lamp hanging above the pool table where two demons battled it out for a stack of cash. I spotted Jereth before anyone spotted me.

He was twice the size of a normal man, if not in height than in pure muscle. His hair was long and pulled back in a ponytail that snaked around his shoulder and down his chest. His arms and neck were heavily tattooed, and he wore actual chains around his body, hooked in crisscross patterns across his chest and legs. His weapon of choice—a semi-automatic rifle he called Lyla—leaned against the arm of his leather recliner.

I counted fifteen other demons besides Jereth in the bar,

including the bartender. Not great odds.

I reached into my pocket and drank down the first potion. Swiftness. For the next twenty minutes, I would move faster than any three of them combined. I had no idea if it would be enough, but at least it was an advantage.

I walked down the steps, letting my boots hit each of the wooden stairs with a loud thump. The music stopped at the flick of Jereth's wrist, and everyone in the dark place turned to look at me.

"You know, next time you send a message that you have information for me, you might want to let your bouncer know I'm coming," I said, taking a handful of pretzels from a bowl on top of the bar and taking my time chewing one up. "You're going to need another one of those, by the way."

The two guys sitting on the leather and chrome stools next to me stood up, their eyes flickering toward the steps as if they expected old redbeard to come walking down. They could stop looking. That guy was gone for good.

Jereth held up a hand and everyone who had bristled at my bouncer comment relaxed and sat back down.

"I see you've been talking to Riley," Jereth said.

"He said you might know something about what happened to Harper," I said. "Do you?"

"Do you have payment worthy of such precious information?" he asked.

"Depends on what you want," I said. I took a leather pouch from the pocket of my hoodie and set it on the bar, making sure I did it hard enough for the gemstones inside to clatter together. There was nothing off-the-grid demons wanted here in the human world more than gemstones. The rarer they were, the better.

For most demons, traveling between worlds was difficult. Portals were hard to come by unless you were prepared to wait for the Order to open one. And even then, you had to be ready to fight an entire coven of powerful witches in order to use it. Not everyone had a magical rose garden like we did.

"Name your price," I said.

"It's going to take a lot more than a handful of gemstones for this information," he said. "If I tell you what I know, it could put my entire crew in danger."

"What do you want?" I asked.

A slow smile crept across his face and he shared a look with the demon woman sitting on the arm of his chair. He nodded to her, and she walked into the next room, shutting the door behind her. He'd either sent her to retrieve something, or he was trying to get her out of the way for whatever came next.

I rested my hand on a small dagger tucked into the waistband of my jeans. It wasn't much, but it was pure demon steel and would kill a demon faster than any bullet or poison they could make here in the human world.

"Come have a seat," Jereth said, motioning to the worn black leather couch across from him. "Let's negotiate."

"I'd rather stand," I said.

"No. You want what I have, you follow my rules," he said. "Sit down."

I gritted my teeth and sat down on the couch. I didn't like that there were half a dozen demons behind me where I couldn't see them. It made me anxious.

"Okay, I'm sitting," I said. "Let's talk. What do you have?"

"I may know where Harper is being kept," he said. "But before I tell you, I need to know you're willing to pay up."

"Whatever it takes," I said. But I didn't think this guy

really knew anything important. What he knew was that if he did what the emerald priestess asked of him—get me here alone—she'd pay him a lot more than I ever could. I was just playing along until shit went down.

And apparently, I wouldn't have to wait long.

Two demons wrapped silver chains around my neck from behind, pulling so tight, I could hardly breathe. I had a split second where I could have shifted before the silver touched my skin, but I decided to stay put. Let Jereth believe he had the upper hand on me.

"I want something from you that doesn't fit inside some little leather bag," Jereth said, standing.

His girlfriend returned from the other room with a needle that would have made a nurse pass out. The needle itself was at least six inches long and was attached to a large glass vial. I didn't see anything inside the vial, though, which meant they weren't planning to inject something into me. They were planning to take something out.

Things had just escalated to seriously messed-up. I hadn't expected a fellow free demon to jump right to stealing my power, but I guess I shouldn't have expected anything else from someone like Jereth. He had no qualms about betraying his own if he thought there was a better payday around the corner.

"I knew you were a real bastard, Jereth, but I didn't think you'd stoop this low," I said. I slowly reached toward my left pocket. "We could have agreed on terms before you threatened to steal something from me."

"After the last time we met, I honestly didn't know if you'd come here tonight," he said, standing to take the needle from a tray his girlfriend held out to him. "That's the problem with you do-gooders. You're always underestimating what those of us who don't give a damn about taking the high road are willing to do when the opportunity presents itself. Now stay still. This is going to hurt."

He stepped toward me, and I shoved my hand into my pocket, grabbing hold of a handful of dust. Rend had recently discovered that when he infused certain gemstones with a particular type of magic and ground those gems into dust, it became a powerful weapon. I only hoped it worked.

I threw the dust into the air and held my breath. It hovered above me like a glittering cloud, and everyone's eyes snapped toward it. I closed my own just in time as the cloud exploded in a brilliant light.

The demons holding the chains let go and stumbled backward. Jereth dropped the needle at his feet and cursed, reaching for his eyes.

Yeah, this is going to hurt alright.

I threw off the chains and shifted to smoke, flying through the room to first break the light and then smash the televisions so that the entire place was thrown into complete darkness. I had no idea if any of the demons in the room shared my particular talent, but it was likely that the majority of them couldn't see in the dark. *Advantage number two.*

I took the dagger from my waistband and shifted back to human form behind Jereth's girlfriend. She screamed as I pressed the tip of the blade into her neck against her pulsing artery.

"Make one move, and your girlfriend is dead," I said. "I know you can't see me right now, so you'll have to trust me."

Jereth blinked, his eyes bleeding from the explosion. He fumbled for the rifle next to his chair, and I didn't hesitate. I pushed the blade into the girl's throat as hard as I could, not stopping until it came through the other side of her neck. She went limp in my arms and then fell onto the floor with a thud, her body shimmering briefly with light before she turned to dust and was gone.

I gathered my energy into my hands, the dim blue glow illuminating the room just enough for the others to see what I had done. Blood coated my dagger and my clothes.

"Saki?" Jereth asked, his nostrils flaring as he looked at me. "You're going to pay for this, Wrath."

"I told you not to move," I said.

I sent a single thread of ice through the floor toward his gun. The black exterior froze quickly, and thanks to Rend's swiftness potion, I was able to conjure a sharp icicle and send it flying toward the gun before Jereth's hand even landed on the strap.

The entire thing burst into shards of ice, its bullets pouring onto the floor and rolling across the hardwood.

Jereth motioned toward his crew. "What are you standing there for? Get him," he said. "And make sure he survives."

A breeze blew across my skin as every demon in the room shifted and flew toward me. I was faster, though, and was long gone before they reached me.

I landed on top of the bar, reforming quickly and gathering more power in the palms of my hands. A pitcher of water the bartender had been using to clean glasses sat on the counter, and I grabbed it, quickly throwing it onto the hardwood floor. I didn't need water to create ice, but it would help.

I sucked in a huge breath and waited for the cold to form inside my core. On the count of three, I blew the air from my lungs toward the floor. Frost poured from my mouth and coated everything from the hardwood to the couch and the coffee table in a thick layer of ice. Every demon in the room was standing on it, and before they could react, I stood and lifted my palms toward the sky with a sudden jerk.

Jereth and five others were quick enough to shift and move away from the ice, but the nine who weren't so lucky were impaled with sharp spikes that rose from the floor and through their feet. It wasn't enough to kill them, but the pain was significant enough to keep them from casting magic for a while. Blood poured onto the ice, melting it quickly. And as the ice melted, the blue glow it emitted went with it, throwing the place into darkness once again.

I needed to move.

I leapt off the bar, shifting in mid-air and flying toward the dusty ceiling of the bar. As I flew, I reached into my right pocket and took out another of Rend's potions. This one was a shielding potion.

In order for my plan to work, I was going to have to let them catch me. I wasn't looking forward to that part. I downed the potion and prayed it would be enough to keep me from losing any valuable part of myself. Like an arm. Or my foot.

Or worse.

Several demons cast orbs of light into the air, and the ones who were uninjured and ready to fight searched the darkness for signs of movement.

I darted quickly between the shadows, but a beast of a demon I recognized from my last encounter with Jereth spotted me. Great big black snakes slithered out of his palms, their jaws opening to reveal long white fangs that dripped with poison. He threw a snake at me and one of its fangs nicked the side of my arm as it soared past. It ripped my favorite hoodie but didn't touch my skin.

In seconds, snakes covered the entire floor in a writhing mass. I searched for a safe place to land, finally deciding on the pool table.

Jereth's eyes searched mine, red and angry. He hadn't expected me to put up this much of a fight, and he intended to make me pay.

Good. I needed him to be irrationally angry. I needed him to want to take it too far before the emerald priestess was ready. His actions would draw her out. All I had to do was keep pissing him off, which was pretty darn easy.

I reached into the inside pocket that Essex had sewn into my hoodie for me and took out a handful of green dust this time: emeralds mixed with poison magic.

I threw it into the air as far as I could and backed away. A green cloud formed in the center of the room over several of the injured demons. Thunder rumbled from inside it and a streak of lightning lit up the room. Then the rain started. Acid rain, strong enough to rip the flesh off a demon in human form. Possibly strong enough to kill him.

Screams echoed off the walls in the dark room, occasional strikes of lightning illuminating the faces of those caught in the rain and too weak to move. Their flesh bubbled and disintegrated, dripping off their bones like honey.

Jereth roared and reached for the chains across his chest.

I knew he'd reached his limit with most of his loyal crew dying right before his eyes. He wasn't going to let me live, no matter what the emerald priestess had agreed to pay him.

He gathered his chains in his hands, wrapping them around his knuckles twice before shifting and flying toward me. I could have moved, but it took great willpower to stay put. To pretend I wasn't fast enough to dodge him.

Silver exploded in my vision as he reformed right in front of me and punched me in the face. I flew backward ten feet, crashing through the wall on the other side of the room. I winced and reached for my eye. He'd hit it just right, and I'd probably lose my vision in it for a full week or more, even if I still had the power to heal myself.

I knew the guy was strong, but maybe I'd underestimated him. That was just his first blow, and from the look in his eyes as he walked toward me, I knew he had bigger things in store for me.

He threw his chains toward me and they elongated, almost as if the steel could stretch. The ends of the chains wrapped around my wrists, and Jereth yanked me forward, smashing my head against the edge of the pool table before I fell in a heap on the floor.

I struggled to stand, but everything hurt. The steel chains were not human-made, either. They were enchanted with some kind of fire locked inside. When I stared hard enough, I could see the flames flickering through the metal sheen.

The skin on my wrists sizzled, and I tightened my jaw against the pain.

Just hold on. She'll show up. She has to.

Jereth knelt at my side, bringing his face so close to mine I could smell the garlic on his breath from dinner.

"You should have joined my crew back in the day when I invited you," he said. "I could have freed your power from those witches. They owed me a favor, but no. You were too honorable to join a crew like ours."

He looked around at the demons who had fallen. There

were only three standing with him now.

"I never expected you to be able to nearly clear a room like that," he said. "With your little bag of tricks, you have some real strength. But it wasn't enough, Wrath."

He tugged on the chains, and I groaned involuntarily at the pain that ripped through me.

"You're going to die," he said, leaning even closer. "And I'm going to make it last."

"You'll do no such thing," a woman said, her heels clacking against the hardwood floor.

One of my eyes was completely swollen shut, and blood dripped into the other from where I'd hit the pool table, so I couldn't see her very well, but I knew at that moment my plan had worked.

Make her angry enough, and she'll find you.

Kristie had been right.

Every emerald gate Prima who had still been loyal to the Order was sitting in the dungeons of Harper's castle, crippling the emerald gates. I guess I'd finally made the bitch angry.

As the woman stepped over the bodies of the dead and made her way toward us, I could just make out the fiery red of her hair and the green silk of her shirt. It wasn't Priestess Evers, though. It must have been one of her daughters, but that was good enough.

I bent my neck toward my hoodie and wiped the blood from my left eye long enough to get a good look at her wrist. A smile tugged at one corner of my lips.

She was wearing a bracelet with a tiny emerald scarab beetle dangling from a loop in the chain.

As long as I made it out of this alive, I was finally going to find Harper. I was finally going to bring her home.

GAME OVER

JACKSON

"The deal's off," Jereth said, his chest rising and falling with great effort as he clasped the chains tighter in his hands. "There's nothing you can give me now that would be worth giving up the opportunity of killing this demon myself."

The red-haired woman curled her palm as if around a ball, her fingers more like talons with her long, manicured nails. She gathered a bright green energy in the center and stared at Jereth.

"You've seen what I can do," she said. "If you lay one more hand on him, I swear you won't live to see the sunrise."

Giant veins on the side of Jereth's neck bulged against his skin. "But—"

"No. We made a deal, and you're going to stick to it, or I'll personally hunt down every demon in your little gang here and kill them myself," she said. "My mother wants this one. He's ours."

"And if I kill you first?" Jereth asked.

She laughed, the sound amazingly full and unafraid. "Feel free to try," she said.

Jereth dropped his chains and shifted into a dark cloud of shadows. He swirled around the woman, the sound of steel hitting steel coming from somewhere inside the darkness.

The witch threw her ball of green energy into the air and spoke two words of magic. "Statuam lapidis."

Jereth's body dropped to the floor, his demon form gone and his human one returned in an instant. A chalky gray color crept along his skin, and his eyes widened into huge circles. He stretched his hands in front of his face as they solidified into pure stone.

"What have you done to me?" he screamed. "What's happening?"

But before he could say another word, the spell had reached his mouth and completed its path along his body from head to toe. He'd become a statue, but I could still feel his frantic energy in the air around us. The demon inside was terrified.

I looked away, the image reminding me too much of the days when my power and my brother's spirit were both locked away in stone statues back in Peachville.

The chains around my wrists went slack, and I worked myself free and glanced toward the door.

What remained of Jereth's crew was gone in the blink of an eye. The three who were still alive left their leader there on the floor of his own bar, helpless and powerless.

So much for loyalty.

I could have gone, too, but I needed this woman. Unlike all

the hunters I'd killed and all the Primas I'd thrown into the dungeon, this woman had something I needed.

It was so simple, it hadn't even occurred to me. I'd been so focused on finding the emerald priestess's home or hideout that I hadn't realized there might be a more efficient way than searching every dark corner of the earth.

The door with the scarab beetle carved into its wooden surface was the only direct portal to the house of the emerald priestess. Every Prima and powerful member of the Order of Shadows had a Hall of Doorways in their house. And every one of those hallways held a door just like the one she had dragged Harper through.

The only problem was that it was locked.

I'd tried everything in the first weeks following Harper's disappearance. We'd all searched for spells that might unlock the magic. We'd even tried to blow the door off its hinges. But nothing worked.

Once a witch had sealed her door with a particular type of blood magic, the only way inside was to either share that witch's bloodline, or to have a key.

With Priestess Winter, her daughters and granddaughters hadn't needed a key. The blood running through their veins was their key. Harper, however, had been given a special talisman that had served as a key. Zara, assigned to train Harper, had given her a sapphire butterfly pendant on the day of her Heritage Ritual.

Back then, the Order had believed Harper was on their side. What could be the harm in it?

That sapphire key had become extremely valuable to us over the past year, allowing us to travel to Winterhaven whenever we wanted.

Most of the time, however, keys were extremely rare. A witch usually had no reason to trust anyone but the members of her own family, so why put your home in danger by creating a key?

But the emerald priestess was a special case.

She was infertile, and even though she was rumored to have dozens of daughters, none of them shared her blood. None of them could pass through the doorway to her home without a physical key.

When the Prima of Alpine had told me about the priestess's daughters, it all clicked. No shared blood meant there were dozens of keys roaming throughout the world. All I had to do was figure out how to get my hands on one.

The emerald beetle shimmered in the light of the witch's green spell as she crouched beside Jereth's statue.

"You didn't honestly think we'd let you live once you captured him for us, did you?" she asked. "Not after you betrayed us once before, or don't you remember?"

The statue had no way to respond, but I could feel his fear.

"Fifty years ago, my mother asked you to kill a woman— a new mother—and take her baby," she said. "She was the prettiest little thing with a full head of red curls at birth. My mother wanted that baby more than you can imagine. All you had to do was kill a single witch. An easy task for a strong demon like you. But who knew a heartless beast like yourself would turn out to have a soft spot for new mothers?"

I swallowed back the taste of bile. How many children had been stolen in the name of the priestess's collection? How many mothers had died over the years to feed her obsession?

"My mother never forgets, Jereth," she said. "She needed

your help setting a trap for this demon, and you did your job. Now it's time for you to die."

Jereth's fear had risen to full-blown panic. I could smell it in the air like sulfur, burning my nostrils.

I didn't know if it was the fact that my enemy was standing over him or if it was her story about the baby that caused me to do it, but I didn't want to watch a five-hundred-year-old demon die at the hands of this witch. Even he deserved better than that.

The witch wasn't paying any attention to me as she poured more of her power into the green spell hovering in her palm.

I only had one shot at surprising her, and if I missed, I would pay dearly for it.

My dagger lay discarded in a pile of bloody ooze ten feet from me. It was my best shot. I was out of dust, and it would take too long and draw too much attention to try to hit her with ice.

The swiftness potion was already wearing off, so I had to move now or Jereth would die.

I took a deep breath and focused on Harper's face, letting the aches and pains that locked me in this form fade away so I could focus enough to shift. When I felt the power within my reach, I grabbed it, shifting to shadow and flying toward the dagger.

I gripped it tightly in my hand and aimed straight for her heart as I threw the dagger.

But the witch was too fast for me. The green spell dropped from her hand as she turned and caught the blade in her fist. Blood dripped from her palm, but she hardly seemed to notice.

She shook her head and made a clicking sound with her tongue. "Naughty, naughty," she said.

I swallowed and tried to focus on drawing my power into my hands, but she had been the one to surprise me with her quick movements. I was in trouble, and just knowing that made it tough to cast.

She dropped the dagger to the ground and stepped aside as my ice spell reached her. I missed and cursed.

"Why is it that you demons always think you're stronger than us?" she asked, shaking her head. She gathered another spell of green energy in her claw-like hand. "But don't worry. I won't kill you."

She smiled and threw the energy toward me. I managed to shift and spin out of the way, but the spell didn't simply fly past me and dissipate like most normal spells. It curved like a boomerang and slammed into my back, stealing the breath from my lungs.

I fell to my knees as pain blossomed through my body, radiating outward from the point of impact. I struggled to breathe, but only wheezed as a tiny bit of air made it through the muscles constricting my throat. My body was paralyzed, and I suddenly understood with great intimacy the panic emitting from Jereth's statue.

The witch laughed and walked in a circle around me, her heels clacking against the floor as my vision blurred.

She crouched beside me, resting a hand on my shoulder as she leaned toward my ear.

"As much as I would love to kill you myself, my mother has something very special planned for you. Something she wants your precious Harper to see."

I fell over, my face hitting the bloody floor. I was losing consciousness, but it wasn't over yet. It couldn't be. Harper was still alive, and I was so close to getting her back.

"She's been a tough case to crack," the witch said. "Every method of torture, every memory spell in the book, couldn't break her. Sure, she lost most of her memories, but for some reason, she refused to let go of you. Mother thinks that if she sees you die with her own eyes, that will be the end of her. Game over. She'll forget you to numb the pain, and we'll start her torture all over again. When she's fully destroyed, we'll sweep in with new memories, giving her a new family and a new home. In six months, she'll be a Prima, just as she was always meant to be. She'll be working for us now, Jackson. Loyal to us. Poetic justice, if you ask me."

My eyes closed, but I refused to give up hope. I refused to give up on us.

This witch thought that demons underestimated the power of witches? Well, witches like her always underestimated the power of true love and friendship. Their loyalty was bought with threats and tricks, but true loyalty came from love, not fear. That was the one thing the Order of Shadows would never understand.

I smiled as the darkness threatened to pull me into its embrace.

"Why are you smiling?" she asked, annoyance clear from her tone.

I didn't have the breath or the energy to speak, but if I could, I would have told her that I was smiling because I had just heard the distinct flapping of crow's wings.

THE ONLY WAY WE DO THIS IS TOGETHER

JACKSON

Bright light exploded in the room, and demons swirled like shadows across the walls.

A crow landed two feet behind the witch and when it landed, the figure shifted into a teenage girl with pale skin and clear blue eyes.

The witch stood, her mouth open in a silent scream as Mary Anne gathered her magic in her hands. Red light shone from her fingertips. Demons shifted and walked to join her.

Essex, Rend, Joost, Mordecai, and everyone who'd been able to join us was there.

"Release him from whatever spell you have on him, or your life ends now," Mary Anne said.

For the first time since she'd entered the room, the witch's confidence disappeared.

"I'll kill him," she said, her voice wavering. "Drop your

weapons and spells, or I'll kill him so fast, you won't have time to stop me."

"Cut the crap," Mary Anne said, rolling her eyes. "You and I both know what happens to you if you kill him. Even if we let you go, your mother would have your head for this, and you know it. Trust me, from what I hear, you'd rather die at my hands than hers, anyway."

The witch began to sob, and she raised a trembling hand to her mouth. "Okay," she said. "I'll do it, but you have to promise not to hurt me."

"I promise I won't hurt you," Mary Anne said.

The witch nodded and knelt down beside me. She placed her hand flat on my back. "Solvo," she said.

Instantly, whatever magic had constricted my lungs and airways released. I gulped in air and pushed up to my hands and knees. Blood dripped from the wound on my forehead, and I swiped at it.

"What took you so long?" I asked, glancing up at Mary Anne. "I was dying over here."

"I expected you to be able to hold your own for a little longer than this," she said, reaching a hand out to help me stand. "All your big talk of wrath and making them pay. Sheesh."

I laughed and pulled her into a hug. "Thank you for coming," I said. "You were right. The only way we do this is together."

"I wouldn't have missed it for the world," she said.

The witch took a step sideways, but Rend quickly sent a shadowy black rope streaming toward her. The shadows wrapped around her arms and legs and throat, stopping her in her tracks.

"I wouldn't take another step if I were you," he said.

Tears streaming down her face, the witch's eyes darted from one person to the next. "Who are you all?" she asked. She looked at me. "You were told to come alone."

"I did come alone," I said. "I can't help it if my friends decided to follow me."

Mary Anne laughed and shook her head. "I have to admit, when you told me your plan, I thought you'd lost your mind," she said. "All those Primas in the basement? I was scared you'd go crazy with rage and slit their throats overnight. But you were right. Hit them hard enough and they'll come looking for you instead of the other way around."

The witch shook her head. "I don't understand," she said.

"Priestess Evers is not an easy woman to find," I said. "I've been searching for information on her house and her hideouts for months with no luck. Everyone was too afraid to talk to me. Even her hunters would rather die than face her anger. But then, thanks to a new friend, I started thinking what might happen if I made my actions impossible to ignore."

I walked in a circle around the witch.

"Killing hunters was one thing," I said. "Annoying, maybe, but not extreme. Not when the priestess could just make more. But taking away her Primas? Crippling her entire network of gates? Now that was something she wouldn't be able to overlook."

"You knew I would be here," she whispered.

"After we'd captured all the most loyal and powerful Primas, it was only a matter of time," I said. "I waited in the one place I knew would be safe. Venom. And sure enough, you came to me. You set your trap and foolishly expected me to come alone and vulnerable."

"I'm not going to tell you where she is," the witch said, lifting her chin. "You can kill me right now. I don't care. I'll never betray my mother."

"You won't have to," I said. I lifted her arm. The beetle charm dangled just beneath the edge of her silk blouse. "I know exactly where to find her. I just needed the key to get in."

The witch's eyelids fluttered closed and she fell back against the leather couch as the truth finally sunk in.

"Now, if you'll kindly release Jereth from that block of stone, we can be on our way," I said. "I have someone very important to rescue."

AT LEAST I WILL DIE FIGHTING

HARPER

Nurse Melody finished her rounds and locked us in our room, but I couldn't sleep. It was too dangerous to sneak out tonight or even to use my astral projection. I was exhausted from the last time I'd used it, so I probably wouldn't have gotten very far, anyway.

I turned my body toward Judith and our eyes met through the darkness.

How much had she seen earlier in the courtyard? Had she seen the tiny birds? Was she going to tell on me again?

It was stupid to risk it. I never should have cast my magic in the courtyard where anyone could be watching.

But Mary Ellen had looked so sad. I had the feeling she'd had a very hard life, but that inside her there was a sweet girl with a good heart. She didn't deserve to be here. None of us did.

I had to figure out how I was going to escape this place, and if I had the chance, I would take as many girls with me as I could.

If Judith had seen me cast that spell, she was a ticking time bomb. One word from her to any of the nurses, and I would be in serious trouble. If the punishment for simply leaving my room in the middle of the night was shock treatments, what would they do if they learned I'd been casting magic?

The things I knew put everything they'd built here in danger. They wouldn't allow it, no matter how important I was to them.

I needed a plan. Just in case. And if things got bad or it seemed someone knew what I could do, I would leave. I would find a way.

Heels clacked against the floor in the hallway, the footsteps fast and frantic.

I sat straight up in bed, my heart leaping into my throat.

"Judith?" I asked, my voice a strangled cry.

She pulled her covers up around her neck. "I didn't tell anyone, I swear," she said. "I didn't say a word about what you did."

I flipped my head toward Mary Ellen, who was now sitting up on the other side of the room. She shook her head furiously, her black hair flying around her.

"What's going on?" Nora asked. "Harper?"

I closed my eyes and tried to think, but the footsteps were growing closer. Faster.

The woman was coming for me. Dr. Evers's mother. Somehow, she'd discovered my stash of spell books, or maybe someone else had seen me cast that spell. I didn't know how she knew, but she was coming for me.

My mind ran through a list of the spells I knew how to

cast. Glamours and lights were nothing right now. I was getting good at lifting and moving objects with my mind, but our room was bare of everything except our beds. I could move them to block the door, but that was just a temporary solution.

There was only one way out of this room, and eventually, she would get in.

Besides, if I could cast a little bit of magic with my limited memories of the past, I could only imagine what powers this woman possessed. She'd turned actual human beings into dolls, for God's sake. She could probably kill me with a flick of her wrist.

"Mother, wait. I can still do this," Dr. Evers said, her voice carrying down the hall. "I can still turn her to our side. I need more time."

"Your time is up," the woman shouted. "You failed me like my daughters always fail me. Why can't I just have one talented and devoted daughter like my sisters? Why?"

"I'm sorry," Dr. Evers said. "Please."

A green light flashed across the small window in the doorway, and Dr. Evers screamed.

I stood and stared at the door, waiting for it to open. I was trapped in here with no way out. That door was the only escape route, but the sound of footsteps was so close. I wasn't sure I'd have time.

Still, I had to try. I couldn't sit in here and wait. I should have run the second I heard those shoes against the tile floor.

I lifted my palm into the air and focused on the lock. I twisted my hand to the left and the lock clicked open. I gripped the doorknob with my magic and turned hard, yanking the door open.

"Harper, don't," Nora said. "They'll kill you."

"Then at least I will die fighting," I said.

I ran from the room, my bare feet slapping against the cold tiles. I only took a second to glance toward the woman, to check and see how far away she was, and then I ran in the opposite direction. She had been only two doors down from our room, but the moment she saw me, she began to run, too.

"Nurses, stop her," the woman shouted.

Two nurses stood up from their desk at the end of the hallway and blocked my path. Their hands glowed with green, pulsing light, but I didn't stop. I would rather face them than whatever the woman behind me had in mind.

I had never tried to move anything heavier than a book or a candle with my magic, but it was the only defense I could think of. I brought both hands in front of my body and focused on the two nurses as I ran toward them. I imagined my power wrapping around them like a giant hand, and when I could feel their energy clearly touching my own, I jerked my arms to the left.

Both women lifted off the floor and crashed into the wall just as I reached them.

I jumped over them and kept running.

Patients were never allowed to go past the nurse's station into this area of the building, but I had been down here a handful of times in the past week or so when I'd been exploring the asylum with my new ability.

I ran through the floor plan in my mind, my heart pumping so hard my lungs hurt.

Right down this hallway, and then left. Another right would take me to a stairwell that went up to the second floor. If I could make it to the middle of that second-floor-hallway, there was a large window there I could smash through. I could jump. It was the only way.

I grabbed the edge of the wall as I hurled my body to the right and down the next corridor. The sound of the witch's shoes against the tile was fading. She was too slow. I could do this.

I turned left and ran, pushing myself harder. I had worked to strengthen my body, and it was going to pay off. I just had to keep running.

When I made it to the T at the end of the hall, I dared a glance behind me. No one was there. Not a single nurse. Not the woman in heels. No one. Had I lost them?

I shook my head and continued on to the stairwell, pulling the door open and racing up the steps. They wouldn't stop until they'd found me. I just had to make it to that window. A two-story drop would hurt, but it wouldn't kill me. If I could get out of here, I could run for help.

Outside, there had been other houses along this street. I could run to one of them and bang on the door until they let me in. I'd tell them to call the police, and then I would be safe.

My lungs burned, and a headache pounded in my skull, but I didn't slow down. I made it to the top of the stairs and ran down the hallway toward the window.

But just as the light from a passing car on the street below came into view, a streak of green shot through the air. I lifted my hands to shield my face, and the green arrow shimmered for a moment on some invisible barrier and slid down to the ground.

I opened my eyes wide, my lips parting as I struggled to catch my breath.

I had no idea how I'd done it, but I'd created a shield to

protect myself. I could taste the bitter poison from the arrow on the back of my tongue, as if I'd somehow absorbed a part of the magic into myself.

I squinted through the half-darkness, trying to see where the spell had come from, but I didn't see any movement. I ran forward and was just steps from the window when another arrow shot toward me. I lifted my hands again, but just as the arrow hit my shield, a net of glowing green rope fell from the ceiling, knocking me to the ground.

I struggled against it, but the rope seemed to constrict itself, forming to my body and wrapping me in a tight ball. I tried to think of any magic that could save me from this, but I was out of ideas. The rope grew tighter the more I struggled, bending me forward at an awkward angle.

I sat very still, trying to breathe and think. There had to be something I could do. Anything.

But when I heard the familiar click of the woman's heels on the floor, I knew it was over. She would kill me for what I had done.

A tear rolled down my cheek as the woman crouched beside me.

"Do you have any idea what kind of mess you've caused for me tonight?" she asked. "There isn't a girl on your wing who didn't see and hear everything. It will take me weeks to purge this memory from their brains. Weeks."

She sighed and stood up, motioning to Dr. Evers, who had followed close behind her.

"At least your traps were useful tonight," she said. "That's one thing you did right for a change."

"Thank you, Mother."

I closed my eyes. *Traps. Dammit. Why didn't I think of that as a possibility?*

My spectral presence wouldn't have set them off, but in my physical form, I had tripped the traps and delivered myself right to them.

The witch crouched again, staring at me with her emerald-green eyes. "I tried," she said. "I tried to save you and make you mine. You would have been my crowning achievement. A half-demon, half-human princess? The murderer of my conceited sister on my side. Fighting for me. Loyal only to me."

I turned my head toward her. *Half-demon? Princess?* She couldn't be talking about me. But something clicked inside my mind, a memory so close to the edge, it nearly sang to me. My father—the man with the impossibly silver eyes—had been king once. A demon king. Was that right?

She slapped her hands across her thighs.

"It would have changed everything for me," she said. "But you just couldn't let go of him, could you? You couldn't be forced to forget him."

She shook her head and sighed.

"And now he has my precious girl. My Isabella," she said. "We had the perfect trap set for him, and he still captured her. He's on his way right now, if you must know."

I gasped and searched her face, trying to see if she was telling me the truth. Jackson was on his way here to me?

"Don't look so hopeful," she said. "As soon as he walks through my door, I'll kill him and anyone dumb enough to follow him. But first, I have something very special in store for you."

She placed her hand on the net of green rope, and it disappeared, finally allowing me to sit up and draw a full breath. The woman grabbed my hair and lifted me from the ground, her grip brutal. She nodded to her daughter, and Dr. Evers took something from her pocket. A solid black stone hanging from a string. She placed it around my neck, and my body tensed as pain forked through my chest, spreading quickly down my arms and legs.

I screamed, and the woman laughed.

"As disappointed as I am to lose you as a potential daughter," she said, "you're going to be a great addition to my collection. After I drain all the power from you, of course. I can't have you figuring out how to cast, and besides, I can use this power for decades to keep me alive. It's a wonderful gift you're giving me, Harper."

"What are you going to do to me?" I asked, wincing through the pain. The stone was drawing energy from my body, sucking through my chest like a straw.

She leaned close to my ear, almost kissing it.

"I couldn't break your mind," she said. "So now, I'm going to take it from you."

THIS IS WHO YOU ARE

HARPER

One of the nurses raced forward with a gurney, and lowered me onto it. She secured leather straps around my wrists and ankles, but it was useless to struggle now. It was over. I'd done everything I could, but they were stronger than I was. I was outnumbered.

They wheeled me down the hall and down two flights of stairs, lifting the gurney with magic when they needed to. I knew the route they were taking, even if I couldn't lift my head to see it clearly.

They were taking me down to the basement.

I'd seen the room where they performed the procedure, as they called it. It was next door to where they had shocked my mind and body. I'd seen the tools they used, and they were crude and terrifying.

I closed my eyes and pictured the ice pick instrument, with its worn wooden handle and pointed steel spear. I pictured the hammer that lay next to it on the surgical tray.

In a few weeks, would they wheel me out into the court-yard to sit in the sun? Would the others look at me in fear, vowing never to speak out against the torture they all knew was happening here?

Or would she dress me up in pink bows and stretch me out on her window seat?

I had so wanted to be an inspiration. A hero. I'd wanted to destroy this place and save them all, but I'd been a fool. I should have kept my head down and waited. Jackson was on his way, and by the time he arrived, it would already be too late for me. I wouldn't even know him anymore.

Tears slid down the side of my face as they wheeled me toward the room. It was much colder down here in the base-ment, and I shivered in my thin nightgown.

All the hours I'd spent down here practicing had been for nothing, and I wanted to scream. Why had Brooke even brought me down here? I was no one special. I was nothing. Whoever I had once been was gone, and anything I had left of that girl who had been brave enough to kill this witch's sister was about to be taken from me.

I couldn't bear it. It wasn't fair.

I deserved better than this. Every girl in this institution deserved better than this, but what could I do? I was strapped to this gurney and only minutes away from having an ice pick shoved into my brain. The black stone around my neck was drawing my energy into it, leaving me even weaker than I'd been when I first woke up here.

I was going to die. Maybe not in body, but in mind and spirit. And I never even had the chance to say good-bye to the people I loved most.

Mary Anne. Jackson. There had to be others, too, and I

longed to remember them. Just this once before they were stolen from me forever.

A door opened, and the nurses pushed me through a narrow doorway to the operating room.

"Where are my instruments?" Dr. Evers said. She rushed by me in a panic, throwing open every cabinet in the room. "They're not here. Where are they?"

I tried to lift my head from the gurney, but the pain of the stone forced my head back down.

"Find them," the woman said. "Now."

"Someone get Melody," Dr. Evers said. "She was supposed to lay them out for me. I sent her down here twenty minutes ago."

The door to the room opened again, and the nurse gasped.

"What are you girls doing down here?" she asked. "Get back to your rooms. This doesn't concern you."

"I'm afraid it does," Brooke said.

Tears flowed from my eyes. Brooke had come? She had risked her life for me?

I struggled against the restraints, but it was no use. They were too tight, fastened with metal buckles in three places.

Dr. Evers and her mother shared a look of concern and anger, and then ran toward the door, both of them shouting for the girls to return to their rooms or be punished for disobeying the rules of this institution.

Someone else stepped into the room, and I craned my neck to see. Nurse Melody rushed to my side. She wrapped her hand in a white towel and flipped the black stone over. Warmth flowed into my body as my power returned. She had somehow reversed its effects.

"Thank you," I said as she went to work on the buckles that held my wrists and ankles to the gurney.

"You have to fight, Harper," she said, out of breath and glancing toward the door. "You have to remember who you are. What you're capable of."

"I can't," I said. "I've been trying for months, but the memories are locked away somewhere. I don't know what to do."

She released my left arm and went to work on my ankle, but her hands were trembling. They kept slipping.

"I don't know how to tell you to fight against the magic," she said. "But that's all it is. Magic. You have to be stronger than the spells she cast against you. You have to open your heart."

She released the straps holding my left ankle and moved to the next.

"Those girls out there, most of them barely have the strength to cast the simplest spells," she said. "They aren't like you. Priestess Evers will kill them in a heartbeat if she wants to. We need you."

"Priestess Evers?" I asked.

"The emerald priestess," she said. "Dr. Evers's mother. She's the one who runs this place. She runs everything here. She's the one who kidnapped you and brought you to this place. Don't you remember her at all?"

I closed my eyes, picturing the woman's face. I could see her now, standing above me, her body covered in blood as she ripped a chain from my neck and threw it against the wall.

My mother's necklace. My engagement locket.

She dragged me up the stairs and down a hall filled with doorways. I remembered.

The door flew open and the emerald priestess stepped into the room, her eyes wild and her magic glowing a dark emerald-green all around her. In her hands, she held an ice pick-shaped instrument and a hammer.

"I'll do it myself if I have to," she said.

She slammed the door behind her and locked it with a wave of her wrist. She jerked her gaze from one side of the room to the other, and the heavy cabinets scraped across the floor to block the doorway.

One side of my body was free of restraints, but the other was still strapped to the gurney.

Melody ripped the hem of my dress, tearing a single long strip of fabric away. She quickly wrapped it around my wrist and tied it off, placing both hands on top of it.

"This is who you are," she said, her eyes shining with tears. "You're the kind of person who doesn't give up, no matter how bad it seems. You're the girl who fights with her whole heart. You're the girl who believes that anyone can change the world if she stands up for what's right."

A glowing green arrow pierced Melody's chest, and blood spattered from her lips and onto my white nightgown. Blood covered the front of her nurse's uniform, and she fell to the floor, unmoving. She had sacrificed her own life for mine.

Priestess Evers set the instruments on the surgical table and went to work securing the straps again, pulling them even tighter this time.

I stretched my fingertips and touched the edge of the torn fabric Melody had tied around my wrist. It was so familiar. A symbol of defiance, even in the darkest moments.

I closed my eyes, shutting out the sounds of struggle behind the door. Forgetting the instruments on the table. I went deep into myself, to the core of what made me who I was. I tapped into that running river of strength that lived inside of me. I breathed new life into it, drawing from the earth beneath the basement floor. I could feel the trees blowing in the wind outside and the birds soaring high above the streets.

I drew my strength from life. From hope.

I fought against the poison that ran through my veins, and I reached inside my own heart. Because the mind may be where we kept our memories, but the heart was where we kept our souls. Every event in my life—my greatest sorrows and my happiest moments—were imprinted on my soul. They were a part of me. They had created me and turned me into the woman I was.

I drew on their strength and focused on their truth.

And suddenly, I remembered everything.

A WOMAN WITH NO HEART

HARPER

My eyes snapped open. The steel tip of the ice pick hovered just above my right eye. The priestess leaned over me, hatred seeping from her pores.

I understood now what this woman was capable of. I knew what she had done to me. To thousands.

I grabbed the ice pick with my mind and ripped it from her hands. It hit the wall behind her, and she gasped. I wrapped my magic around her and threw her across the room, her body landing at an awkward angle on the floor.

I focused on the metal buckles of the restraints, unhooking each of them simultaneously and threading the leather straps through them. I pulled my arms free just as the priestess regained her footing and gathered a new spell in her hands.

I breathed in, connecting to my power. Wind whipped my hair around my face, and I moved my hands in a circle in front of me as I slipped off the gurney to stand on my own two feet.

I created a storm in the small surgical room. A furious tornado circled the edge of the room with me standing in the eye, my feet hovering just above the ground.

The priestess stumbled, her body thrown by the wind. She threw her spell toward me, but it blew sideways and crashed into the wall. Cement blocks disintegrated, and green ooze dripped down the white walls.

The gurney flew into the air and slammed against the brick, toppling sideways, its wheels spinning.

She pushed her palms flat against the side of the wall and walked forward into the wind, her laughter rising above the sound.

"You can't kill me, Harper," she said. "You tried that, remember?"

I narrowed my eyes at her, remembering that night in the halls of Winterhaven. I had plunged my hand into her chest to rip her heart out, only to find that she had no heart. She'd hidden it somewhere.

The priestess reached into her pockets and drew out a fist, gleaming shards of emerald glass peeking through her knuckles.

I lifted my hands and created a shield, but something tugged at me. Something important.

You have my heart.

Chills ran down my spine. I'd heard her say those words to her daughter. To Dr. Evers. Last night in the house across the street, I'd seen the priestess lay her palm flat against her daughter's chest.

"You have my heart," she'd said.

As the shards of glass pierced through my shield, I looked up and smiled at the priestess.

She thought she was invincible. Immortal. But without her stone heart, she was nothing more than a rotting pile of bones.

I turned my attention to the cabinets that blocked the door. I had to get to Dr. Evers before the priestess realized what I knew. The storm was making it difficult for her to cast, but she was making her way toward me. I had to hurry.

I reached one hand to the side and lifted the large cabinet off the floor. I threw it toward the priestess, the wood cracking as it hit the floor and flipped over, separating us.

I ran forward and yanked the door open. Smoke billowed through the hallway, and I coughed, nearly choking on it. Flames consumed the other end of the hallway, where boxes of books and gowns had been stacked against the walls. I lifted the front of my gown to cover my nose and mouth and stepped forward. The ice pick rolled across the floor, bumping against the edge of my bare foot. I bent down to retrieve it, gripping it tightly in my fist.

In the hallway, a group of girls in white nightgowns fought against the remaining nurses and the doctor. Two of the younger girls lay still on the floor, their eyes closed and blood dripping from various wounds.

Dr. Evers had Brooke by the throat. Her hand was covered in emerald ivy that grew rapidly, its vines wrapping all the way around Brooke's body like a rope.

I gathered a new spell in my hands and rushed toward my friend, but a searing heat tore through my side as a green light flashed behind me.

I flew forward, falling face-first to the ground.

The pain blossomed, poison spreading like wildfire through my body. I pushed against it, holding it at bay as best I could. I crawled across the floor, my hands stretching toward the doctor's ankles.

I grabbed onto her and pulled myself up, spinning her around and pressing the point of the ice pick into her chest just above her heart.

Priestess Evers stood in the doorway of the surgical room, her hair wild and her eyes glowing.

"No," she said, finally understanding.

She stretched her arms out and stumbled toward us.

"I'll give you anything you want," she said. "Power. Money. Anything. Don't do this."

I raised an eyebrow. "Tell me where all of your sisters are hiding," I said. "I want details. Names, locations, everything you know. And tell me where I can find the High Priestess. Help me kill them all, and I'll let you live."

She shook her head and grabbed her hair, pulling it hard and screaming. She fell to her knees, emerald-colored tears falling down her cheeks.

Everyone in the hallway stopped fighting and grew silent. The only sounds were the crackling of flames and the sobs of the witch on her knees at my feet.

"I can't," she said. Her face crumpled, and she beat her fists against the floor. "I'll do anything else you want, but not that."

"I didn't think so," I said. I pressed the ice pick deeper into Dr. Evers's chest. I could feel the pounding of her human heart against my arm.

"Wait," Priestess Evers screamed. She drew her lips into a snarl and gathered her skirts in her hand. She stood slowly, her eyes locked on mine. "If you kill me, you'll never see him again. I swear it."

"Jackson?" I shook my head. "You said it yourself. He's on his way here now."

"He won't be able to get to you," she said, laughing and sobbing at the same time. "Kill me and you'll never find each other."

"You're wrong," I said. "But then, how could I expect a woman with no heart to understand the power of true love?"

I pushed the ice pick deep into Dr. Evers' heart until it hit something rock-hard just behind it. She slumped against me as her heart stopped beating, and I lowered her to the floor.

"No," Priestess Evers screamed. She shook her head violently from side to side. She gathered a new spell into her hands and poured all of her power into it. Her body lifted off the ground as the brilliant light traveled up her arms and around her body like a halo.

I only had one chance to get this right.

I placed my hand over the small hole in the doctor's chest. I embraced my demon half, sending a rope of white smoke through the wound until I felt the energy press against the solid surface of the stone.

Each of the Order's priestesses had kept themselves alive for centuries through the use of a master stone. It was a piece of the original portal stone that severed the veil between the human world and the Shadow World. Without it, she was nothing.

I closed my demon fist around the stone and pulled it from the dead woman's chest just as Priestess Evers unleashed the full force of her power.

IT WAS NEVER JUST ME

HARPER

Priestess Evers screamed, but the sound was muffled by the explosion that rocked the entire building.

I acted on instinct, tapping into the raw power of the stone in my hand. I stretched a powerful shield of dark energy down the hallway as far as I could, protecting everyone from the blast.

I could feel the depth of her evil heart inside that final spell. It burned my throat, and I fell to my knees.

Pieces of the ceiling caved in around us, and emerald flames consumed the basement. I forced myself to my feet. I lifted debris and created a pathway toward the stairwell.

"Run," I shouted, my voice hoarse. "The flames are spreading."

Girls screamed and ran, stepping over pieces of brick and ceiling that littered the floor. Two of them paused to lift the injured girls into their arms.

I collapsed, the source of my power exhausted.

A hand reached down to me, and I looked up.

Brooke smiled. "You did it," she said.

"Not without you," I said with a smile. "Come on. Let's get out of here."

She helped me to my feet, and I threw an arm around her shoulder. We pushed toward the stairwell as the flames grew higher and hotter around us.

I glanced back once, just in time to see Hazel Evers's flesh turn to dust and her ancient bones scatter among the flames.

"We have to get everyone out of the building," I said. "They're all still locked in their rooms."

"Spread out," Brooke said when we reached the top of the stairs. A cluster of girls in nightgowns stood in the dark hallway, their hands clasped tightly to one another. "Anyone who can open locks, get as many as you can."

I wanted to help, but I was exhausted and injured, the priestess's poison still coursing through my veins.

Together, we ran down each of the hallways, unlocking doors and shouting at the sleeping girls to wake up and get out of the building.

No sprinklers came on, and no fire alarm sounded. We had to get to everyone before it was too late.

The floor grew hot beneath my feet as the flames consumed the basement level of the building. "We have to hurry," I said. "Is that everyone?"

"That's everyone," Brooke said.

Mary Ellen took my hand. Tears shimmered in her eyes.

"Let's go," she said, and I nodded.

"Follow me," I shouted to the mass of more than seventy or eighty girls huddled together in the semi-darkness. Those in wheelchairs were being pushed by those who could walk, and everyone who could was holding the hand of the person next to them.

I led them through the maze of corridors and out through the front door of the Evers Institute for Troubled Girls. We emerged as an army, victors against an evil that had no rightful place in this world. The night air was clean and warm, and I breathed in the smell of freedom and ash.

We stood as a group on the lawn of the asylum, nearly a hundred girls and women in thin nightgowns and awed expressions. We watched as the flames grew higher, burning through the sides and roof of the building.

"Look," someone said.

I turned and saw that a young girl at the edge of the group was pointing to the house across the street.

Sobs of relief shook my body as more than a dozen girls in bonnets and frilly dresses walked out of the old Victorian home and into the streets. I let go of Mary Ellen's hand and ran toward the girl who led them.

"Robin," I said, taking her hand in mine.

She pulled me into a hug, her body trembling with relief. "Was this you?" she asked.

"Not just me," I said. "It was never just me. It was all of us."

Along the street, the doors to several houses opened and people stepped onto their porches, pointing toward the fire.

I limped to the nearest one and an elderly woman in a robe, her hair in curlers, stepped forward to offer me her hand.

"My goodness, dear, are you alright?" she asked. "What happened in there?"

"I need to call for help," I said, making my way up the steps. "Do you have a cell phone?"

Her forehead wrinkled, and she shared a curious look with the man standing beside her. "A what, dear?"

"A phone," I said, holding my hand out.

She stared at me as if I'd lost my mind. "Come inside, sweetheart," she said. "Ralph can call the fire department, though I suspect someone already has. What a fright you must have had."

"I'm fine," I said. I winced at the pain in my side. At least I hoped I was fine. I needed to find Jackson. My sister Angela. They could help me heal quickly, and hopefully they were already on their way.

I couldn't wait to wrap my arms around Jackson and feel his lips on mine. God, I'd missed him.

I followed the couple into their home, noticing the antique car in the driveway before I stepped across the threshold. It had been perfectly restored, the paint reflecting the emerald flames that burned through the asylum across the street.

"Come on, let me get you a glass of milk," the woman said.

Stepping into their home was like stepping back in time. The velvet couch. The ceramic painted dog on the side table. Even the lamp shade was retro.

The old man sat down on the couch and picked up the receiver on an old black phone with a rotary dial. He flipped through a phone book, licking his fingers between each page turn before he finally found the one he'd been looking for. He slowly dialed the number, placing a finger in the hole of each number and spinning the little plastic wheel around.

Of course, I'd ended up at the weirdest house on the block.

I wrapped my arms around my body, shivering. I still couldn't believe she was dead.

"Sit down," the woman said, placing a glass of milk on the

table. Everything in the kitchen, from the cabinets to the refrigerator, was a bright teal color, like something out of a retro design catalog.

I shook my head. *Something isn't right here.*

I spun around, taking in each of the pieces as a whole, dread filling my heart. The restored antique car. The decor. The funny look on her face when I'd mentioned the word cell phone.

I stumbled forward, the pain in my side throbbing with heat.

"Oh, my," the old man said. He dropped the phone and rushed to catch me. "Here, please. Sit down."

He ushered me to an olive-green plastic chair. I sat down and took a deep breath. Everything was fine. Jackson was on his way, and this whole nightmare was almost over.

I still had the emerald stone clutched in my fist, and I held it in my lap. As long as I had this stone, everything was going to be okay.

But when I looked up, my lips parted in surprise.

The couple's television sat on a plain box of a stand, the volume turned down. Black and white images moved silently across the screen. I shook my head, my hands trembling as I stared at the antique box. I didn't care how old they were, no one still had a TV like that these days, with its boxy shape and round dials.

I struggled to stand, waving the man's hand away when he tried to help me.

"What on earth is wrong?" the woman asked, rushing to the living room.

"She's not right in the head," the man said. "I told you it

was a mistake to buy this place with that crazy-house next door."

"Ralph, hush," she said. "She's scared. Anyone can see that, plain as day."

I slowly turned back toward the door, understanding for the first time.

"All those poor girls," the woman said with a sigh. "I hope they got everyone out in time. What will they do with them, Ralph?"

I stepped out into the night, my body trembling despite the warm spring air.

I sat down on the top step and watched as the fire trucks parked across the street and men raced to extinguish the flames.

I stared down at the large emerald stone in my hand.

No wonder she'd brought us here. No wonder no one protested the shock therapies and the lobotomies going on at Evers.

Tears streamed down my face. She'd said that if I killed her, Jackson wouldn't be able to get to me. I didn't believe her.

I'd just killed the one person who knew how to get me back home.

***

The End

Continue this series with Beyond The Darkness. Buy now.

SET THEM FREE

JACKSON

We used the closest doorway we could find, breaking into a Prima's house in a small town in Tennessee and waking her up. She shouted at us, but as soon as she saw our sheer numbers—more than fifty demons and witches in total—she backed away and let us pass.

My heart was light, and a smile played on my lips as we climbed the stairs to the third floor and stepped into the Hall of Doorways. We still had a fight in front of us, but I was closer to Harper than I'd been in months.

We searched for the familiar door of the emerald priestess with its green scarab beetle etched into the wood.

Rend carried the priestess's daughter in his arms. She was still alive for now. I wasn't sure the key would work otherwise. But as soon as we opened the door, she was fair game to any of the thirsty vampires in our group.

The moment the door appeared, my heart began to race.

The past few months had been torture without Harper,

but she was just on the other side of that door somewhere. I had no idea what state I'd find her in, but the witch had said Harper had refused to let go of her memories of me. They'd been unable to break her.

My heart pounded against my ribs. I couldn't wait to see her.

My life was nothing without her at my side. These past few months had been devastating, and I longed to hold her in my arms for hours and kiss every inch of her body. I wanted to marry her.

We had decided to wait until the war was over, but I didn't want to wait. I was going to marry the woman I loved, and I was never going to let her go.

Rend stepped toward the door and nodded. I took the witch's hand and placed it against the wood. Something deep inside clicked, and the door fell open.

I raced inside and ran through the five-sided room to the staircase that led down to the main part of the house.

"Slow down," Mary Anne shouted. "You don't want to have to fight the emerald priestess alone, do you?"

But I'd stopped at the bottom of the stairs. She nearly ran into me.

"What's wrong?" she asked.

"This isn't right," I said, fear taking hold. "Look at this."

I stepped forward and picked a broken mirror off the floor. The place was in shambles. Furniture was toppled over. Dust covered every surface. A roach crawled across the floor at my feet.

"Does this look like the house of a priestess to you?"

"It's disgusting in here," she said.

"It is looking a bit rough around the surfaces," Essex said.

"Edges," Mary Anne corrected, bumping him with her elbow.

He shrugged and they laughed, but I couldn't find any laughter inside my heart.

Something was wrong. No priestess would let her home fall into ruin like this.

"Harper," I shouted, panic creeping through my veins.

I shifted and flew down the grand staircase. The first floor was in even worse condition than the second. The roof was leaking in the entryway and the hardwood floors were warped and covered in mold. Graffiti covered the walls.

Fear drowned me, and I could hardly breathe. Please say we hadn't just walked into another trap. Or worse. The wrong house. Where was she? Where was her creepy doll collection?

What kind of trick was the emerald priestess pulling on us, anyway?

I opened the front door and stepped out into a quiet neighborhood. The porch creaked beneath my feet, and I stepped carefully around broken boards and shards of glass. Harper was being kept in an asylum near here, I was sure of it.

But when I saw the large building across the street, my heart broke all over again. The roof had caved in and black scars marred the brick. Ivy clung to the outside of the building, and a tree grew through a hole in the roof. A wrought-iron fence surrounded the front of the property, and the grass on the lawn was overgrown.

I shook my head. This couldn't be right. Harper was supposed to be here. I flew down the steps and across the street, not stopping until I'd reached the fence. A plaque welded to the front gate read *Evers Institute for Troubled Girls.* This had to be it. I didn't understand.

Harper was being kept in that asylum. I'd seen it in my dreams. Everything I'd learned had led me here to this place. She should be here.

It's not where you find her. It's when you find her.

The words of the Alpine Prima echoed in my mind, and goose bumps broke out on my arms. She'd known more than she had let on.

I shifted and flew through the iron bars toward the building. I pulled on the front doors, but a heavy rope of chains was looped around the handles, locked with a heavy metal lock. A weathered NO TRESPASSING sign was taped to the door. I cupped my hands around my face and peered inside.

The walls were charred, and debris littered the floor. It looked as though no one had even set foot inside this place in years.

The priestess had to be keeping the girls in the basement somewhere. I refused to believe she wasn't here. I needed her to be here.

I searched the yard for a stick or something I could use to break the glass, but when I bent down, something blowing in the breeze caught my attention, and my heart tightened in my chest.

A single white rose grew among the thick ivy. I took a deep breath and crouched near the flower. A rose had no business growing in a place like this.

I touched its silky leaves and pulled back the veil of ivy, my heart sinking the moment I saw the large wooden box hidden behind it.

I pulled it from the ground and sat on the bottom steps of the ruined building. I set the box beside me and wiped away the thick layer of dirt that covered the top. A large ornate *H* was carved into the wood.

I didn't want to open it. I wanted to believe that she was locked somewhere downstairs and that all I had to do was go down and find her.

But a part of me knew the journey back to each other wasn't over yet.

With trembling hands, I lifted the lid of the box.

On the very top was a yellowed newspaper clipping that had been folded in half. I prayed this was just some nightmare, and not the truth. I unfolded the article, and the headline split my heart into a million pieces.

"EVERS INSTITUTE CONDEMNED DUE TO FIRE"

At the top of the page was a date: April 2, 1951.

I clutched the newspaper in my hand and fought back fresh rage and confusion. I had lost her all over again.

Across the street, Mary Anne walked out of the weathered Victorian house, and when she saw me, I think she knew. She held a hand out to tell the others to stay put and shifted to her crow form. She landed beside me and sat down, not saying a word.

I took a deep breath to still my heart, and I handed her the newspaper clipping. "She's not here," I said.

"No," she whispered, tears forming in her blue eyes. She read the article several times, and then placed a hand on my shoulder. "What else is in the box? Did she explain what happened?"

I ran my hand across a layer of bright green silk. Underneath were the five items needed to close the emerald gates:

A dagger.

A chalice.

A ring.

A necklace.

And finally, a large round stone. The master stone. The life-support of the emerald priestess herself.

Mary Anne gasped, and I pressed the back of my palm to my lips, understanding what she had done. Harper had killed the priestess. She'd ended the life of another witch who had terrorized so many for so long.

At the bottom of the box was a faded note, the page covered in Harper's handwriting. I ran my fingers across it, wanting more than anything to feel closer to her. To be with her. To tell her how much I loved her.

I wiped tears from my eyes and read her message to me.

My dearest Jackson,

As I write this letter, I'm sitting on the same steps you are likely sitting on now. It isn't distance that separates us. It's decades.

The emerald priestess is dead, but I didn't realize at the time that killing her would keep me from you for a little while longer. We're alive and another priestess of the Order is dead. That's what matters.

I hope you know how much I love you. How much I miss you. I long for you every moment we're apart.

Through this entire ordeal, you were my anchor. My savior. My sanity in a place of lies. She tried to break my mind but never understood that you are a part of my heart and soul. We share a love that transcends magic and distance and yes, even time.

We have to be stronger now than ever. We have important work to do.

Set them free, my love.

And then come find me.

YOURS THROUGH ETERNITY,
Harper

I FOLDED the letter and placed it inside the box, my heart aching for her. I missed her more than any words could describe. I missed our whole family.

But she was right. We couldn't let this destroy us. We had to be strong now. We still had work to do.

I watched as the group of demons and witches who had followed me into battle gathered on the porch of the old Victorian, and I realized that we would survive this. I'd spent months mourning her loss and distancing myself from everyone else.

But we were in this together. All of us. There was enormous power in that.

When you truly loved someone—when they became a part of you—nothing could ever take that away.

Not even time.

I closed the box and gathered it in my arms, lingering for just a moment longer in the place where she had once been.

Someday, we would find our way back to each other.

Someday, we would be free to live the life we'd dreamed of.

But for now, there was work to do.

"What's going on?" Rend asked as we climbed the steps to the priestess's old house. "Where's Harper?"

"She's not here," I said. I glanced at the asylum and wondered what horrors had been laid to rest as this place burned to the ground. "Not anymore."

"I don't understand," he said. "Is she okay?"

"She is. And she left us a present," I said.

I ran my hand across the letter carved into the wood.

"Come on," I said, throwing one arm around Mary Anne's shoulder. "Let's go free some demons."

ABOUT THE AUTHOR

Sarra Cannon is the author of several series featuring young adult and college-aged characters, including the bestselling Shadow Demons Saga. Her novels often stem from her own experiences growing up in the small town of Hawkinsville, Georgia, where she learned that being popular always comes at a price and relationships are rarely as simple as they seem.

Sarra recently celebrated eight years in indie publishing and has sold over half a million copies of her books. She currently lives in Charleston, South Carolina with her programmer husband and adorable redheaded son.

Love Sarra's books? Join Sarra's Mailing List to be notified of new releases and giveaways!

Also, please come hang out with me in my Facebook Fan Group: Sarra Cannon's Coven. We have a lot of fun in there, and I often share exclusive short stories and teasers in the group. Join now.

Want more? Get insider information on my writing process, inspiration, and what it's like to be an author with weekly videos on my YouTube channel.

Connect With Sarra Online:
www.sarracannon.com

37932538R00211

Printed in Poland
by Amazon Fulfillment
Poland Sp. z o.o., Wrocław